THE GRAYWOLF ANNUAL SEVEN:

STORIES FROM THE AMERICAN MOSAIC

1 9 9 0

THE GRAYWOLF

ANNUAL SEVEN

STORIES

FROM THE

AMERICAN

MOSAIC

Edited by Scott Walker

GRAYWOLF PRESS : SAINT PAUL

Publication of this volume is made possible in part by grants from the
National Endowment for the Arts, the Grotto Foundation, and the
Minnesota State Arts Board. Graywolf Press is the recipient of a McKnight Foundation Award administered by the Minnesota State Arts Board and receives generous contributions from corporations, foundations, and individuals. Graywolf Press
is a member agency of United Arts, Saint Paul.

This book was designed by Tree Swenson. It is set in Baskerville type by
The Typeworks.

ISBN 1-55597-136-9
ISSN 0743-7471

9   8   7   6   5   4   3   2
First Printing, 1990

Published by Graywolf Press, 2402 University Avenue, Suite 203,
Saint Paul, Minnesota 55114. All rights reserved.

Cover by Laura Popenoe

ACKNOWLEDGMENTS

Most of the stories collected in this *Graywolf Annual* have appeared previously in publications, as noted below. We gratefully acknowledge the cooperation of editors, agents, and the authors for their permission to reprint the stories here.

Kim Chi-wŏn's "A Certain Beginning" is from *Words of Farewell: Stories by Korean Women Writers* (Seal Press, 1989). Copyright © 1989 by Kim Chi-wŏn.

Ekoneskaka's "Chicapoo Juice" is from *Fiction Network* magazine, no. 13, Fall/Winter 1989/90. Copyright © 1989 by Ekoneskaka and Jim Salvator.

Louise Erdrich's "American Horse" is originally from *Earth Power Coming: Short Fiction in Native American Literature* (Navajo Community College Press, 1983) and was reprinted in *Spider Woman's Granddaughter* (Beacon Press, 1989). Copyright © 1983 by Louise Erdrich.

K.C. Frederick's "What Can You Do With a Fish?" is from *Concert at Chopin's House* (New Rivers Press, 1987). Copyright © 1987 by K.C. Frederick.

Joseph Geha's "Monkey Business" is from *Through and Through: Toledo Stories* (Graywolf Press, 1990). Copyright © 1990 by Joseph Geha.

Gayl Jones's "Asylum" is from her collection *White Rat: Short Stories* (Random House, 1977). Copyright © 1977 by Gayl Jones.

Jamaica Kincaid's "Mariah" was first published in the *New Yorker* and appears in her new book, *Lucy* (Farrar, Straus & Giroux, 1990). Copyright © 1990 by Jamaica Kincaid.

Salvatore La Puma's "Inside the Fire" was first published in the *Kenyon Review.* Copyright © 1989 by Salvatore La Puma.

Bharati Mukherjee's "The Tenant" is from her collection *The Middleman and Other Stories* (Grove Press, 1988). Copyright © 1988 by Bharati Mukherjee.

Susan Nunes's "A Moving Day" was originally published in *Home to Stay: Asian American Women's Fiction*, edited by Sylvia Watanbe and Carol Bruchac and published by the Greenfield Review Press. Reprinted by permission of the author. Copyright © 1990 by Susan Nunes.

Mary Helen Ponce's "Enero" is published here for the first time. Copyright © 1990 by Mary Helen Ponce.

Nahid Rachlin's "Journey of Love" was first published in *Redbook*. Copyright © 1988 by Nahid Rachlin.

Jim Sagel's "The Holy Cheese" is from *El Santo Queso/The Holy Cheese* (Ediciones del Norte, 1990). Copyright © 1990 by Jim Sagel.

Amy Tan's "Two Kinds" first appeared in the *Atlantic Monthly* and then as part of *The Joy Luck Club* (Ballantine Books, 1989). Copyright © 1989 by Amy Tan.

Yoshiko Uchida's "Tears of Autumn" was published in *The Forbidden Stitch* (Calyx Books, 1989). Copyright © 1989 by Yoshiko Uchida.

CONTENTS

FOREWORD

✳

WE THINK of our newest *Graywolf Annual* as a fiction companion to our *Graywolf Annual Five: Multi-Cultural Literacy.* Both of these annual explorations are attempts to understand and celebrate our nation's cultural diversity.

Our *Annual Five* (co-edited by Rick Simonson and Scott Walker) presented a number of essays that directly or indirectly expanded the prevailing notion of "cultural literacy." The United States has been and continues to be settled by immigrants. If the notion of the United States as a cultural "melting pot" was ever valid, it certainly is no longer. The newest metaphors that help us understand ourselves are those of a cultural 'salad bowl' or 'mosaic,' in which richly diverse cultures maintain their own characteristics while adding immeasurably to the whole. Population groups that once might have "melted" and lost some of their cultural identities are now rediscovering and embracing their origins. Newer immigrants are finding they can maintain their own culture and succeed in mainstream American culture, despite the mainstream's obstacles to entry and success.

In the two years since we published our *Graywolf Annual Five: Multi-Cultural Literacy,* issues of cultural diversity have grown in urgency and in popular recognition. At the same time that mainstream American culture has quite amazingly come to realize the importance of these issues and taken steps to promote understanding, we have seen an alarming increase in the number of racial "incidents."

It is heartening to note the number of major corporations that have instituted cultural diversity programs (and the number of corporations that now have vice presidents of cultural diversity!). What is most encouraging about this is that the programs are not instituted as the result of ephemeral corporate idealism, but because people in business know that diversity is an economic reality – it is here to stay – and steps must be taken to assure that the transition to an ethnically diverse work force is a positive one.

At another level of our society, fears of the racial "other" have erupted in many forms: violent confrontation, censorship, that seems in some cases to be racially motivated, positive and negative challenges to affirmative action. . . . It was Plato who said something like "Beware of the society which is not at war, for it will find its enemies within." Perhaps a post-Cold-War need for enemies has heightened our tribal fears of "the stranger," at the same time that economic policies that benefit the wealthy have intensified class tensions.

We have gathered together the fifteen stories of this *Graywolf Annual Seven: Stories from the American Mosaic* to help ourselves understand how the many cultures of the United States interact and intersect with the mainstream culture. As never before, it is important for all of us to cultivate an openness to and understanding of our neighbors. We must consciously counter any fears and anxieties we have about "otherness" by remaining curious about and interested in the people with whom we live and work.

It is our hope that the stories included here will help foster curiosity and interest. They are stories of people who are struggling to understand mainstream American culture; of confrontations, and the beginnings of mutual understanding. Through such works of individual imagination we can come to recognize common characteristics and lose our natural fear of the unknown.

We gladly acknowledge how partial this accounting is. This anthology, like other Graywolf *Annuals,* is meant to act as a starting point or as a stop along the way to greater understanding.

We make no claim to be fully or adequately representative of all cultural groups. We encourage our readers to seek out other stories and novels and memoirs from the authors included here, and to work consciously to extend their knowledge of the extraordinary literary and cultural diversity of the United States.

This anthology was compiled with the help and advice and assistance of a good many people. David Chow, Ingrid Erickson, and Rosie O'Brien deserve special mention for their intelligent contributions to this process.

S.W.

KIM CHI-WŎN

✳

A Certain Beginning

Translated by Bruce and Ju-Chan Fulton

YUN-JA floated on the blue swells, her face toward the dazzling sun. At first the water had chilled her, but now it felt agreeable, almost responding to her touch. Ripples slapped about her ears, and a breeze brushed the wet tip of her nose. Sailboats eased out of the corner of her eye and into the distance. She heard the drone of powerboats, the laughter of children, and the babble of English, Spanish, and other tongues blending indistinguishably like faraway sounds in a dream. Her only reaction to all this was an occasional blink. She felt drugged by the sun.

Yun-ja straightened herself in the water and looked for Chŏng-il. There he was, sitting under the beach umbrella with his head tilted back, drinking something. From her distant vantage point, twenty-seven-year-old Chŏng-il looked as small as a Boy Scout. He reminded her of a houseboy she had seen in a photo of some American soldiers during the Korean War.

"Life begins all over after today," Yun-ja thought. She had read in a women's magazine that it was natural for a woman who was alone after a divorce, even a long-awaited one, to be lonely, to feel she had failed, because in any society a happy marriage is considered a sign of a successful life. And so a divorced woman ought to make radical changes in her life-style. The magazine article had suggested getting out of the daily routine – sleeping as late as you want, eating what you want, throwing a party in the middle of the week, getting involved in new activities. "My case is a bit different, but like the writer says, I've got to start over again. But how? How is my life going to be different?" Yun-ja hadn't the slightest idea how to start a completely new life. Even if she were to begin sleeping all day and staying up all night, what difference would it make if she hadn't changed inwardly? Without a real change the days ahead would be boring and just blend together, she thought. Day would drift into night; she would find herself hardly able to sleep and another empty day would dawn. And how tasteless the food eaten alone; how unbearable to hear only the sound of her own chewing. These thoughts hadn't occurred to her before. "He won't be coming anymore starting tomorrow," she thought. The approaching days began to look meaningless.

Several days earlier, Chŏng-il had brought some soybean sprouts and tofu to Yun-ja's apartment and had begun making soybean-paste soup. Yun-ja was sitting on the old sofa, knitting.

"Mrs. Lee, how about a trip to the beach to celebrate our 'marriage'? A honeymoon, you know?"

Yun-ja laughed. She and Chŏng-il found nothing as funny as the word *marriage*. Chŏng-il also laughed, to show that his joke was innocent.

"Marriage" to Chŏng-il meant the permanent resident card he was obtaining. He and Yun-ja were already formally married, but it was the day he was to receive the green card he had been waiting for that Chŏng-il called his "wedding day."

Chŏng-il had paid Yun-ja fifteen hundred dollars to marry him so that he could apply for permanent residency in the U.S. Until his marriage he had been pursued by the American immigration authorities for working without the proper visa.

"Americans talk about things like inflation, but they're still a superpower. Don't they have anything better to do than track down foreign students?" Chŏng-il had said the day he met Yun-ja. His eyes had been moist with tears.

Now, almost two months later, Chŏng-il had his permanent

resident card and Yun-ja the fifteen hundred dollars. And today their relationship would come to an end.

Chŏng-il ambled down the beach toward the water, his smooth bronze skin gleaming in the sun. He shouted to Yun-ja and smiled, but she couldn't make out the words. Perhaps he was challenging her to a race, or asking how the water was.

Yun-ja had been delighted when Ki-yŏng's mother, who had been working with her at a clothing factory in Chinatown, sounded her out about a contract marriage with Chŏng-il. "He came here on a student visa," the woman had explained. "My husband tells me his older brother makes a decent living in Seoul. . . . The boy's been told to leave the country, so his bags are packed and he's about to move to a different state. . . . It's been only seven months since he came to America. . . . Just his luck – other Korean students work here without getting caught. . . . "

"Why not?" Yun-ja had thought. If only she could get out of that sunless, roach-infested Manhattan basement apartment that she had been sharing with a young Chinese woman. And her lower back had become stiff as a board from too many hours of piecework at the sewing machine. All day long she was engulfed by Chinese speaking in strange tones and sewing machines whirring at full tilt. Yun-ja had trod the pedals of her sewing machine in the dusty air of the factory, the pieces of cloth she handled feeling unbearably heavy. Yes, life in America had not been easy for Yun-ja, and so she decided to give herself a vacation. With the fifteen hundred dollars from a contract marriage she could get a sunny room where she could open the window and look out on the street.

And now her wish had come true. She had gotten a studio apartment on the West Side, twenty minutes by foot from the end of a subway line, and received Chŏng-il as a "customer," as Ki-yŏng's mother had put it.

After quitting her job Yun-ja stayed in bed in the morning, listening to the traffic on the street below. In the evening,

Chŏng-il would return from his temporary accounting job. Yun-ja would greet him like a boardinghouse mistress, and they would share the meal she had prepared. Her day was divided between the time before he arrived and the time after.

Thankful for his meals, Chŏng-il would sometimes go grocery shopping and occasionally he would do the cooking, not wishing to feel obligated to Yun-ja.

Chŏng-il swam near. "Going to stay in forever?" he joked. His lips had turned blue.

"Anything left to drink?" she asked.

"There's some Coke, and I got some water just now."

Chŏng-il had bought everything for this outing – Korean-style grilled beef, some Korean delicacies, even paper napkins.

"Mrs. Lee, this is a good place for clams – big ones too. A couple of them will fill you up – or so they say. Let's go dig a few. Then we can go home, steam them up, and have them with rice. A simple meal, just right for a couple of tired bodies. What do you think?"

Instead of answering, Yun-ja watched Chŏng-il's head bobbing like a watermelon. "So he's thinking about dropping by my place. . . . Will he leave at eleven-thirty again, on our last day? Well, he has to go there anyway to pick up his things." While eating lunch, she had mentally rehearsed some possible farewells at her apartment: "I guess you'll be busy with school again pretty soon," or "Are you moving into a dorm?"

Yun-ja was worried about giving Chŏng-il the impression that she was making a play for him. At times she had wanted to hand Chŏng-il a fresh towel or some lotion when he returned sopping wet from the shower down the hall, but she would end up simply ignoring him.

Yun-ja thought about the past two months. Each night after dinner at her apartment Chŏng-il would remain at the table and read a book or newspaper. At eleven-thirty he would leave to spend the night with a friend who lived two blocks away. Chŏng-il had been told by his lawyer that a person ordered out of the country who then got married and applied for a permanent resident card could expect to be investigated by the Immigration and Naturalization Service. And so he and Yun-ja had tried to look like a married couple. This meant that Chŏng-il had to be seen with Yun-ja. He would stay as late as he could at her apartment, and he kept a pair of pajamas, some old shoes, and other belongings there.

Tick, tick, tick. . . . Yun-ja would sit knitting or listening to a record, while Chŏng-il read a book or wrote a letter. Pretending to be absorbed in whatever they were doing, both would keep stealing glances at their watches. . . . Tick, tick, tick. . . .

At eleven-thirty Chŏng-il would strap on his watch and get up. Jingling his keys, he would mumble "Good night" or "I'm going." Yun-ja would remain where she was and pretend to be preoccupied until his lanky, boyish figure had disappeared out the door.

It hadn't always been that way. During the first few days after their marriage they would exchange news of Korea or talk about life in America – U.S. immigration policy, the high prices, the unemployment, or whatever. And when Chŏng-il left, Yun-ja would see him to the door. The silent evenings had begun the night she had suggested they live together. That night Chŏng-il had brought some beer and they had sung some children's ditties, popular tunes, and other songs they both knew. The people in the next apartment had pounded on the wall in protest. Chŏng-il and Yun-ja had lowered their voices, but only temporarily. It was while Chŏng-il was bringing tears of laughter to Yun-ja, as he sang and clowned around, that she had broached the subject: Why did Chŏng-il want to leave right at eleven-thirty every night only to sleep at a friend's apartment where he wasn't really welcome? He could just as easily curl up in a corner of her apartment at night and the two of them could live together like a big sister and her little brother – now wouldn't that be great? Immediately Chŏng-il's face had hardened and Yun-ja had realized her blunder. That was the last time Chŏng-il had brought beer to the apartment. The lengthy conversations had stopped and Chŏng-il no longer entertained Yun-ja with songs.

Yun-ja had begun to feel resentful as Chŏng-il rose and left like clockwork each night. "Afraid I'm going to bite, you little stinker!" she would think, pouting at the sound of the key turning in the door. "It's a tug-of-war. You want to keep on my good side, so you sneak looks at me to see how I'm feeling. You're scared I might call off the marriage. It's true, isn't it – if I said I didn't want to go through with it, what would you do? Where would you find another unmarried woman with a green card? Would you run off to another state? Fat chance!"

The evening following her ill-advised proposal to live together, Yun-ja had left her apartment around the time Chŏng-il was to arrive. She didn't want him to think she was sitting around the apartment waiting for him. She walked to a nearby playground that she had never visited before and watched a couple of Asian children playing with some other children. She wondered if being gone when Chŏng-il arrived would make things even more awkward between them. She wanted to return and tell him that her suggestion the previous evening had had no hidden meaning. Yun-ja had no desire to become emotionally involved with Chŏng-il. This was not so much because of their thirteen-year age difference (though Yun-ja still wasn't used to the idea that she was forty), but because Yun-ja had no illusions about marriage.

The man Yun-ja had married upon graduating from college had done well in business, and around the time of their divorce seven years later he had become a wealthy man, with a car and the finest house in Seoul's Hwagok neighborhood.

"Let's get a divorce; you can have the house," he had said one day.

Yun-ja was terribly shocked.

"But why?. . . Is there another woman?"

"No, it's not that. I just don't think I'm cut out for marriage."

In desperation Yun-ja had suggested a trial separation. But her husband had insisted on the divorce, and one day he left, taking only a toiletry kit and some clothes. Yun-ja had wept for days afterward. She was convinced that another woman had come on the scene, and sometimes she secretly kept an eye on her husband's office on T'oegye Avenue to try to confirm this.

"Was there really no other woman?" she asked herself at the playground. "Did he want the divorce because he was tired of living with me?" Their only baby had been placed in an incubator at birth, but the sickly child had died. Being a first-time mother had overwhelmed Yun-ja. "Maybe he just got sick and tired of everything. Or maybe he just wanted to stop living with me and go somewhere far away – that's how I felt toward him when he stayed out late." She had heard recently that he had remarried.

"Are you Korean?"

Yun-ja looked up to see a withered old Korean woman whose hair was drawn into a bun the size of a walnut. Yun-ja was delighted to see another Korean, though she couldn't help feeling conspicuous because of the older woman's traditional Korean clothing, which was made of fine nylon gauze.

Before Yun-ja could answer, the woman plopped herself down and drew a crimson pack of cigarettes from the pocket of her bloomers.

"Care for one, miss?"

"No, thank you."

The old woman lit a cigarette and began talking as if she were ripe for a quarrel: "Ah me, this city isn't fit for people to live in. It's a place for animals, that's what. In Korea I had a nice warm room with a laminated floor, but here no one takes their shoes off and the floors are all messy."

"Can't you go back to Korea?"

"Are you kidding? Those darn sons of mine won't let me. I have to babysit their kids all day long. Whenever I see a plane I start crying – I tell you! To think that I flew over here on one of those damned things!"

The old woman's eyes were inflamed, as if she cried every day, and now fresh tears gathered. Yun-ja looked up and watched the plane they had spotted. It had taken off from the nearby airport and seemed to float just above them as it climbed into the sky. Its crimson and emerald green landing lights winked.

"I don't miss my hometown the way this grandmother does. And I don't feel like crying at the sight of that plane," thought Yun-ja. Her homeland was the source of her shame. She had had to get away from it – there was no other way.

It was around seven when Yun-ja returned from the playground.

Chŏng-il opened the door. "Did you go somewhere?" he asked politely, like a schoolboy addressing his teacher.

Yun-ja was relieved to have been spoken to first.

"I was talking with an elderly Korean woman."

"The one who goes around in Korean clothes? Was she telling you how bad it is here in America?"

"You know her?"

"Oh, she's notorious – latches on to every Korean she sees."

This ordinary beginning to the evening would eventually yield to a silent standoff, taut like the rope in a tug-of-war.

Chŏng-il's joking reference to "marriage" the evening he had offered to take Yun-ja to the beach had come easily because his immigration papers had finally been processed. All he had to do was see his lawyer and sign them, and he would get his permanent resident card.

Though it was six o'clock, it was still bright as midday. It was a muggy August evening, and the small fan in the wall next to the window stuttered, as if it were panting in the heat of Yun-ja's top-floor apartment.

Realizing that Chŏng-il was only joking, Yun-ja stopped knitting. She got up and put a record on. The reedy sound of a man's mellow voice unwound from the cheap stereo:

> *Now that we're about to part*
> *Take my hand once again. . . .*

Yun-ja abruptly turned off the stereo. "Listening to songs makes me feel even hotter," she said.

Several days later, after Chŏng-il had obtained his permanent resident card, he borrowed a car and took Yun-ja to the beach, as promised. Yun-ja had thought it a kind of token of his gratitude, like the flowers or wine you give to the doctor who delivered your baby, or a memento you give to your teacher at graduation.

They stayed late at the beach to avoid the Friday afternoon rush hour. As the day turned to evening, the breeze became chilly and the two of them stayed out of the water, sitting together on the cool sand. Whether it was because they were outside or because this was their last day together, Yun-ja somehow felt that the tug-of-war between them had eased. But the parting words a couple might have said to each other were missing: "Give me a call or drop me a line and let me know how things are going." Chŏng-il did most of the talking, and Yun-ja found his small talk refreshing. He told her about getting measles at age nine, practicing martial arts in college, and going around Seoul in the dog days of summer just to get a driver's license so he could work while going to school in America. And he talked about a book he'd read, entitled *Papillon*.

"If you have Papillon's will, the sky's the limit on what you can do in America. You've heard Koreans when they get together here. They're always talking about the Chinese. The first-generation Chinese saved a few pennies doing unskilled labor when the subways were built. The second generation opened up small laundries or noodle stands. Buying houses and educating the kids didn't happen until the third generation. Whenever I hear that, I realize that Koreans want to do everything in a hurry—I'm the same way. They sound like they want to accomplish in a couple of years what it took the Chinese three generations to do. . . . When I left Korea I told my friends and my big brother not to feel bad if I didn't write, because I might not be able to afford the postage. My brother bought me an expensive fountain pen and told me that if I went hungry in the States I should sell it and buy myself a meal. And then my older sister had a gold ring made for me. I put the damned thing on my finger, got myself decked out in a suit for the plane ride, and then on the way over I was so excited I couldn't eat a thing – not a thing. The stewardess was probably saying to herself, 'Here's a guy who's never been on a plane before.' That damned ring – I must have looked like a jerk!"

Yun-ja related a few details about the elderly Korean woman she had met in the park. (Why did her thoughts return so often to this grandmother?) Then she told Chŏng-il a little about herself, realizing he had probably already learned through Kiyŏng's mother that she was just another divorcée with no one to turn to.

The cool wind picked up as the sunlight faded, and they put their clothes on over their swimsuits. Chŏng-il's shirt was inside out, and Yun-ja could read the brand name on the neck tag.

"Your shirt's inside out."

Chŏng-il roughly pulled the shirt off and put it on right side out. Her steady gaze seemed to annoy him.

The beach was deserted except for a few small groups and some young couples lying on the sand nearby, exchanging affections. Hundreds of sea gulls began to gather. The birds frightened Yun-ja. Their wings looked ragged; their sharp, ceaselessly moving eyes seemed treacherous. Yun-ja felt as if their pointed beaks were about to bore into her eyes, maybe even her heart. She folded the towel she had been sitting on and stood up.

"Let's get going."

More gulls had alighted on the nearly empty parking lot, which stretched out as big as a football field.

"Want to get a closer look?" Chŏng-il asked as he started the car.

"They'll fly away."

"Not if we go slow. God, there must be thousands of them."

The car glided in a slow circle around the sea gulls. Just as Chŏng-il had said, the birds stayed where they were. Yun-ja watched them through the window, her fear now gone.

They pulled out onto the highway and the beach grew distant. A grand sunset flared up in the dark blue sky. The outline of distant hills and trees swung behind the car and gradually disappeared. Yun-ja noticed that Chŏng-il had turned on the headlights.

"You must be beat," Chŏng-il said. "Why don't you lean back and make yourself comfortable."

Perhaps because he was silent for a time, Yun-ja somehow felt his firm, quiet manner in the smooth, steady motion of the car. She wondered what to do when they arrived at her apartment. Invite him in? Arrange to meet him somewhere the following day to give him his things? But the second idea would involve seeing him again. . . . The tide hadn't been low, so they hadn't been able to dig clams. . . . "I'll bet I've looked like a nobody to him, a woman who's hungry for love and money." Yun-ja recalled something Chŏng-il had once told her: "After I get my degree here, write a couple of books, and make a name for myself, I'd like to go back to Korea. Right now there are too many Ph.D.'s over there. I know I wouldn't find a job if I went back with just a degree."

"And for the rest of your life," Yun-ja now thought, "I'll be a cheap object for you to gossip about. You'll say, 'I was helpless when they told me to leave the country – so I bought myself a wife who was practically old enough to be my mother. What a pain in the neck – especially when she came up with the idea of living together.' And at some point in the future when you propose to your sweetheart, maybe you'll blabber something like 'I have a confession to make – I've been married before. . . . '"

Chŏng-il drove on silently. His hand on the steering wheel was fine and delicate – a student's hand. Yun-ja felt like yanking that hand, biting it, anything to make him see things her way, to make him always speak respectfully of her in the future.

Chǒng-il felt Yun-ja's gaze and stole a glance at her. The small face that had been angled toward his was now looking straight ahead. "She's no beauty—maybe it's that thin body of hers that makes her look kind of shriveled up—but sometimes she's really pretty. Especially when it's hot. Then that honey-colored skin of hers gets a nice shine to it and her eyelashes look even darker." But Chǒng-il had rarely felt comfortable enough to examine Yun-ja's face.

"Mrs. Lee, did you ever have any children?"

"One—it died."

Chǒng-il lit a cigarette. Her toneless voice rang in his ears. "She doesn't seem to have any feelings. No expression, no interest in others, it even sounds as if her baby's death means nothing to her. True—time has a way of easing the pain. I don't show any emotion either when I tell people that my father died when I was young and my mother passed away when I was in college. Probably it's the same with her. But her own baby? How can she say 'It died' just like that?"

He had known from the beginning, through Ki-yǒng's mother, that Yun-ja was a single woman with no money. It had never occurred to him when he paid Ki-yǒng's mother the first installment of the fifteen hundred dollars that a woman with such a common name as Yun-ja might have special qualities. What had he expected her to be like, this woman who was to become his wife in name only? Well, a woman who had led a hard life, but who would vaguely resemble Ki-yǒng's mother—short permed hair, a calf-length sack dress, white sandals—a woman in her forties who didn't look completely at ease in Western-style clothing. But the woman Ki-yǒng's father had taken him to meet at the bus stop was thin and petite with short, straight hair and a sleeveless dress. Her eyelids had a deep double fold, and her skin had a dusky sheen that reminded Chǒng-il of Southeast Asian women. She was holding a pair of sunglasses, and a large handbag hung from her long, slender arm.

As they walked the short distance to Ki-yǒng's mother's for

dinner that first night, Chŏng-il had felt pity for this woman who didn't even come up to his shoulders. He had also felt guilty and ill at ease. But Yun-ja had spoken nonchalantly: "So you're a student? Well, I just found an apartment yesterday. I'll be moving in three days from now. We can go over a little later and I'll show you around. It's really small—kitchen, bathroom, living room, and bedroom all in one." To Chŏng-il this breezy woman of forty or so acted like an eighteen-year-old girl. "This woman's marrying me for money." He felt regretful, as if he were buying an aging prostitute.

"Why don't you two forget about the business part of it and get married for real?" Ki-yŏng's mother had said at dinner. And when she sang a playful rendition of the wedding march, Chŏng-il had felt like crawling under the table. Yun-ja had merely laughed.

The traffic between the beach and the city was heavy, occasionally coming to a standstill. Among the procession of vehicles Yun-ja and Chŏng-il noticed cars towing boats, cars carrying bicycles, cars with tents and shovels strapped to their roof racks.

As Chŏng-il drove by shops that had closed for the day, he thought of all the time he had spent on the phone with his older brother in Korea, of all the hard-earned money he had managed to scrounge from him (did his sister-in-law know about that?)—all because of this permanent resident card. And now he couldn't even afford tuition for next semester. These thoughts depressed him. But then he bucked up: Now that he had his green card (his chest swelled at the idea), there was no reason he couldn't work. "I'll take next semester off, put my nose to the grindstone, and by the following semester I'll have my tuition." And now that he was a permanent resident, his tuition would be cut in half. He made some mental calculations: How much could he save by cutting his rent and food to the bone? "But you can't cut down on the food too much," Chŏng-il reminded himself. There were students who had ended up sick and run-down, who couldn't study or do other things as a result. "This woman Yun-ja really has it easy – doesn't have to study. All she has to do is eat and sleep, day after day." Chŏng-il felt it was disgraceful that a young, intelligent Korean such as himself was living unproductively in America, as if he had no responsibilities to his family or country. "Why am I busting my butt to be here? Is the education really that wonderful?" In English class back in Korea he had vaguely dreamed of studying in America. Or rather he had liked the idea of hearing people say he had studied there. More shameful than this was the impulse he had to stay on in America. "What about the other people from abroad who live in the States – do they feel guilty about their feelings for their country, too?" He had read diatribes about America's corrupt material civilization. But he couldn't figure out what was so corrupt about it, and that bothered him. He wanted to see just what a young Korean man could accomplish in the world, and he wanted to experience the anger of frustration rather than the calm of complacency. He wanted knowledge, and recognition from others. But this woman Yun-ja didn't even seem to realize she was Korean.

The car pulled up on a street of six-story apartment buildings whose bricks were fading. Children were running and bicycling on the cement sidewalk; elderly couples strolled hand in hand, taking in the evening. Chŏng-il got out, unpacked the cooler and the towels, and loaded them on his shoulder. He and Yun-ja had the elevator to themselves. Yun-ja felt anxious and lonely, as if she had entered an unfamiliar neighborhood at dusk. She braced herself against the side of the elevator as it accelerated and slowed. When she was young it seemed the world belonged to her, but as time went on these "belongings" had disappeared; now she felt as if she had nothing. When it came time to part from someone, her heart ached as if she were separating from a lover. "Am I so dependent on people that I drove my husband away? Nobody wants to be burdened with me, so they all leave – even my baby. . . . I wonder if that old woman at the playground went back to Korea. Maybe she's still smoking American cigarettes and bending the ear of every Korean she sees here. Maybe I'll end up like her when I'm old. Already my body feels like a dead weight because of my neuralgia – God forbid that I latch on to just anybody and start telling a sob story."

Yun-ja unlocked the door to the apartment and turned on the light.

Today the small, perfectly square room looked cozy and intimate to them. They smelled the familiar odors, which had been intensified by the summer heat.

But Chŏng-il felt awkward when he saw that Yun-ja had packed his trunk and set it on the sofa. If only he could unpack it and return the belongings to their places.

"You must feel pretty sticky – why don't you take a shower?" Yun-ja said.

Chŏng-il returned from washing his salt-encrusted body to find Yun-ja cleaning the sand from the doorway. She had changed to a familiar, well-worn yellow dress. The cooler had been emptied and cleaned, the towels put away. Yun-ja had shampooed, and comb marks were still visible in her wet hair. Chŏng-il tried to think of something to say, gave up, and tiptoed to the sofa to sit down. "She's already washed her hair, changed, and started sweeping up," he thought. As Yun-ja bustled about, she looked to Chŏng-il as if she had just blossomed.

"Shouldn't I offer him some dinner?" Yun-ja thought as she swept up the sand. "He went to the trouble of borrowing a car and taking me out – the least I can do is give him a nice meal. And where would he eat if he left now? He'd probably fill up on junk food. . . . But if I offer to feed him, he might think I had something in mind. And when I've paid people for something, they never offered me dinner, did they?"

"How about some music?" Chŏng-il mumbled. He got up, walked stiffly to the stereo, and placed the needle on the record that happened to be on the turntable. The rhythm of a Flamenco guitar filled the room. Although Chŏng-il didn't pay much attention to the music Yun-ja played, it seemed that this was a new record. "Why have I been afraid of this woman? You'd think she was a witch or something."

"If that woman sinks her hooks into you, you've had it." Chŏng-il had heard this from his roommate, Ki-yŏng's father, and goodness knows how many others. "Nothing happened again today?" the roommate would joke when Chŏng-il returned in the evening from Yun-ja's apartment. "When it comes to you-know-what, nothing beats a middle-aged woman. I hope you're offering good service in return for those tasty meals you're getting."

The shrill voices of the children and the noise of airplanes and traffic were drowned out by the guitar music. The odor of something rotten outside wafted in with the heat of the summer night.

Chŏng-il began to feel ashamed. Here he was about to run out on this woman he'd used in return for a measly sum of money – a woman whose life he had touched. He had visited this room for almost two months, and now he wished he could spend that time over again. "Why didn't I try to make it more enjoyable?" he asked himself. He and Yun-ja had rarely listened to music, and when they had gone strolling in the nearby park after dinner he had felt uneasy, knowing that they did this only so that others would see the two of them together.

Yun-ja finished sweeping the sand up and sat down at the round dinner table. "If you're hungry, why don't you help yourself to some leftovers from yesterday's dinner? There's some lettuce and soybean paste and a little rice too."

Yun-ja's hair had dried, and a couple of strands of it drooped over her forehead. She looked pretty to Chŏng-il.

"And some marinated peppers," she continued.

Chŏng-il's body stiffened. This offer of dinner was a signal that it was time for him to leave. He rose and fumbled for something appropriate to say about the past two months. The blood rushed to his head and his face burned. Finally he blurted out, "What would you say if I . . . proposed to you?" Then he flung open the door as if he were being chased out. In his haste to leave he sent one of Yun-ja's sandals flying from the doorway toward the gas range. The door slammed shut behind him.

Yun-ja sprang up from the table. "What did he say?" Her body prickled, as if she were yielding to a long-suppressed urge to urinate. "I don't believe in marriage," she told herself. "Not after what I went through." She rushed to the door and looked through the peephole into the hall. She saw Chŏng-il jab futilely at the elevator button and then run toward the stairway.

"The boy proposed to me – I should be thankful," Yun-ja thought. Like water reviving a dying tree, hot blood began to buzz through her sleepy veins. This long-forgotten sensation of warmth made her think that maybe their relationship had been pointing in this direction all along. "It was fun prettying myself up the day I met him. And before that, didn't I expect some good times with him even though we weren't really married?"

Yun-ja turned and looked around the room. There was Chŏng-il's trunk on the sofa. "But he'd end up leaving me too." Suddenly she felt very vulnerable. Everything about her, starting with her age and the divorce, and then all the little imperfections – the wrinkles around the eyes, the occasional drooling in her sleep – reared up in her mind. "But I'm not going to let my shortcomings get me down," she reassured herself. "It's time to make a stand."

EKONESKAKA

✳

Chicapoo Juice

I WAS STANDING with Chago Maestas. Don't ask me what we were doing. The sun was warm. The air was bright. We had nothing to do but have a smoke and stand there. Maybe it was my chemotherapy day. I had cancer then, and I still do, so maybe we were just waiting around for my doctor's appointment so I could get that shot they like to stab in the vein of my hand. I wouldn't get far after a shot like that. I'd be knocked down for a week with the chemotherapy pulsing through my blood like a drum that has no war to go to.

We could have been waiting around for our class to begin. I mean believe this if you like, we were students then, two forty-year-old guys taking college classes with a bunch of teenagers, lots of teenagers and two old goats, that was us. And so you can imagine how we spent so much time just looking around. A pretty girl would walk by and I'd say, "Somebody did it right." Maestas usually had a good answer like, "Sure, why don't you bring that home to your wife."

I would have liked to bring that home, but not to my wife. I could imagine that pretty girl getting out of her clothes. I'd help her. I could see her lying down on the sofa with her underwear falling soft around her knees, falling soft like storm clouds falling soft around a mountain, and real quiet, and we'd take our time, just suffering.

We'd take a lot of time just suffering with our hands, and my mind would go off running to the days of wild horses blazing across the purple hills, blazing and suffering and suffering and blazing like there was no tomorrow, and there's not, is there? And I couldn't call my mind back because each time I opened my mouth I found that pretty girl's mouth right next to mine. I'd find her legs too, and just about all the different parts of her body kept me from using my mouth to call that wild horse home. So I let it go. You know how.

I wonder why it has to be like that. Why does Kitziata make me see all those pretty girls? Why does he like to play with me and why does he like to see me suffering? And *hombre*, why does he like to see you suffering too? Oh *sí*, and those pretty girls, why do they have to suffer also? *Sí hombre, sí*, everybody's got to be suffering, and that's the truth, but why?

I'd start to get that tingling feeling, you know, and then instead of feeling anything good my hand would touch those crawling plastic tubes from my cancer operation. Those tubes, they were deadly cold, and then in just one second I'd forget that pretty girl because no matter how lucky I could be with any girl I could never do what I wanted to do because my cancer operation left me standing there, just looking dumb. There were so many plastic tubes sticking through my guts. There was a plastic bag of urine riding just below my belt, hidden by the long tail of my shirt.

Who cared if we were going to be late for whatever we had to be on time for. We always came in a little late, somehow we always did, and it was like our style, the thing we had to do, or everyone would have gotten all excited and called up General Custer or something. Just the same we started to get ourselves moving, and I tossed my cigarette onto the sidewalk.

"Hey spic, pick it up." I felt those words burn into my face before I saw who said them. Standing there like the Holy Trinity Itself was Mister *Gabacho*, Mister Gringo, Mister *Huale* all rolled up into one sweet package, One Great Big White Padre, all standing straight as a spindle, and truly this one, he looked about forty years old, like me, like my age, and he had pale hair and stark gray eyes like the eyes of a falcon's ghost.

Maestas was all ready to jump him, but I calmed him down by catching his eye, and he knew right away that this little business was going to be all my business. I didn't have to tell Mister *Gabacho* I wasn't Mexicano. Maybe I am, maybe I'm not, but this one thing is sure, I am a full-blood Kickapoo warrior, I am a pure-blood Kickapoo Indio, but I was born in Mexico, and I speak the language of Mexico second only to my own language, the language of my people, the Me-thu-de-ne-nia, the Ki-ki-ka-pa-wa, and so Mexico is like a second mother to me, and sometimes my Mexico is a good mother and sometimes she is also a wild mother, but my home that I built with my own two hands is right there, *en Mejico*.

So, you see, sometimes I just don't know. I have two names. My Kickapoo name is Ekoneskaka, but my Mexican name is the way most people know me here. That name is Aurelio. Aurelio Valdez Garcia. That's what most people call me around here in Colorado, except for my wife, Marisol, Marysue, because she's Kickapoo and she calls me something else. Yeah, she calls me a lot of things. And my daughter, Eurika, she calls me Daddy. But usually I like to keep the fact secret that I'm a Kickapoo Indio. It's just easier if most people think I'm Mexicano.

Then I don't have to be explaining so much, like they always ask me, "Hey, what does your name mean?"

"It's a name. It's my name, Ekoneskaka. What does your name mean?"

That's how I answer them, and it works. They keep real quiet.

I mean nobody's ever heard of the Kickapoo Indios as a real live people. We're secret. We're unknown. We're quiet. We are. We are a true people, and nobody knows anything about us, and that is how we alone have escaped to remain true to our sacred duty.

Now *hombre, hombrecito*, here is the big problem I was facing that day as I was standing with Chago Maestas. They say I am a sure Mexicano. My great grandpa and a whole bunch of Kickapoos were warriors for the famous Pancho Villa back in the old days. We owned that *frontera* and you better believe we still count it as ours. They say I am also a sure Chicano, whatever that may be. I don't know, but I am one. Or maybe I'm pure blood Chicapoo Juice, and I'm dark-skinned too; bronze-skinned, truly, and to Mister Gabacho that was all that mattered.

"Dirty spic, pick it up." That's what he said to me all right, and he kept saying it, and then he turned, but before he turned he walked back toward me and he spat. He spat right at my feet and when his juice hit the pavement it sounded like glass cracking when it gets too hot. I kept thinking of Mork, you know, the Mork on television, the one who comes from a planet where spitting is kind of a compliment. It means, "Yeah, I like that." But what I got back then was no kind of compliment. I could smell the blood rushing up that white man's throat. Even though he didn't know me, or know anything about me or my people, I could feel the blood rushing out of him like the torn-loose wire from an electric fence.

Maybe it was just that feeling that gave me what I needed. I walked two steps after him and I kicked. The sharp toe of my boot hit him square in the crack of his ass. He didn't turn around. He just stopped like somebody smashed a pie in his face, so I kicked him again.

When he did turn around, Christ, he was really scared. And like I say, I had cancer then and there was a plastic bag hooked onto me and plastic tubes crawling through my guts. I had to be really careful, but then a circle of students who were just standing around folded in to cover just the two of us, like the song says, just me and Mister *Gabacho*, and that circle became like a wall that I couldn't see over or through, a wall with broken glass along the top so I couldn't crawl out and escape.

Chago Maestas was talking to me real fast. "You're wearing that operation, *hombre*. You could die right here. *Basta ya!*

Enough is enough. Let it go. *Mucho gusto,* right?"

But by then I was ready to kick again, and I didn't miss either. I caught him square in the *huevos* and he doubled over and I kicked him in the face and he struck the ground with one more kick for a blanket. I was ready to kick the living shit out of him, starting with his brains, but Maestas grabbed me with his forearm real tight around my throat and dragged me out of there so fast I don't even remember crossing the street. "Why'd you do it, *hombre?*" he said. "You're not Mexicano, why you?"

I was sitting with Chago Maestas, drinking coffee, and if you'd have asked me I'd have said I was feeling pretty calm, too calm, *sabes? Bien tranquilo, y todo eso.* Chago's question was always, "Hey, why you?" I didn't even know "why me?" I wasn't sure and I kept thinking and I lost my calm and I kept scratching that place on my leg, just above my boot top, that place where I was getting real sure the cancer was working into my skin, working all through me and filling my whole body with poison.

Maybe I'd hurt that Mister *Gabacho.* Maybe I had, but I just sat there. Then I thought I heard something like a buzzing in my head, and then a voice. I heard my great grandpa's voice, the one I told you about, the one who was fighting on the side of Pancho Villa back in the old days. It was his *voz* all right, *claro con claro,* and I just closed my eyes to listen.

> *Sa-sa-ke*
> *sing water*
> *sing wish*
> *water moon*
> *yellow wish*
> *water moon*
>
> *open bird*
> *open sun*
> *open bird*
> *sun songs*

It was spring in your village and still you were going to school. The bus driver would stop for the gate and you would jump down to open it for him. Sometimes you would trick him. You would throw open the gate and then you would run down the road away from your bus and away from your school all the way home to the village.

Back there you had you a game. You played by yourself because nobody knew you were there. You would take a plastic bag from Aunt Kika's house and steal away to the trees all around the village. You would climb the trees and look at the little birds in their nests and then you would put the baby birds in your bag. Sometimes you would collect dozens of baby birds in one day.

Then you were taking the birds down to the road. You were waiting until you heard the school bus coming and then you were dumping the birds in front of the tires and running away.

> *open bird*
> *open sun*
> *open bird*
> *sun songs*

Someone had left their saddle on the bridge and you threw it into the quickmud and you watched it sink. You saw the quickmud was pretty strong, but you still went down under the bridge and dug around on your hands and knees and found dozens of turtle eggs in the warm sandy bank. They were round and soft like warm tortillas and you tore some open and played with their yolks in the soft grainy edges of the mud.

You tossed them all in the quickmud, but they bubbled on top and didn't sink. They were too light, so you threw some heavy sticks on top of them, and you threw rocks at them too until they were all sucked down.

This took you all day and then it was night and you were walking home.

> *Sa-sa-ke*
> *sing water*
> *sing wish*
> *water moon*
> *yellow wish*
> *water moon*

I like feathers and I like shells. Maybe because you did those things you have this bad luck today. I make this song to tell the birds that you like feathers too. I make this song to tell the turtles that you also like shells.

> open bird
> open sun
> open bird
> sun songs

I make this song because your body is falling apart. When you die the pieces will be searching for you. Your intestine is looking for you now. Your stomach is looking for you. Maybe the turtle makes a home in your stomach. Maybe the bird eats your intestine. I can see the bird. It's flying by the moon. It's flying by the sun. It has your intestine hanging from its beak, trailing behind it, trailing a long way over the trees and river and through the sun and around the horns of the moon. I can see it there, trailing a long way, touching the mud of the turtle. The turtle has many intestines in its mouth. It wants to eat. The turtle and the bird are eating your intestine. The turtle is digging around in your stomach. The turtle buries her eggs in the mud of your stomach. We like feathers. We like shells. We want the turtle and the bird to bring you the pieces of your body.

> say
> say a sun
> open soft
> grainy edges
> of the sun
> of the mud
>
> say
> say a moon
> open soft
> water tree
> of the moon
> in a shell
>
> Sa-sa-ke
> sing water

sing wish
water moon
yellow wish
water moon

open bird
open sun
open bird
sun songs

"Hey man, you acting kinda strange. You better come on back inside and drink up the *café*, you know?"

I guess I'd walked out the door. I didn't know that Chago had followed me, but there he was, standing right next to me, looking dumb.

"Hey *hombre*, don't just get up and run like I'm the *policía*. Don't just leave me sitting there, and when you gotta leave someplace, how come you forget to pay? That waitress, you know, the one you like, she wants a little silver, *hombre, pura plata*."

I just looked at him a minute, feeling funny, then I looked back toward a van as it curved downhill.

"Oh yeah, *hombre*. Really neat. I like that van too. But hey, come on, let's go back inside, drink *café*, make everybody and everything *tranquilo*."

"Hey Chago," I finally said, "You know what!"

"*Qué?*"

"I'm interested in that van, *hombre*, I really am."

"Yeah, I know. That's cool. That's real slick."

"You know what?"

"What the fuck?"

"I heard me some *voces en mi cabeza*."

"Yeah, sure *hombre*. Fuckin-A."

"No kidding, *hombre*, it was my great *granpacito*, but his *voz* faded off real fast and then another *voz* was just starting to scream in my head like a white tornado."

"Jeezus Cristos' nails, let's get our fuckin' asses off this fuckin' street, *sabes?* Fuckin' *policía* might come around here fuckin' lookin' for you! Maybe you just castrated that *gabacho* mother, you know? *Fuímanos!*"

But I just stood there looking out at the street, following with my eyes the place where I'd seen the van had disappeared. And I wanted to keep talking.

"You know what, Chago, I think maybe that second *voz* I heard come straight from that cherry van."

"Oh yeah, sure *hombre, seguro,* like you maybe got a fuckin' C.B. right inside your fuckin' brain? You crazier than shit."

"*Sí,* I think you're right. I agree. I'm real crazy. I'm Chicapoo Juice."

"What kinda goddamn shit you talking about?"

"*Sí,* I maybe do have a brand new C.B. in my brain, and what I'm pickin' up must be comin' from right inside that cherry van."

Hey Tonto, como estás? This is your ol' good buddy, El Lone Rangerino. How's the wife and kid? How's the stealing and robbing and killing? How's the taste of human flesh? How's the blond tresses swaying from your war belt?

They tell me to feel my conscience because I have treated thee, Poor Tonto, in a barbarous manner, but I've seen one thing they haven't seen. I've seen a wild Indio. I've seen my whole family broken and butchered by wild Indios. I've seen my own little children carried away by wild Indios and brought up to believe that robbery was meritorious, that cold-blooded murder was a praiseworthy act.

I've had my own dear and rugged limbs beaten and bruised and burnt with fiendish ingenuity by yet gentle savages. My own scalp was ruthlessly torn from my head. And I am one of the few to survive such an operation, so I can personally tell you, Poor Tonto, ye gentle savage, that my naked brain was subject to the wind and weather, but before I sealed it up tight once again with polyurethane crystal I installed herein a super-duper power pack C.B. transmitter to which end I am hereby torturing you with the power of my righteous megawatts. And Tonto, no doubt ye wonder how that C.B. receive was so secretly installed inside your brain. I was right there in the operating room when they put you under the knife. I personally wired you from the guts up, señor, so happy trails.

"Hey man, you really crazy. You Chicapoo Juice all right, but what the fuck?"

There was Chago, standing right next to me again, looking dumb. I guess I hadn't gone so far. I was down a few blocks, that's all. I just didn't remember how I got there or how long I'd been there or what I'd been doing. We turned around and started walking back to the coffee shop. I was rubbing my head, looking kind of dumb myself.

"Yeah man, what happenin'? You look like you just got mauled by a pretty *señorita, qué no?* You doin' okay, *hombre?*" I couldn't answer right. I was still buzzing on some C.B. frequency I didn't even want to hear, and Chago's voice rolled under like a soft wind. It felt good. I know it's hard to believe that Chago's voice could ever sound good. Usually it sounded like he was chewing shit, you know, but now, somehow, it sounded okay. I couldn't answer, though, because I kept listening for my great *granpacito's voz.* I kept wondering if he'd come back and explain what the hell was going on. I wanted to hear from him and I wanted to pay him my respects. I didn't believe this was happening to me. I didn't believe one word of it, and I still don't.

Jesus Christ, *hombre,* what was I doing there?

I guess I was up by a university because I was a student. It's hard to believe, I know. Why is anyone a student? Don't ask me. I was the first one of my people to ever get through high school. Maybe I was a student because there was a chance for me to help my people, if they wanted my help. I was pretty sure they didn't.

I was a student because for a short time there was plenty of grant money and those whites needed a few of us around to make them look good. But I knew I didn't belong there. It was really hard to say where I belonged. I was partly educated along the white man's way, but because of this my own people didn't trust me.

Maybe I was going to a university just to see what would happen. Sure, yeah *hombre,* that's why. *Seguro.* So there I was, standing where I didn't belong, which could have been anywhere, waiting, I guess, for something to happen.

That same bright red cherry sports van with chrome mag wheels cruised by me again real fast. That *voz* shouted in my brain, "Hey you, dirty spic, get off the street!" I knew I was getting pretty crazy when I started to believe that. Sure, I'd been in the hospital. I'd had an operation on my cancer, but that was in my guts, not in my head. Nobody put a damn C.B. in my head.

"Hey spic, dirty spic, what'd you steal today?" I kept hearing it. I watched the van turn west and I started walking west too. I never expected to see it again, but just in case the van made a turn I could maybe get a good bead on the driver. I'd ask him his name. I really wanted to find out.

After walking four blocks I saw the van again. It had turned and the driver was parking on the slope of a street lined with big trees and houses, and he got out and started walking like he had somewhere to go. I was surprised when I got a good look at him. He was a paleface all right, but it was pretty funny because he looked exactly like the other *gabacho* I'd almost killed that day, like he was his twin brother. I waited for him where he couldn't see me.

I just wanted to ask him who he was. I didn't want any trouble, *hombre,* I swear I didn't, but I was pretty confused, you know, and I think maybe also I just wanted to scare him a little. When he got about one foot from where I was hiding I just stepped out and greeted him face to face. "*Ay, buenas tardes, señor,*" I said, and he just stopped walking like he had somewhere to go.

I smelled something funny then, like Mister *Gabacho* had built himself a fire in his pants. It made me want to back off. Wouldn't you? But then all of a sudden he turned and ran, and for some damn reason I started to run after him. I pursued him. You got to pursue, you always got to pursue, but I had that cancer bag hanging there from my colostomy and just like before, I had to be plenty careful that it didn't get busted.

I grabbed the back of his shirt and it slowed him down and then he made his big goof. I mean if he'd kept running and let his shirt tear then it would have been okay. I would have stopped. I know I would have. I bet you right now, *hombre*, I would have stopped and just stood there holding on to the torn-off piece of his shirt. Maybe I would have waved to him, kind of smiling, you know, or shook my fist, kind of threatening, but I would have let him go. Probably, *hombre*. That would have been enough for me. But he really goofed. He didn't keep running. He turned around fast and caught me in the ear with his fist.

I don't carry a knife, and I don't know why but for some reason I was carrying my pen in my hand like it was a knife, and as he turned around and struck me you better believe I rammed that pen clean into his guts and I felt it pop and glide.

He looked funny. His mouth opened like a hole. He looked down at his belly and that was his second big goof because I kicked him in the chest and he went down hard on his back and there was nobody around to pull me away.

I guess there was pretty much blood on the street. I guess there was. I got him real good, too good, but I don't know why I dragged him over to his van. Maybe I wanted to check out the radio in there. I got the keys to the van out of his pocket and, like I say, he was a real mess. I yanked him up by his hair and threw him back inside that van of his and then I jumped in the driver's seat and drove around for a while, you know, just driving around, playing with the radio, calling up every good buddy I could think of, and listening in on what the *policía* were up to. I was okay. I felt pretty good, you know. Don't ask me why. Crazy, you know? Maybe just crazy.

I'd never had a C.B. that could pick up *policía* before. I learned no one had reported me or called in about the blood all over the street. I was glad it was getting dark. It would be night soon, but I got a little afraid. I thought maybe a friend of this guy would recognize his van and report that something funny was going on. Also, to tell the truth, I was getting a little tired. After the *policía* report there was nothing really interesting coming in on the C.B., and also nobody was really interested in making radio contact with me. But my head was clear; the radio was in my hand and I was in control of it and I sure didn't hear any more C.B. voices in my head.

I drove that pretty van up into the mountains and I was going to leave it there in a parking area. I was just going to leave it there and walk home. I love to walk, even a long way, even at night; I can walk for miles and miles, all day and all night long. But, you know, *hombre:* that van was just too pretty to leave up there for anybody to come along and steal. So I just slipped myself back in and headed for a cliff that I knew had a pretty deep drop. I stopped by the edge of the cliff and waited for a chance when I couldn't see or hear no other vehicles in the area. It was dark. All dark, just like the lights from the city were glowing a deep kind of orange like the throat of a fish. A lot of people were in their houses watching TV and eating their food. That's where I should have been. I kept wishing I was just at home eating *blanquillos* and watching TV.

I shifted that fine pretty van into neutral and got out and gave it a shove. It sort of hurt my colostomy to push so hard but I just kept pushing and sure enough that van rolled right over and off the edge and crashed down on some rocks.

It didn't burn up, and I was kind of glad about that. I'd seen most vehicles burn when they went over cliffs on television, but now I know what it's really like and I can tell you they don't always burn and they don't always make a hell of a lot of noise. This pretty van just went down nose first and then it went over and over and then it just stopped. I learned something that day.

I walked back home because, like I say, I love to walk. I watched the news and I read the paper, but I never heard anything.

I don't know what to think. Maybe it never really happened. Maybe I dreamed it all, just standing with Chago Maestas.

LOUISE ERDRICH

✳

American Horse

THE WOMAN SLEEPING on the cot in the woodshed was Albertine American Horse. The name was left over from her mother's short marriage. The boy was the son of the man she had loved and let go. Buddy was on the cot too, sitting on the edge because he'd been awake three hours watching out for his mother and besides, she took up the whole cot. Her feet hung over the edge, limp and brown as two trout. Her long arms reached out and slapped at things she saw in her dreams.

Buddy had been knocked awake out of hiding in a washing machine while herds of policemen with dogs searched through a large building with many tiny rooms. When the arm came down, Buddy screamed because it had a blue cuff and sharp silver buttons. "Tss," his mother mumbled, half awake, "wasn't nothing." But Buddy sat up after her breathing went deep again, and he watched.

There was something coming and he knew it.

It was coming from very far off but he had a picture of it in his mind. It was a large thing made of metal with many barbed hooks, points, and drag chains on it, something like a giant potato peeler that rolled out of the sky, scraping clouds down with it and jabbing or crushing everything that lay in its path on the ground.

Buddy watched his mother. If he woke her up, she would

know what to do about the thing, but he thought he'd wait until he saw it for sure before he shook her. She was pretty, sleeping, and he liked knowing he could look at her as long and close up as he wanted. He took a strand of her hair and held it in his hands as if it was the rein to a delicate beast. She was strong enough and could pull him along like the horse their name was.

Buddy had his mother's and his grandmother's name because his father had been a big mistake.

"They're all mistakes, even your father. But *you* are the best thing that ever happened to me."

That was what she said when he asked.

Even Kadie, the boyfriend crippled from being in a car wreck, was not as good a thing that had happened to his mother as Buddy was. "He was a medium-sized mistake," she said. "He's hurt and I shouldn't even say that, but it's the truth." At the moment, Buddy knew that being the best thing in his mother's life, he was also the reason they were hiding from the cops.

He wanted to touch the satin roses sewed on her pink tee shirt, but he knew he shouldn't do that even in her sleep. If she woke up and found him touching the roses, she would say, "Quit that, Buddy." Sometimes she told him to stop hugging her like a gorilla. She never said that in the mean voice she used when he oppressed her, but when she said that he loosened up anyway.

There were times he felt like hugging her so hard and in such a special way that she would say to him, "Let's get married." There were also times he closed his eyes and wished that she would die, only a few times, but still it haunted him that his wish might come true. He and Uncle Lawrence would be left alone. Buddy wasn't worried, though, about his mother getting married to somebody else. She had said to her friend, Madonna, "All men suck," when she thought Buddy wasn't listening. He had made an uncertain sound, and when they heard him they took him in their arms.

"Except for you, Buddy," his mother said. "All except for

you and maybe Uncle Lawrence, although he's pushing it."

"The cops suck the worst, though," Buddy whispered to his mother's sleeping face, "because they're after us."He felt tired again, slumped down, and put his legs beneath the blanket. He closed his eyes and got the feeling that the cot was lifting up beneath him, that it was arching its canvas back and then traveling, traveling very fast and in the wrong direction for when he looked up he saw the three of them were advancing to meet the great metal thing with hooks and barbs and all sorts of sharp equipment to catch their bodies and draw their blood. He heard its insides as it rushed toward them, purring softly like a powerful motor and then they were right in its shadow. He pulled the reins as hard as he could and the beast reared, lifting him. His mother clapped her hand across his mouth.

"Okay," she said. "Lay low. They're outside and they're gonna hunt."

She touched his shoulder and Buddy leaned over with her to look through a crack in the boards.

They were out there all right, Albertine saw them. Two officers and that social worker woman. Vicki Koob. There had been no whistle, no dream, no voice to warn her that they were coming. There was only the crunching sound of cinders in the yard, the engine purring, the dust sifting off their car in a fine light brownish cloud and settling around them.

The three people came to a halt in their husk of metal – the car emblazoned with the North Dakota State Highway Patrol emblem which is the glowing profile of the Sioux policeman, Red Tomahawk, the one who killed Sitting Bull. Albertine gave Buddy the blanket and told him that he might have to wrap it around him and hide underneath the cot.

"We're gonna wait and see what they do." She took him in her lap and hunched her arms around him. "Don't you worry," she whispered against his ear. "Lawrence knows how to fool them."

Buddy didn't want to look at the car and the people. He felt his mother's heart beating beneath his ear so fast it seemed to push the satin roses in and out. He put his face to them carefully and breathed the deep, soft powdery woman smell of her. That smell was also in her little face cream bottles, in her brushes, and around the washbowl after she used it. The satin felt so unbearably smooth against his cheek that he had to press closer. She didn't push him away, like he expected, but hugged him still tighter until he felt as close as he had ever been to back inside her again where she said he came from. Within the smells of her things, her soft skin, and the satin of her roses, he closed his eyes then, and took his breaths softly and quickly with her heart.

They were out there, but they didn't dare get out of the car yet because of Lawrence's big, ragged dogs. Three of these dogs had loped up the dirt driveway with the car. They were rangy, alert, and bounced up and down on their cushioned paws like wolves. They didn't waste their energy barking, but positioned themselves quietly, one at either car door and the third in front of the bellied-out screen door to Uncle Lawrence's house. It was six in the morning but the wind was up already, blowing dust, ruffling their short moth-eaten coats. The big brown one on Vicki Koob's side had unusual black and white markings, stripes almost, like a hyena and he grinned at her, tongue out and teeth showing.

"Shoo!" Miss Koob opened her door with a quick jerk.

The brown dog sidestepped the door and jumped before her, tiptoeing. Its dirty white muzzle curled and its eyes crossed suddenly as if it was zeroing its cross-hair sights in on the exact place it would bite her. She ducked back and slammed the door.

"It's mean," she told Officer Brackett. He was printing out some type of form. The other officer, Harmony, a slow man, had not yet reacted to the car's halt. He had been sitting quietly in the back seat, but now he rolled down his window and with no change in expression unsnapped his holster and drew his pistol out and pointed it at the dog on his side. The dog smacked down on its belly, wiggled under the car and was out and around the back of the house before Harmony drew his gun back. The other dogs vanished with him. From wherever they had disappeared to they began to yap and howl, and the door to the low shoebox-style house fell open.

"Heya, what's going on?"

Uncle Lawrence put his head out the door and opened wide the one eye he had in working order. The eye bulged impossibly wider in outrage when he saw the police car. But the eyes of the two officers and Miss Vicki Koob were wide open too because they had never seen Uncle Lawrence in his sleeping get up or, indeed, witnessed anything like it. For his ribs, which were cracked from a bad fall and still mending, Uncle Lawrence wore a thick white corset laced up the front with a striped sneakers' lace. His glass eye and his set of dentures were still out for the night so his face puckered here and there, around its absences and scars, like a damaged but fierce little cake. Although he had a few gray streaks now, Uncle Lawrence's hair was still thick, and because he wore a special contraption of elastic straps around his head every night, two oiled waves always crested on either side of his middle part. All of this would have been sufficient to astonish, even without the most striking part of his outfit – the smoking jacket. It was made of black satin and hung open around his corset, dragging a tasseled belt. Gold thread dragons struggled up the lapels and blasted their furry red breath around his neck. As Lawrence walked down the steps, he put his arms up in surrender and the gold tassels in the inner seams of his sleeves dropped into view.

"My heavens, what a sight." Vicki Koob was impressed.

"A character," apologized Officer Harmony04.

As a tribal police officer who could be counted on to help out the State Patrol, Harmony thought he always had to explain about Indians or get twice as tough to show he did not favor them. He was slow-moving and shy but two jumps ahead of other people all the same, and now, as he watched Uncle Lawrence's splendid approach, he gazed speculatively at the torn and bulging pocket of the smoking jacket. Harmony had been inside Uncle Lawrence's house before and knew that above his draped orange-crate shelf of war medals a blue-black German luger was hung carefully in a net of flat-headed nails and fishing line. Thinking of this deadly exhibition, he got out of the car and shambled toward Lawrence with a dreamy little smile of welcome on his face. But when he searched Lawrence, he found that the bulging pocket held only the lonesome-looking dentures from Lawrence's empty jaw. They were still dripping denture polish.

"I had been cleaning them when you arrived," Uncle Lawrence explained with acid dignity.

He took the toothbrush from his other pocket and aimed it like a rifle.

"Quit that, you old idiot." Harmony tossed the toothbrush away. "For once you ain't done nothing. We came for your nephew."

Lawrence looked at Harmony with a faint air of puzzlement.

"Ma Frere, listen," threatened Harmony amiably, "those two white people in the car came to get him for the welfare. They got papers on your nephew that give them the right to take him."

"Papers?" Uncle Lawrence puffed out his deeply pitted cheeks. "Let me see them papers."

The two of them walked over to Vicki's side of the car and she pulled a copy of the court order from her purse. Lawrence put his teeth back in and adjusted them with busy workings of his jaw.

"Just a minute," he reached into his breast pocket as he bent close to Miss Vicki Koob. "I can't read these without I have in my eye."

He took the eye from his breast pocket delicately, and as he popped it into his face the social worker's mouth fell open in a consternated O.

"What is this," she cried in a little voice.

Uncle Lawrence looked at her mildly. The white glass of the eye was cold as lard. The black iris was strangely charged and menacing.

"He's nuts," Brackett huffed along the side of Vicki's neck. "Never mind him."

Vicki's hair had sweated down her nape in tiny corkscrews and some of the hairs were so long and dangly now that they disappeared into the zippered back of her dress. Brackett noticed this as he spoke into her ear. His face grew red and the backs of his hands prickled. He slid under the steering wheel and got out of the car. He walked around the hood to stand with Leo Harmony.

"We could take you in too," said Brackett roughly. Lawrence eyed the officers in what was taken as defiance. "If you don't cooperate, we'll get out the handcuffs," they warned.

One of Lawrence's arms was stiff and would not move until he'd rubbed it with witch hazel in the morning. His other arm worked fine though, and he stuck it out in front of Brackett.

"Get them handcuffs," he urged them. "Put me in a welfare home."

Bracket snapped one side of the handcuffs on Lawrence's good arm and the other to the handle of the police car.

"That's to hold you," he said. "We're wasting our time. Harmony, you search that little shed over by the tall grass and Miss Koob and myself will search the house."

"My rights is violated!" Lawrence shrieked suddenly. They ignored him. He tugged at the handcuff and thought of the good heavy file he kept in his tool box and the German luger oiled and ready but never loaded, because of Buddy, over his shelf. He should have used it on these bad ones, even Harmony in his big-time white man job. He wouldn't last long in that job anyway before somebody gave him what for.

"It's a damn scheme," said Uncle Lawrence, rattling his chains against the car. He looked over at the shed and thought maybe Albertine and Buddy had sneaked away before the car pulled into the yard. But he sagged, seeing Albertine move like a shadow within the boards. "Oh, it's all a damn scheme," he muttered again.

"I want to find that boy and salvage him," Vicki Koob explained to Officer Brackett as they walked into the house. "Look at his family life – the old man crazy as a bedbug, the mother intoxicated somewhere."

Brackett nodded, energetic, eager. He was a short hopeful redhead who failed consistently to win the hearts of women. Vicki Koob intrigued him. Now, as he watched, she pulled a tiny pen out of an ornamental clip on her blouse. It was attached to a retractable line that would suck the pen back, like a child eating one strand of spaghetti. Something about the pen on its line excited Brackett to the point of discomfort. His hand shook as he opened the screendoor and stepped in, beckoning Miss Koob to follow.

They could see the house was empty at first glance. It was only one rectangular room with whitewashed walls and a little gas stove in the middle. They had already come through the cooking lean-to with the other stove and washstand and rusty old refrigerator. That refrigerator had nothing in it but some wrinkled potatoes and a package of turkey necks. Vicki Koob noted in her perfect-bound notebook. The beds along the walls of the big room were covered with quilts that Albertine's mother, Sophie, had made from bits of old wool coats and pants that the Sisters sold in bundles at the mission. There was no one hiding beneath the beds. No one was under the little aluminum dinette table covered with a green oilcloth, or the soft brown wood chairs tucked up to it. One wall of the big room was filled with neatly stacked crates of things – old tools and springs and small half-dismantled appliances. Five or six television sets were stacked against the wall. Their control panels spewed colored wires and at least one was cracked all the way across. Only the topmost set, with coathanger antenna angled sensitively to catch the bounding signals around Little Shell, looked like it could possibly work.

Not one thing escaped Vicki Koob's trained and cataloguing gaze. She made note of the cupboard that held only commodity flour and coffee. The unsanitary tin oil drum beneath the kitchen window, full of empty surplus pork cans and beer bottles, caught her eye as did Uncle Lawrence's physical and mental deteriorations. She quickly described these "benchmarks of alcoholic dependency within the extended family of Woodrow (Buddy) American Horse" as she walked around the room with the little notebook open, pushed against her belly to steady it. Although Vicki had been there before, Albertine's presence had always made it difficult for her to take notes.

"Twice the maximum allowable space between door and threshold," she wrote now. "Probably no insulation. Two three-inch cracks in walls inadequately sealed with whitewashed mud." She made a mental note but could see no point in describing Lawrence's stuffed reclining chair that only reclined, the shadeless lamp with its plastic orchid in the bubble glass base, or the three-dimensional picture of Jesus that Lawrence had once demonstrated to her. When plugged in, lights rolled behind the water the Lord stood on so that he seemed to be strolling although he never actually went forward, of course, but only pushed the glowing waves behind him forever like a poor tame rat in a treadmill.

Brackett cleared his throat with a nervous rasp and touched Vicki's shoulder.

"What are you writing?"

She moved away and continued to scribble as if thoroughly absorbed in her work. "Officer Brackett displays an undue amount of interest in my person," she wrote. "Perhaps?"

He snatched playfully at the book, but she hugged it to her chest and moved off smiling. More curls had fallen, wetted to the base of her neck. Looking out the window, she sighed long and loud.

"All night on brush rollers for this. What a joke."

Brackett shoved his hands in his pockets. His mouth opened slightly, then shut with a small throttled cluck.

When Albertine saw Harmony ambling across the yard with his big brown thumbs in his belt, his placid smile, and his tiny black eyes moving back and forth, she put Buddy under the cot. Harmony stopped at the shed and stood quietly. He spread his arms to show her he hadn't drawn his big police gun.

"Ma Cousin," he said in the Michif dialect that people used if they were relatives or sometimes if they needed gas or a couple of dollars, "why don't you come out here and stop this foolishness?"

"I ain't your cousin," Albertine said. Anger boiled up in her suddenly. "I ain't related to no pigs."

She bit her lip and watched him through the cracks, circling, a big tan punching dummy with his boots full of sand so he never stayed down once he fell. He was empty inside, all stale air. But he knew how to get to her so much better than a white cop could. And now he was circling because he wasn't sure she didn't have a weapon, maybe a knife or the German luger that was the only thing that her father, Albert American Horse, had left his wife and daughter besides his name. Harmony knew that Albertine was a tall strong woman who took two big men to subdue when she didn't want to go in the drunk tank. She had hard hips, broad shoulders, and stood tall like her Sioux father, the American Horse who was killed threshing in Belle Prairie.

"I feel bad to have to do this," Harmony said to Albertine. "But for godsakes, let's nobody get hurt. Come on out with the boy, why don't you? I know you got him in there."

Albertine did not give herself away this time. She let him wonder. Slowly and quietly she pulled her belt through its loops and wrapped it around and around her hand until only the big oval buckle with turquoise chunks shaped into a butterfly stuck out over her knuckles. Harmony was talking but she wasn't listening to what he said. She was listening to the pitch of his voice, the tone of it that would tighten or tremble at a certain moment when he decided to rush the shed. He kept talking slowly and reasonably, flexing the dialect from time to time, even mentioning her father.

"He was a damn good man. I don't care what they say, Albertine, I knew him."

Albertine looked at the stone butterfly that spread its wings across her fist. The wings looked light and cool, not heavy. It almost looked like it was ready to fly. Harmony wanted to get to Albertine through her father but she would not think about American Horse. She concentrated on the sky blue stone.

Yet the shape of the stone, the color, betrayed her.

She saw her father suddenly, bending at the grille of their old gray car. She was small then. The memory came from so long ago it seemed like a dream – narrowly focused, snapshot-clear. He was bending by the grille in the sun. It was hot summer. Wings of sweat, dark blue, spread across the back of his work shirt. He always wore soft blue shirts, the color of shade cloudier than this stone. His stiff hair had grown out of its short haircut and flopped over his forehead. When he stood up and turned away from the car, Albertine saw that he had a butterfly.

"It's dead," he told her. "Broke its wings and died on the grille."

She must have been five, maybe six, wearing one of the boy's tee shirts Mama bleached in Hilex-water. American Horse took the butterfly, a black and yellow one, and rubbed it on Albertine's collarbone and chest and arms until the color and the powder of it were blended into her skin.

"For grace," he said.

And Albertine had felt a strange lightening in her arms, in her chest, when he did this and said, "For grace." The way he said it, grace meant everything the butterfly was. The sharp delicate wings. The way it floated over grass. The way its wings seemed to breathe fanning in the sun. The wisdom of the way it blended into flowers or changed into a leaf. In herself she felt the same kind of possibilities and closed her eyes almost in shock or pain, she felt so light and powerful at that moment.

Then her father had caught her and thrown her high into the air. She could not remember landing in his arms or landing at all. She only remembered the sun filling her eyes and the world tipping crazily behind her, out of sight.

"He was a damn good man," Harmony said again.

Albertine heard his starched uniform gathering before his boots hit the ground. Once, twice, three times. It took him four solid jumps to get right where she wanted him. She kicked the plank door open when he reached for the handle and the corner caught him on the jaw. He faltered, and Albertine hit him flat on the chin with the butterfly. She hit him so hard the shock of it went up her arm like a string pulled taut. Her fist opened, numb, and she let the belt unloop before she closed her hand on the tip end of it and sent the stone butterfly swooping out in a wide circle around her as if it was on the end of a leash. Harmony reeled backward as she walked toward him swinging the belt. She expected him to fall but he just stumbled. And then he took the gun from his hip.

Albertine let the belt go limp. She and Harmony stood within feet of each other, breathing. Each heard the human sound of air going in and out of the other person's lungs. Each read the face of the other as if deciphering letters carved into softly eroding veins of stone. Albertine saw the pattern of tiny arteries that age, drink, and hard living had blown to the surface of the man's face. She saw the spoked wheels of his iris and the arteries like tangled threads that sewed him up. She saw the living net of springs and tissue that held him together, and trapped him. She saw the random, intimate plan of his person.

She took a quick shallow breath and her face went strange and tight. She saw the black veins in the wings of the butterfly, roads burnt into a map, and then she was located somewhere in the net of veins and sinew that was the tragic complexity of the world so she did not see Officer Brackett and Vicki Koob rushing toward her, but felt them instead like flies caught in the same web, rocking it.

"Albertine!" Vicki Koob had stopped in the grass. Her voice was shrill and tight. "It's better this way, Albertine. We're going to help you."

Albertine straightened, threw her shoulders back. Her father's hand was on her chest and shoulders lightening her wonderfully. Then on wings of her father's hands, on dead butterfly wings, Albertine lifted into the air and flew toward the others. The light powerful feeling swept her up the way she had floated higher, seeing the grass below. It was her father throwing her up into the air and out of danger. Her arms opened for bullets but no bullets came. Harmony did not shoot. Instead, he raised his fist and brought it down hard on her head.

Albertine did not fall immediately, but stood in his arms a moment. Perhaps she gazed still farther back behind the covering of his face. Perhaps she was completely stunned and did not think as she sagged and fell. Her face rolled forward and hair covered her features, so it was impossible for Harmony to see with just what particular expression she gazed into the head-splitting wheel of light, or blackness, that overcame her.

Harmony turned the vehicle onto the gravel road that led back to town. He had convinced the other two that Albertine was more trouble than she was worth, and so they left her behind, and Lawrence too. He stood swearing in his cinder driveway as the car rolled out of sight. Buddy sat between the social worker and Officer Brackett. Vicki tried to hold Buddy fast and keep her arm down at the same time, for the words she'd screamed at Albertine had broken the seal of antiperspirant beneath her arms. She was sweating now as though she'd stored an ocean up inside of her. Sweat rolled down her back in a shallow river and pooled at her waist and between her breasts. A thin sheen of water came out on her forearms, her face. Vicki gave an irritated moan but Brackett seemed not to take notice, or take offense at least. Air-conditioned breezes were sweeping over the seat any-way, and very soon they would be comfortable. She smiled at Brackett over Buddy's head. The man grinned back. Buddy stirred. Vicki remembered the emergency chocolate bar she kept in her purse, fished it out, and offered it to Buddy. He did not react, so she closed his fingers over the package and peeled the paper off one end.

The car accelerated. Buddy felt the road and wheels pum-meling each other and the rush of the heavy motor purring in high gear. Buddy knew that what he'd seen in his mind that morning, the thing coming out of the sky with barbs and chains, had hooked him. Somehow he was caught and held in the sour tin smell of the pale woman's armpit. Somehow he was pinned between their pounds of breathless flesh. He looked at the choc-olate in his hand. He was squeezing the bar so hard that a thin brown trickle had melted down his arm. Automatically he put the bar in his mouth.

As he bit down he saw his mother very clearly, just as she had been when she carried him from the shed. She was stretched flat on the ground, on her stomach, and her arms were curled around her head as if in sleep. One leg was drawn up and it looked for all the world like she was running full tilt into the ground, as though she had been trying to pass into the earth, to bury herself, but at the last moment something had stopped her.

There was no blood on Albertine, but Buddy tasted blood now at the sight of her, for he bit down hard and cut his own lip. He ate the chocolate, every bit of it, tasting his mother's blood. And when he had the chocolate down inside him and all licked off his hands, he opened his mouth to say thank you to the woman, as his mother had taught him. But instead of a thank you coming out he was astonished to hear a great rattling scream, and then another, rip out of him like pieces of his own body and whirl onto the sharp things all around him.

K.C. FREDERICK

✳

What Can You Do With a Fish?

OH, SWEET CHRIST, Art sang to himself, relaxing at last, lying against the cool bark of a willow. He could hardly believe it was there on the grass; but for a while he kept from looking because he wanted to hold it in his mind. Sweet Christ, he repeated, feeling his cut hand already beginning to heal, his soggy trousers drying in the warm air, his run-down nerves and muscles recharging in the rich blank moment of complete exhaustion. Finally he looked and saw it, large and strange like a hunk of meteorite, but even seeing it didn't convince him it was really his: it couldn't be his because the old Polacks who came out there every weekend never caught anything that big, and he was no fisherman. And to have gotten it with that old rod and reel, weak line, no net, so that he had to get into the water after it and cut his hand on its gill – no, it couldn't be his, but there it was, lying there as long as a man's leg, powerful, vicious-looking, a strange thing to find in the grass with its hard, pirate's eye that was designed to search out swimming perch and frogs, its strong tail and fins slapping pointlessly now at the thin air.

It belonged in the cold water far below the river's green skin, not in the soft, bright, late afternoon heat. When he first glimpsed it it had looked like a fully preserved dinosaur under the ice – now he closed his eyes and saw it glowing in the high grass like an oddly shaped moon, and the moment hung: he could feel the tree shift its weight in the breeze. He pressed the cool grass to his cut hand and tried to recapture appropriate phrases from those hundreds of stories he'd read when he was thirteen, in magazines like *Field and Stream* and *Sports Afield*, but the words just reminded him of the barbershops he'd read them in. He opened his eyes and saw the water again. He reached cautiously toward his shirt pocket. There was one twisted cigarette left – he would have been willing to trade the contents of his wallet for that one smoke – and he lit it hungrily. Now, sucking down the dry, friendly smoke, he had everything: if the bomb came he wouldn't flinch. But it would be even better if the bomb held off for a while yet. He watched a dragonfly silently grasp a blade of grass. It stuck there, wings extended stiffly like transparent jackknife blades. Somewhere in the distance a motorboat was droning in a hidden bay. A breath of wind cooled his face. He inhaled again and looked at the fish.

But he started to remember his troubles again and all the empty crates that filled his mind: he and Rita were through for good and nothing had taken its place; high school was over and he had nothing to do; he was going into the Navy for no good reason; and he'd come out here only because he was bored, and it would be a way of killing time. He bent forward and looked steadily at the pike – it was at least a yard long; the white, rectangular spots gleamed like coins on its green sides. He was tired, but he suddenly felt he should be doing something, so he picked himself up. When the fish smacked at the grass with its tail, he used the rake to pull it into the shade. Then he ripped out some of the longer tufts, soaked them, the closed cut pinching a little, and threw them over the fish. The shade and moisture would keep it alive longer. He stood there a few moments looking at the long white dock extending into the deep, swift part of the river where he'd first hooked it. He tried to judge how long it had actually taken to land the fish: the incredible, nervewringing experience had seemed to take forever, but once it was over, he could only think of it as quick and surprising, it had caught him before he was ready for it. He realized it couldn't have taken more than ten minutes. It was hard to believe, and he realized that already he was losing the experience, that all he had left was a story in his own mind that was becoming blurred. All he had was his own word for it. But of course, he had the fish.

The pike flapped again, the grass sticking to its sides. Art saw that it was dying. All at once he felt a need to get back to Detroit while it was still alive, as if the fish were a wounded gangster who had to be taken to the cops so he could talk before he died. He tossed away his cigarette and ripped out more grass, soaked it, strewed it all around the pike: it looked like a fancy meal. Satisfied he had enough covering, he filled his cupped hands with water and poured it over the grass. He got some newspaper and wrapped the fish in it so that the moisture would be held in. He wished he'd had a tarpaulin, that would have been even better. When he picked up the wrapped fish, he felt its full weight for the first time. It was heavy; once again he wondered that he'd been able to land it. He put it in the car's trunk, where at least it would be protected from the sun.

He was ready to go now, and he should have got into the car, but he felt a hesitation. Everything was so perfect that any change could only be for the worse. He leaned against his uncle's old car, and the warm metal felt good. He felt lucky, rewarded. Every break had gone right in his fight with the fish, and even the things that had made it hard just added to the victory. Everything he'd done had been smart. The shaggy willows swayed in the warm breeze, and he wished he could stop time for five minutes or so while he added things up. This was the kind of experience that might start a lucky streak. He must have done something in the last hour that was the key to everything, if he could only remember it. Something inside his head had clicked – a broken windshield wiper had got working for a moment. He was used to having the glass blurred, and he couldn't be sure the wipers would keep working. He touched the warm door of the car's trunk: he had a trophy. He felt like an especially smart crook.

But once he was under way, his mood began to sink. As he

drove over the quiet, dusty road to the ferry, as the orange ferry pulled him across the swift, deep river (he could never forget when he crossed that there was supposed to be a boatload of bootleg whiskey down there, ninety feet below), as he started along the curve of the lake toward the city, his mind kept nibbling away at the question: what do you do with something like this, a trophy, a prize? There was a bar in Detroit that served things like buffalo burgers and rattlesnake steaks. He'd seen a menu once, and what he remembered best was that for a whole group that rented the place for a banquet of, say, lion meat, they'd show films of the hunt. Art had forgotten whether the films came before or after the meal, and he wasn't sure which would have made him sicker. But for a moment he imagined himself presiding over a big fish dinner (except that he didn't eat fish) and then, when they'd cleared away the plates, they'd roll down the screen and show him catching his monster pike, jumping in after it, cutting his hand on the inside of the fish's gill (it had been a small cut, but as he imagined it in the film it was like an oil leak), and finally pulling the pike out of the water with the rake.

But it was too much—he had to work too hard at it—it was like the football banquets he used to imagine before he started high school: the All-State awards he got there never really consoled him for barely being a regular on the actual team. It seemed, now that high school was over, just as incredible that those long, boring years were past, as that the catching of the fish had actually taken just a few minutes: before high school he'd dreamed of being a football star, of doing vaguely exciting things with the same kids he'd known all his life, but when it happened, it was all wrong. Even if he had been a football star, no one would have cared very much—it was the tough guys who were the heroes, the guys who started fights after the games, and would become numbers men when they left school—and Art wasn't tough. In fact, he knew that by his senior year he was considered pretty dull—you were either one or the other—and though he tried to hide it, and never got very good grades, the other kids knew he actually liked to read, and to learn. And so, with high school over, all his imaginary football banquets were ended, and he was just another Polack in Detroit.

The trouble with everything was, no matter how good it might make you feel, sooner or later you had to come back to Detroit, and that spoiled it. Detroit was the taste in his mouth as he chewed on a greasy hamburger in the drive-in, slowly, without appetite, because he found now that he was in no hurry to get anywhere, he was no longer bringing his fish in against a deadline. He watched a short blonde carhop dancing by herself in the corner to the blaring jukebox music and somehow it seemed sad. He was still feeling this way by the time he got to the city. As he moved along one of the big streets, the traffic was mostly gone, and only a few cars raced noisily past him on the broad asphalt plain between dull, slouching buildings. High windows were stuffed full of liquor, lawnmowers, baseball bats, and cars that looked shiny and dead. Everywhere were giant letters and numbers, big enough to be read even as you zipped by. There were words like Avco, Goldman, Nova, Northeast – pasted on windows – objects in themselves, blotting out the merchandise as though the words themselves were for sale. Art knew that if he were to stop the car in the middle of the street right now and lay the fish down there, on the pavement, no one would even notice this not very large cylinder with a head and tail. The cars would pass it, run right over it (he could hear the thunks), flattening it, dulling it, until it was just a thin layer on the pavement, to be washed away in the next good rainstorm and less durable than Avco or Nova.

Turning off the wide street, he was in the city of houses. Everything was quiet, just after dinner, and people were sitting around their tables, digesting their food. It was still bright but there was no energy behind the light now. House after wooden house was crossed by the shadow of the house next door, the shapes moving past thickly, opening out at corners and intersections where a few kids sat blankly on the steps of neighborhood groceries or bakeries. Then the house-shapes again, hung with wedges of shadow. Lines of tired cars sprawled before porches. Steel, wood, glass, brick, rubber. There were smells in the street, too: asphalt, the dead rotting heat – even the trees and grass gave off the smell of intersection. He was tired, and he tried to remember if there was a Tiger's game on TV tonight that he could use to wipe out the night.

By the time he was back in the neighborhood his lonely excitement over the fish embarrassed him. He felt he'd been driving a hearse all day and all he wanted to do was get rid of the body. Halfheartedly he tried Eddie Galicki's place, but as he guessed, Eddie was out with Virge somewhere. So much for showing off his catch. Even so he was a little relieved. It seemed pretty stupid now to be driving around with a fish, trying to show it to someone. What could you expect them to say? All that was left was to go to his Uncle Gabby's to return the car. It was as good a place as any to get rid of the pike. Not that his uncle needed it or could use it: Art had already had to give him two dollars for the use of his car, and that was enough for him to get drunk on, which was his only real need. Except for the odd electrical jobs he did, he hadn't worked in years; yet somehow he always managed to pick up enough change to be able to buy a few drinks at Connie's bar, get a few bought for him, and sit around complaining. He insulted all the customers but nobody took him seriously enough to fight him; though if they had, he probably wouldn't have been hurt, scrawny as he was. He stepped into a passing car once and he wasn't even scratched; and another time he completely wrecked his brother's car but walked away clean. Everybody called him a loser but he was a funny kind of loser. In his own way, he had it made, except for his wife, who was as big as a barn and really mean when she got drunk, and once pushed him down his front steps. He survived that too, but sometimes when he limped you could tell he was thinking about it.

In front of his uncle's house, he opened the trunk and saw that the fish was still alive though all it could manage now was a slow, mechanical opening and closing of its gills. The water still glistened. As he lifted his prize, Art marveled again at how heavy it was; it was amazing that something that big shouldn't be worth more. His uncle ought to at least give him back a dollar for the fish, or maybe let him use the car free tomorrow. But Art knew better: with the few people he had any power over, his uncle wasn't soft.

Art was on the porch Uncle Gabby had been pushed from. (It had only happened once, but in his mind he saw the old man getting thrown down again and again, slow motion, his mouth a dark cave with curses escaping like flying bats.) Holding the soggy bundle across his arms, his pants still damp below the knees, Art knocked on the door but no one answered, and he had to keep knocking, which was hard to do with the fish in his arms. He was getting angry now. He knew his uncle was home. All he wanted to do was to get rid of the damned fish – the thought of dumping it in the garbage can in the alley crossed his mind – he'd leave his uncle's keys on the porch and go home, take a shower and change. But he knew he couldn't do it, so he suffered and rapped, still louder, until at last he heard the sudden snapping open of the door and saw his uncle, hunched over, squinting, trying to squirm free of sleep, and holding the doorknob for support, "Aw, for Christ's sake, it's you," he croaked, shaking the fuzz out of his head. His body seemed to be falling slowly in several directions at once, but his bloodshot eyes made a quick, suspicious leap past Art toward the car. "Goddam car's covered with dust," he mumbled. "What'd you do? Race it over that dirt road?" He always assumed that everyone was trying to screw him. Even while he talked, though, his eyes crawled back into their red webs and he seemed to have forgotten where he was. His sing-song voice trailed off into a distant humming, and Art continued to stand there, with the wet, heavy fish in his arms. The man hadn't even noticed it: Art felt like taking it by the tail and bringing it down on his uncle's head; but the old man finally staggered back into the dark house, leaving the door open behind him, and Art could do nothing but follow.

Inside, the house smelled thickly of his uncle's failure. Art moved through the dark living room full of holy pictures Aunt Sophie collected, and sometimes threw at her husband. Even when she wasn't home, she left her presence all over the place, like the tracks of some large animal. In the kitchen, Uncle Gabby had dropped himself before a tableful of dirty dishes. The place was a mess as usual. The evening light illuminated a little star of cellophane under the table and a powder of crumbs shining on a chair. "Oh, Christ," his uncle slurred, and took a sip of cold coffee. "What the hell have you got there?" he suddenly asked, noticing the wet hulk that Art carried awkwardly before him.

"It's a fish," Art said, not too hopefully.

"A fish?" The older man frowned. "What the hell you bring it in here for?"

Though it was clumsy with one hand, Art managed to pull away the mushy paper and brush back the grass, revealing the huge, vicious head of the pike, near dead, the long slits of mouth open enough to show the dangerously plentiful teeth. "Look," he said, pushing it toward his uncle like a proud mother showing a baby. Just a glimpse of the head was enough to recall the fear he'd felt just before dropping off the dock into the water. "You want it?" he asked, trying to act casual.

"What the hell do I want with a goddamned fish?" he shouted. "Get that thing out of here." He waved it away, hardly looking at it, and took up his coffee cup. "Put it down somewhere," he growled. "Don't just stand there like an idiot. Put it in the sink."

Art carried his load to the sink full of dirty dishes and set it down noisily atop the half-full cups and watermelon rind. It was so long its uncovered tail hung out over one edge; he'd had to move the dish-drying tray and set its head on the dirty rubber mat with little channels that caught its runoff. "It's too big," he said, knowing his uncle wasn't listening, and he half-hoped that with one final surge of life the pike would knock the cups flying and fling the tray to the floor. But it just lay there while his uncle moaned curses into his coffee cup. From the alley behind the house came shouts of black kids playing.

"Here's the keys," Art muttered, dropping them to the table. But his uncle, lost, in his own world, didn't hear him. He raised his head and looked out toward the front door. Just across the street the yellow bricks of the rectory shone through the screen. "Goddamned monsignor," he spat, hitting the table with his palm. He ran his hand through his hair. "Listen, kid, don't let those priests make a monkey out of you." Art was still wondering what brought that up when the old man switched directions, as if he'd just remembered something: "When the hell you going to the Navy, anyway?"

He wished he knew. "They said I could go on active duty in a couple of months." He looked at the sink: the fish had already become part of the mess.

"You'll see," his uncle said, his voice reaching for the moralistic pitch. "All this free and easy stuff's going to be over. You're going to have to get up early in the morning. . . . " But he suddenly lost interest and let it drop. Art was already far away. The sudden mention of the Navy reminded him that someday he'd be out of here.

He was trying to hold on to this feeling when suddenly his uncle wheeled back to another topic: "Motherfucking priests." His voice blazed. "Goddamned monsignor don't care if you don't go to church. But he sure knows if you're not putting something in the collection basket." Silently he meditated on some grievance with the monsignor: probably the pastor had been trying to influence some of the women of the parish not to do business with his uncle. "The bastard," he exclaimed.

"Oh, screw the monsignor," Art said quietly, not because he sided with his uncle, but because he was bored with his uncle's problems; he was like a bug, and almost anyone could step on him from his wife to the monsignor, and for his uncle to talk to him about it made it somehow Art's problem too.

"What should I do with the fish?" he asked.

"Get it out of here." His uncle's face sagged like a wet dishrag. "I don't want any goddamned fish. Give it to one of those sports in the bar. . . . " Suddenly his voice straightened as if it had been pinched. Without any transition he was saying excitedly, "Wait a minute. . . . "

The last thing Art wanted to do was wait a minute. But his uncle got up now, laughing to himself, and looked at the oversized fish squeezed in among the dishes. "Hot damn," he said, slapping his hands, and he turned to Art with a sudden look of approval on his face. "Say, that *is* a mighty big fish, isn't it?" He walked to the sink and touched its tail. He stood before the pike, his head tilted as if it had become unscrewed. Art realized he should have guessed from the beginning what would happen: his uncle wanted to take the fish to Connie's bar and show it to the numbers men who'd be there – it might be worth a few free drinks. Art was tired; he saw now that from the moment he'd hooked it the fish had been getting its silent revenge. It had caused him nothing but trouble. Now he was to be turned over to this old man, to act as his altar boy, carrying the fish before him in their little procession. "No," he would have liked to say, "damn it, no. It's your fucking fish now; carry it yourself." But somehow he didn't. "I don't know," he said. The old man wasn't paying attention. As Art watched his uncle's calculating face, his curiosity was roused. He knew he'd deliver this package to the bar. But then what would his uncle do with the fish? Art saw it lying on the floor of the bar, dead, beginning to smell, and Uncle Gabby stopping every newcomer with the same story, hoping to get one last free drink before the bones began to show. In a way it would be interesting to see what happened: if the guys from the bar clouted him, that would be worth seeing too. But as he wet the grass and wrapped the fish in fresh newspaper, he realized that he too had been thinking of those numbers men in the bar, the high school tough guys of a few years ago. Maybe he'd wanted all along to show the fish to them. Was it possible that even as he lay back against the tree with the fish on the grass he was secretly hoping to use Uncle Gabby to get it into the bar, so that they could see it? Because he knew he was as much of a blank to the numbers men as his uncle: when he'd won a citywide essay contest in his junior year, they'd acted as if he'd been caught in some perversion.

It burned him to think, as he picked up the fish again, that his uncle was more real to them than he was. But one thing he was sure of: they couldn't ignore an actual fish this big.

When the two of them entered the bar, his blood thickened. The jukebox that washed over the buzz of voices, the smell of liquor and smoke, faint traces of perfume, the points of light and color softened by the haze, gave the place a kind of underwater feeling, and Art found himself, even with the heavy fish in his arms, adjusting to the rhythm of the place by relaxing his stance. He hesitated just inside the threshold for a moment, but his uncle pushed at him from behind. "Here, here," he rasped, and springing ahead, he pointed to a table. "Put it down there." But he seemed to forget about Art immediately, and stood there vacantly, waiting for someone to turn around. Art continued to hold the wrapped fish. Near them were four numbers men playing cards almost wordlessly. They were all big, and the tiny table squeezed between them like someone they'd jumped and knocked down, made them look even bigger. For a few seconds after Art's arrival, they remained locked in their game. Except for the flicker of their eyes when the door had been opened, they all stared down at the little table, intent, only breaking their silence with a grunt or half-audible curses, their broad backsides uneasy in the chairs while their big hands hid the little cards. Even Art's uncle seemed to have forgotten his plans for the moment, and stared over the thick backs of the players at their cards. Art remembered those backs, and the white hats that rose above them like shark fins, in the crowds after basketball games a few years ago. He suddenly felt embarrassed, standing before the table with his dripping package wrapped in newspaper. The bartender had noticed him and had started down the bar to find out what Art, a minor, was doing here. "I'm a paperboy," he felt like saying. "I've got some good news." Just then the hand ended with one of the men slamming his cards to the table, which set off a crack of laughter and swearing, and as the men pushed their chairs away from the table, Uncle Gabby stepped forward. "Hey, look at this," he called.

The card players turned skeptically toward the intruders, as though they feared Art was going to deliver a speech. They looked as if they expected to be bored, sitting there heavily, even their big relaxed fists sneering at him and his essay contests. He felt inadequately armed, even guilty. One of the men moved in his chair impatiently, as if he was about to say, "Hey. What the shit: let's get on with this game." So Art stepped forward and, not knowing what to say, he held the covered fish before him. The water had turned the print into an indecipherable blur.

"Here, you dumb asshole," his uncle barked. Art clenched his fist but his uncle didn't even know he was there. He grabbed at the paper and began tearing at it. "Look," he cried, ripping off the covering so that the fish's scales began to show. To Art, they seemed disappointingly dull. "There," his uncle said when he'd got the head free. The pike was dead now. "There. Look."

"Motherfuck," one of the cardplayers grunted, pushing back his chair so he could get up. The others did the same.

"Christ, where'd that come from?" another asked. They were really impressed. Taken by surprise, they forgot all about their cards and bottles.

"The kid got it at Big Johnny's," His uncle answered for him. Art was grateful at least that he didn't claim it for himself.

"At Big Johnny's? Where?" A large man bent over the fish but kept a careful space between himself and the pike's mouth.

"I was casting off the dock." It seemed like years ago.

By now they were all gathered around him and his uncle motioned for him to put the fish on the table, which he was glad to do. He'd had enough weight lifting for one day.

"What is it? A muskie?" someone asked. A skinny old man at the pool table wanted to keep playing, but his partner came over to join the crowd, and he just stood beside the pool table leaning on his stick.

"That's a pike, isn't it, Artie?"

Men came up from the bar to look at the fish and they all paid
their tribute with hushed, reverent swearing. For the time being
everyone seemed to have forgotten the presence of everyone else
in the bar, including Art. They were all fascinated by the dead
creature stretched across the table. It was like the time when
there'd been a long streetcar strike and he and his friends had
been standing on the corner talking: because he was facing the
right way he was the only one to see an orange length slide into
an intersection blocks away. When he pointed they all turned
around and shouted the word for him: "A streetcar. A streetcar.
For Christ's sake, it's a streetcar."

For a while, the customers were so interested in the fish that
Uncle Gabby began to look around nervously, afraid they'd lost
their taste for liquor. But at last someone ordered a round of
drinks, and his face was rung dry of worry. "Want a Coke?" he
offered bigheartedly, but one of the numbers men cut him off:
"Shit, man, he caught that fish; he can have a real drink." The
bartender wasn't comfortable about serving minors but at last
he let Art down a quick shot in the back room. When he came
back the numbers men were excitedly talking about going to
Big Johnny's tomorrow. "You know," one of them said, "the
mate to that thing'll be right there, in the same spot." Anything
that had to do with the outdoors would set off a bunch of
Polacks. The old ones were always fooling with gardens and
getting up at the crack of dawn to hunt mushrooms; and even
when they went to Big Johnny's and sat on the dock all day listening to the ballgame and drinking beer, so that it was just like
being in a bar, they felt better because it was outdoors. So it was
no surprise that the younger numbers men would feel challenged by anything that had to do with hunting or fishing and
would come out with statements like the one about the pike's
mate, that even Art knew was nonsense. The fish lay on the
table like a stick of firewood and for a few moments the bar was
transformed into a hunting and fishing lodge and all of Detroit
outside the bar's walls was a Northern wilderness. Even the reluctant pool player had been drawn into the fish stories and

only Uncle Gabby was silent, though contented: his uncle was really an indoor person. He could have been born in a bar.

The dead fish looked smaller and duller, as if its effect on the group had cost it its remaining luster. It seemed all but forgotten as the numbers men competed with tales of their fishing prowess or their strategies for getting the mate they'd convinced themselves was lurking just off Big Johnny's dock. Occasionally someone would ask Art about details of his catch, and he gave back remembered phrases from outdoor magazines. They bought another round of drinks and Art went to the back room once more. He felt light now, not good, not elated. But not bad. He saw the numbers men talking with quick gestures; he saw his uncle drinking alone and thinking hard about something; he saw the fish lying on the newspaper, stone dead, its eye vacant: a fly was walking across its sticky side.

Suddenly his uncle rapped the table, poured down his drink and called to him. "Come on," he said, "I just had an idea." Art lifted himself, the whole day's weariness coming back to him. When he picked up the fish nobody noticed. The jukebox was blasting away and all over the bar people were busy talking to each other. Some of the customers turned their heads for a moment when Art covered the fish again, but the break in the bar's rhythm was slight, just as it had been when they'd entered, and he and his uncle slipped out quietly. When they were out in the dark street, the sounds from the bar, though quieter, seemed gayer, more emphatic on the warm night air. From the moment he'd gotten up, Art's spirits had been sinking. The liquor had given him an expansive feeling, but now he was aware of how empty those expanses were: it was like being in a giant phone booth. He regretted the drinks too, since there was no point to getting high if you couldn't do anything with it. From habit his mind turned toward Rita, but he knew that was a closed book. All he could do was to grit his teeth and stick it out to the end with this fish – it couldn't be long now. He was puzzled, though: why had his uncle left the bar, when there was probably at least one more free drink in it for him? The move had been so unpredictable that Art didn't even have any guesses handy, and would have to find out from the old man himself. He didn't have long to wait. "Listen," his uncle said, "I want you to take that fish to the monsignor."

Though they were near the bar, and some of the light reached out into the street, it was dark, and since his uncle had dropped his head when he stepped back, Art couldn't see his expression. Still, he could imagine the smile of triumph. His own face tightened in a reflection of that smile. The bastard! What a move! It was brilliant. It would get the monsignor off his back beautifully. Art thought of the biblical passage that had troubled him as a kid, about loving your enemies and heaping burning coals on them. Now he realized what he'd been carrying in his uncle's procession all this while: a couple of armsful of burning coals.

Art stood in the hall of the rectory, waiting for the monsignor. The warm, enclosed air had its own particular smell. Art had known it all his life: faintly sweet from incense, it was smooth, cleaned, empty of food, an impressive official aroma, unlike any other. It seemed to come from the paintings in the hall of Christ and the saints, pale, sad but quietly commanding men, thoughtful in their dim garments that blended into fading landscapes. It was the smell of power, of an efficient, womanless world of crosses, triangles, circles – clean symbols of an order visible everywhere in the ranks of priests, even in the makes of the cars they drove. There was a time when Art had wanted to be a priest: he'd been attracted to the Jesuits with their military rigor, with their generals and provincials. Now he was going to the Navy only because Detroit was on no ocean. It had been four years ago that he'd come close to entering the seminary's high school, and his last-minute switch had been a disappointment to the monsignor: a priest from the parish would have been a feather in his cap. It was strange to think of himself as a priest, but even stranger to realize as he waited for him that the monsignor had his losses too, and that Art was surely one of them. Maybe the pastor would think Art owed him the fish for his desertion. It didn't matter. The important thing was that someone was getting the thing at last and the involvements it had gotten him into would be over. The need to get out of Detroit suddenly attacked him like heartburn. In the bar he'd thought he was a big deal for about thirteen seconds, but even as he'd downed the second drink in the back room he'd known that things don't change just because you catch a fish. It embarrassed him to think that he had. Now he wondered, did things ever change?

The monsignor came down the steps gravely, followed by Father Boris, who'd answered the door. He was a little gray priest from Poland, and he followed his boss at a respectful distance. Seeing him again, Art uttered a little prayer of thanks that he'd escaped that fate. It made him realize not everything was lost.

"Well, well, good evening, Arthur," the monsignor said impressively. The tall, smooth-looking priest wore his black cassock with a purple sash, but he had no power over Art.

"Hello, monsignor," he said quickly. "I've got this pike. My uncle Mr. Sendlik asked me to take it to you, monsignor." It was probably the liquor, but Art felt like saying "monsignor" again and again. When he'd mentioned his uncle's name, the priest's face, which was the color of strawberry ice cream, lost its official smile of greeting, and just hovered there without any expression at all for a moment. He seemed to be weighing the possibilities of halting the affair now, before Art could unveil the fish, so he could keep his hold on Uncle Gabby; but the priest was a fisherman too, and his eyes betrayed his curiosity about what was obviously a giant fish under the paper. All at once something in the monsignor's face gave Art the idea that the pastor was getting some heat from the bishop, and was already thinking of using the pike in his own way. At last, bringing his hands together, the priest exclaimed, "Well, let's see it."

Once again Art displayed his fish. He was getting to be like a magician with his act, and this time he did it more slowly, deliberately. When he saw that dead familiar face again, Art was supremely bored: it was getting to be like the face of a relative. The pike seemed to him one of the dullest of God's creatures, but its

power still worked on the priests. The monsignor's eyes en-
larged quietly and Father Boris darted toward the revealed fish
as if he was going to race his superior to a relic they both wanted
to kiss; but, catching himself in time, he was content to stand on
tiptoe just beside and slightly behind the monsignor.

The taller priest bent over the fish. "Oh, my. I'll say *that's* a
big one." He rubbed his pink hands thoughtfully. "Mmm," he
hummed softly, "I've been fishing thirty years and I've never
got one that big."

"Just luck, monsignor," Art consoled him.

"Mmm... Your uncle sent... " He was looking at the dead
fish, as if measuring it for his freezer, where he could keep it until he needed to spring it on the bishop.

"Yes, monsignor," Art doled out his words solemnly. "Mr.
Sendlik said it was only right that you should have it." He
paused. "You're the fisherman in the parish, he said. . . . " And
then Art added, "monsignor."

The priest snorted a little laugh. "Tell your uncle," he said
ceremoniously, "that I thank him in the name of the parish."
His face assumed a look that was supposed to express the whole
parish: it was like a proud pink kite beaming charitably down
on the neighborhood. "Father Boris," he muttered, "take the
fish," hardly moving his lips because he was hooked now. When
the little priest bent under the weight of the pike Art was free at
last.

It was only as he came down the last step from the rectory
that he realized the fish was gone as suddenly as it had come
and again he'd been caught unprepared. It had gotten away
from him after all. Now, for the first time in hours, he was without occupation: an unemployed fish-carrier. Actions and
people had supported him like sticks throughout the day, but
now there was nothing left to do and no one more to see. All he
had left was the liquor that had inflated him like a balloon and
now the air was quickly escaping. He could only speculate on
what would happen to his pike (or what had been his pike):
probably it would be kept in the rectory freezer until one day

when the monsignor needed it badly, he and Father Boris would hurry down the steps two at a time to the monsignor's Chrysler, Father Boris trudging behind with a big bass fiddle case, and they'd speed off toward the cathedral. And there was no reason why the fish should stop there. Why shouldn't the bishop keep it in *his* freezer? Bishops had bosses. . . . In his mind Art saw the fish going all the way to the Vatican. Who knew what would happen once it was there? Maybe the Pope could work a miracle with it and convert the Jews.

Art walked around the block. Once more he was before the rectory. Looking in at the light on the second floor it occurred to him that he'd been robbed. The pike was gone, and all he was left with was the neighborhood he'd known all his life, the dark houses standing heavily across the street, the church's hulk confronting them like a wall. The black trees rocked softly in the warm night breeze that carried from the corner the sagging, broken music of the jukebox and the voices of merry thieves in the bar. His world was complete again: even the stars above Detroit, which looked like holes punched into the roof of sky, were part of it—just burning coals cooling to ice. Worse still, he knew that soon he'd be sick. A greasy feeling had been filling his throat. (He thought of his hamburger and it didn't make him feel better.) The unpleasant taste of liquor was rising. Soon, he feared, he was going to have to throw up; but there was even some consolation in that. He'd probably have to force it up with his fingers, and he didn't like to think of it. But when it was over, he'd feel better: scraped clean, eyes watering, but alert again, unencumbered; maybe he could once more see things clearly.

JOSEPH GEHA

✻

Monkey Business

MAKE WAY! MAKE WAY! the marriage song begins. Its
words, its slow, circular rhythms catch in the back of Zizi's
mind as he waits for the streetcar – *the bridegroom walks with sure-
ness* – and, absently he begins to twist his wife's wedding ring
around the knuckle of his little finger. *Make way.* Across the
street the bums are waiting too, standing or leaning motionless
beneath the green canvas awnings until the taverns open their
doors for the evening. Zizi's eye follows the line of them, dirty
feet in dirty shoes, as it stretches all the way to the Yankee Cafe
on the corner.

And there, rounding the corner yet once more, comes the
man in the sandwich sign, the bum they call Asfoori. He limps
as he walks, one side of his face gripped by palsy into a blank
and rigid smile. And he is filthy. Even from across the street Zizi
can see where the sign (YAKOUB'S YANKEE CAFE AND GRILLE)
is stained dark from bobbing up and down against his chin. Asfoori has circled the block a half-dozen times since Zizi began
waiting for the streetcar. But this time a little boy is following
him. It is Zizi's son, Jameel, limping and half-smiling in perfect
imitation.

"You!" Zizi calls out. "Jimmy!"

The boy refuses to turn. He keeps his eyes fixed in a flat,
downward stare like the eyes of the man in the sandwich sign.

"Monkey!" Zizi shouts, but the two ignore him – the man because he is somewhat deaf, the boy because he is pretending to be – and they limp on past the line of bums, on to the opposite corner where they turn and disappear.

Zizi lets them go. What good would one more strapping do? The boy needs a mama; and now, across town this very minute, Zizi's bride-to-be is expecting him, waiting to receive the wedding ring of his dead wife.

Samira died in November, not quite five months ago, and Zizi realizes that his impatience to remarry is causing talk among the *ibn Arab*, whose families run most of the neighborhood's stores and taverns. Some are saying that Zizi's eagerness is nothing more than lust, and therefore improper. But not as improper, others are quick to add, as his choice in a new wife. Braheem Yakoub, Zizi's boss at the Yankee Cafe, has been against it from the first day he met the woman.

"Listen to me, Cousin," he told Zizi that day. "Every man pays for the love in bed – that's life – but the practical man doesn't pay too much."

And yet the love in bed has nothing to do with it. Even after all this time Zizi still does not miss it much. Frankly, it gave him nothing but trouble, especially at the start. It was the old country in the old days, and Zizi a son obedient to his father: the marriage had been arranged. On the wedding night Samira was expected to know nothing, like most brides in the old country. Zizi, for his part, simply thought that there was nothing much to know, presuming a kind of miraculous ease which is taken for granted in the stories boys overhear. But whatever it was was no miracle, and it certainly wasn't easy. Samira cried all that night and the next, and on the third night they didn't even try. Zizi dared not confess his failure; even so he quickly became the subject of village jokes. At last, a married cousin who was visiting from America – and who didn't think any of this was funny – took Zizi aside and explained everything, answered every question until both their faces were red: the how, the why, the when you do this or that. And he told him, too, to stop calling his penis by the baby name his mother had used and to call it instead his "Oldsmobile." That night Zizi showed his wife. And so much for the love in bed.

The streetcar is late. Zizi glances up at the sky, its single sheet of cloud lowering now with the promise of rain. It has rained every day this week; tonight will be no different. Even the air smells wet, and across the street the bums are huddling beneath the awnings like dirty children afraid of a bath. Zizi looks away from them, up to the top windows of the apartment building two streets beyond. A bedroom, a front room, a tiny kitchen, but when Samira was alive it had been a home. It had been a place where Zizi rediscovered what he'd had once before in his own father's house – the quiet, childlike confidence that here things would always be clean and, no matter what, he would be taken care of. It is this Zizi misses far more than the love in bed. Even now the memory of it remains, centered and epitomized in the one remembered image of a cup of coffee, Samira sitting at the kitchen table, drinking a cup of coffee.

And in his home she used to call him Nazir, his true name. What kind of a nickname is Zizi! A boyish diminutive, yet another reminder that he alone of the *ibn Arab* is not what they call "a practical man," the kind who earns his living in the employ of no other man; who has a home, a wife, children who obey his word; the kind of man who knows how to do things.

". . . Watch me and I'll show you how. Watch. Watch," Braheem Yakoub keeps saying as he carves the meat from the bone. "Watch – " and his fingers dance so effortlessly as they mix spices with fat and filler, pressing it all into the funnel of the meat grinder. But Zizi cannot do it. Awed beneath the cold eye of a practical man, an impatient man nicknamed the Green Devil for his shrewdness in business, Zizi is always too slow or too clumsy, too easily confused. Usually, Braheem would have to take over the job himself. ("Go on, move over.") Then he would send Zizi off to do something simple, to bus dishes or wipe down the lunch counter.

He used to walk home after a day like that, and Samira would be there. She unlaced his shoes for him. She poured the coffee – always there was coffee – then she would sit with him at the kitchen table. Little Jameel was still in diapers when they came to America (in 1945, on the first ship to leave Beirut after the war), and the child used to sit like a puppy on the newspaper that covered the bare floor then, watching the two of them as they talked, his wet mouth working in silent imitation. Sometimes they laughed, and when they did, little Jameel would laugh too. . . .

And it is for Jameel, almost six years old now, that Zizi has decided to put Samira's ring on the finger of a strange woman. So that the boy will have a mama. *Make way*. He swats at the song as if it were a mosquito humming in his ear. The humming fades, then immediately sputters into the electric crackle of the approaching streetcar. As he steps out to wave it down, Zizi once again catches sight of Asfoori, the half-smile and the sandwich sign, still limping his way around the block. And there, still following behind him, is Jameel.

"Jimmy!" Zizi shouts.

This time the boy looks, and Zizi gives him the warning gesture, thumb against the fingertips: Just you wait. Jameel promptly returns the gesture, then he too shouts something, but it is lost as the streetcar door hisses open.

("Monkey business," Braheem Yakoub calls it. "Monkey see, monkey do – that's all it is. Don't worry, Cousin, he'll catch on.")

But sometimes the boy even acts like a monkey. Jumping and scratching at his ribs, making monkey sounds that he calls "Ingleez" even though he can speak English better than any of them, without the slightest accent. No, it's more than simple childishness. Zizi had first noticed it just before Samira died, during those last weeks that she was in the hospital. Every morning and every afternoon he took an hour off work to visit her. Braheem Yakoub could have objected but he didn't. He understood. Even so, like a practical man, he hardly ever mentioned Samira. He talked business instead.

"Cousin, the day will come," he said one morning after Zizi and Jameel had returned from the hospital, "when the customers will order everything from machines, all of it wrapped up in waxed paper. They won't even see the waitress."

Zizi nodded. The doctors had told him not to expect miracles, and there were none. Samira was dying. He slipped the apron over his head and said nothing. Then after a minute Jameel spoke. Someday, he said, he would own a place like this. And when that day came he would sell everything in waxed paper – the burgers, the pie, even the chili. "God willing," Braheem Yakoub said, pleased. But the boy went on. He would marry an *Amerkani* woman, he said, and teach his children to speak only Ingleez, like the other monkeys. The pleasure immediately drained from Braheem's face, and he gave Zizi a quick glance.

Even at the funeral Jameel had acted strange, a boy of five standing tearless in front of his own mother's coffin, while Zizi himself had to be supported on either side by an uncle.

That was November. In February, after the commemoration ceremony, Zizi removed the black armband from his jacket, and that very night he spoke with Braheem Yakoub about finding another mama for the boy. Eventually, Braheem consulted Aunt Afifie; such things were, after all, really her business. The letters she wrote to the old country were shrewdly worded, never mentioning marriage, and yet their message was clear: a widower in America, a man of good family, has ended his mourning.

Cousins talked to cousins, and they agreed on just the girl, the daughter of a man in Aunt Afifie's old village overlooking the Syrian hills. In their letter of response they wrote that she was still young, not yet twenty-two. (So what if she was really closer to forty-two? In the mountains there were only church records, so who would know the difference?) The matter was quickly arranged, documents were signed on both sides of the ocean. The cousins, after payment to the father and the taking of their share, sent the old women to find the girl and inform her of the good news. They were told she would be somewhere in the nearby fields, sitting with a rifle, watching over her father's goats.

Uhdrah was staring hard at the brown hills when they came for her. Beyond those hills was Damascus where Holy Boulos was knocked from his horse and blinded by the light of Jesus. She did not hear them at first. She was talking with the saints, listening to their sad, premonitory voices when the old women came singing the marriage song.

> *Make way! Make way!*
> *The bridegroom is tall,*
> *He walks with sureness. . . .*

They told her, laughing and singing, that she was to be married, that she was to be sent to live in America.

No! the voices said. But she found herself smiling in her surprise. She let go the voice and laughed to hear the news.

> *Nazir is his name.*
> *His house is famous. . . .*

No! But she said yes to her father and brothers, blushing like a young girl as she said it.

After getting off the streetcar, Zizi still has a long walk ahead of him to Aunt Afifie's house. There, Uhdrah has been waiting since her arrival in America nearly a month ago, awaiting the ring that should have been hers that first week.

Zizi walks quickly along the darkening pavement, but within several blocks of the house, he stops short. There is a faint smell in the air, like incense. No, it couldn't carry this far, his mind must be playing tricks. He swats the thought away and continues walking. Then, thinking anyway: it's not just the incense, there's the rest of it too. Right at first he'd realized there was something odd about the woman. It wasn't that she was older than he expected her to be, nor that she was as heavy in the hips and breasts as a mother of many children. On the contrary, he found all this somewhat attractive. In a way it was even exciting – a grown woman, a stranger, crossing an ocean for no other man but him. What was odd, he discovered gradually that first week, were her ways and the strange stories she told.

"She's new here," Braheem Yakoub shrugged when Zizi mentioned the holy pictures that Uhdrah had hung in Aunt Afifie's house, the rosaries and incense and little figures of Jesus and Mary. "Besides, she comes from the mountains. They're all that way in the mountains."

But Braheem was never around when Uhdrah told her stories about how she had seen and actually spoken with the Virgin, and about how, with the help of Saint Maron, she had raised a dead goat to life. During those first days Braheem accused Zizi of making something out of nothing. "All right," Zizi said, "then see for yourself."

And Braheem did see. It was at the welcoming dinner in Uhdrah's honor. Salibah the butcher and Toufiq the mortician from Detroit – both of them cousins who would do anything for a joke – asked her about the stories. They kept their faces serious, as if truly interested, but the rest knew what was really going on. All except Uhdrah. She told them the stories, putting down her knife and fork so she could use her hands. She described the Virgin's voice, which was like gentle water, and the little goat, so still, then trembling back to life. And she told a new story about how the voices of Holy Mikhail and Holy Raphael had directed her to a little pouch of Turkish gold buried in her father's field. The whole time Zizi's mouth hung open.

Then Toufiq, called Taffy up in Detroit, turned away and winked, and that was the signal. All around the table there were the snorts and chuckles of suppressed laughter. Even Jameel, whose face had been as serious as Taffy's, was snickering so that he had to spit back the milk he held in his mouth.

Uhdrah seemed oblivious to it all. She was looking at the

light above the table, whispering to something up there as if in
deep conversation. That made Zizi's spine tingle. Braheem
Yakoub, too, was not laughing. He threw his fork into his plate,
then stared at Aunt Afifie. Aunt Afifie ducked her head a little
and shrugged. . . .

Afterward, for nearly a month now, Braheem has been saying
no, the practical man doesn't pay too much. Aunt Afifie says
nothing at all. She doesn't have to because, finally, she is right.
Each week Zizi pays Uhdrah a formal visit, each week Aunt
Afifie gives him the fish eye, and her meaning is clear: a man like
other men doesn't waste time; a man like other men makes a
home for his son.

And so now, like any other man, Zizi climbs the porch steps
and presses the doorbell. The porch, the whole neighborhood
smells of incense. He presses the bell again.

"Awl ride! Awl ride!" It is Aunt Afifie's voice. "I yam coming!"

The old woman opens the door, and immediately her glance
recedes into that look of bored disdain, the fish eye. Stepping
aside, she takes Zizi's jacket and tells him to wait in the front
room. Then, to show that there is nothing more to be said between them, she turns her back and goes into the kitchen.

Inside, the incense is stronger than he ever smelled it in
church. Atop the mantel Uhdrah has placed a row of holy pictures rimmed in tooled leather frames from the old country:
Saint Maron, patron of Lebanon; the Virgin of Fatima and of
Lourdes; the Sacred Heart. And there is a new one that Zizi
doesn't recognize. It is unframed, ragged on one edge as if taken
from a book. A woman, near naked, but a saint – he can tell by
the glow around her head – lies smiling on a pallet while gold
coins fall toward her lap from a golden cloud.

Vigil candles flicker at each end of the mantel, like an altar.
On the coffee table are tiny statuettes of the Holy Family, plas-
ter things you win at parish fiestas. In the center, three cones of
incense smoulder on a silver dollar.

A door closes, and Uhdrah steps out of the hall bathroom,

smoothing her hair with the palms of her hands. She who has crossed an ocean for his sake.

"Sit down, *Khawaja* Nazir." She uses the formal "Mister." Zizi knows what this means: We are strangers until you give me the ring.

He does not sit down. "Uhdrah . . . " he begins, then falters. Her eyes remain on him like the eyes of Jesus in the Sacred Heart picture, staring straight at you, waiting for the answer you have. Promising everything. He bows his head.

"Yes, *Khawaja?*"

His hand fumbles toward the ring in his pocket. Then, abruptly, he clasps his hands together and sits down.

"Do you have coffee?"

"Of course, *Khawaja*. If that is what you want."

After she is out of the room, Zizi sits perfectly still a while, listening to the cup-and-saucer sounds from the kitchen, the anxious, pigeonlike murmuring of the two women. It is April, past Easter, yet here next to an ashtray is the Christ Child in a manger. Thoughts come but he does not want to think them. He swats at them with his hand. "That is all," he says to drive them away. Then, taking Samira's ring out of his pocket, he places it on the table at the feet of the Christ Child.

Immediately Uhdrah sees it. She stops short in the hall, coffee sloshing onto the tray. She sets the tray down on the telephone table and hurries into the room, embracing Zizi before he can stand up. The ring is already on her finger. He did not see her put it on.

"My sweet one, Nazir," she is muttering in Familiar Arabic, "my eyes, my heart, Nazir!" She kisses him on both cheeks and on the forehead. "My baby, Nazir!" she says.

Samira, too, used to call him that. The coincidence thrills him, and he starts to smile. But, he reminds himself, this is for the boy's sake.

In the kitchen something clangs to the floor, bounces, and breaks. "Allah!" It is Aunt Afifie, a shout and a laugh at the same time. "Al-LAH!" She is thanking God.

Uhdrah sits back against the sofa cushions and, as if a dam has burst, begins talking rapidly of the arrangements to be made, the wedding dress, the church, food for the guests. Zizi continues to smile. He nods his head now and then to show that he is a polite man, interested in what is, after all, women's business. He can hear Aunt Afifie singing in the kitchen. No, not singing, not words anyway—more like a humming chuckle. After a time the smile grows tight on his face.

Uhdrah has forgotten the coffee, beginning to cool by now. As she talks—flowers, witnesses, invitations, gifts—her fingers brush back and forth across Samira's ring. It is on her right hand, according to custom. On the wedding day she will wear it on her left.

Zizi does not want to smile anymore. He wonders if it's started to rain yet. Then he thinks of the streetcar schedule, but to look at his watch would be rude. Staring at the picture of the Sacred Heart, he makes a silent request, and just as he does the telephone rings in the hallway. By way of thanks, he lowers his eyes before the picture.

"Awl ride!" Aunt Afifie shouts as the phone continues to ring. "I yam coming!"

Using this as an excuse to stand up and look at his watch, Zizi explains that it is getting late, it might rain any minute, and he dare not miss the last streetcar because if he does he'll have to call Braheem Yakoub—he forces a knowing chuckle—and Braheem won't enjoy having to drive all the way across town and back again.

Uhdrah glares at him, not even trying to mask her displeasure. And why should she anymore?—the ring is on her finger. Zizi is about to sit down again when Aunt Afifie looks into the room.

"Nazir," she says, her face grim. "Braheem, he's onna telephone. Asfoori's dead."

Instantly, Uhdrah makes the sign of the cross and drops to her knees. Zizi cocks his head to show that he does not understand. Asfoori is dead, too bad. Still, he was no relative, no rea-

son to be making phone calls with the news. And Uhdrah, pray-
ing aloud on her knees doesn't even know the man.

He takes the receiver, and Braheem tells him that Asfoori was
walking the sandwich sign when, just a few minutes ago, he
bent over to tie a shoelace, and simply died.

Zizi still doesn't understand. "After all, he's better
off – right?"

"Right, Cousin. But that's not it. Your son was standing behind him when it happened. The boy saw it all."

Zizi stiffens and holds the receiver tight against his ear. "Is he
scared bad?"

"No. But I don't think it's hit him yet. You better get here
quick."

Uhdrah is still on her knees when he hangs up. "The man is
only sleeping," she says, almost smiling. "Like Lazarus – "

"Quiet," Aunt Afifie says.

"When I was little, a baby goat they gave me died. My father
was going to carve it up, but I took it and carried it into the
fields. I ran until I heard a voice say, 'Your little goat is not dead
but only sleeping.'" Uhdrah's face lights up with the memory.
"It was Saint Maron's voice. He told me to put my hands on the
goat, like this." She strokes the air back and forth with her
hands.

"Stop that," Aunt Afifie says.

"And the little goat awoke from the dead." There is triumph
in her voice. "Sometimes God gives the power."

"Hush, woman," Aunt Afifie says as she helps Zizi with his
jacket.

"To those who truly believe, sometimes He gives the power."

*Poor monkeys. That is what they are like with their big ears and the faces
they make. Just like monkeys he has seen in the zoo and in jungle movies.
The way they use their back legs to walk. And he is a monkey, too.*

". . . I tell you, Cousin, customers want to believe. That's
why a practical man can fool them. They want to believe what

their mama told them about everything. If their mamas put dogshit on a plate and said it was good, they'll eat it up and lick the spoon! The businessman says 'Look, I am just like your mama.'"

"How?" his father had asked. . . .

Braheem Yakoub's ears do not stick out, but if you look at them and only at them, they stick out. His nose is not large, but if you stare at it, his face is all nose.

"'How?' Watch the practical man. Do like he does. Don't ask how. Does the man slicing the liver know how he does it? Can he tell you? No. So don't ask, watch. Do like he does, Cousin, and then you'll know how."

"I still don't understand." His father still did not understand. . . .

They are just like monkeys if you look at them that way, making noises with their mouths, showing their teeth, using their hands to pick things up. Laughing sometimes and chattering, and sometimes looking sad. Scratching the sides of their faces when they are thinking, shaking their heads when they do not understand. Walking up and down the pavement, turning white when they are old. Making little noises when they are old. When they are dead, rolling over with their eyes shut. Lying very still, mouths open against pavement, against hospital pillows, poor monkeys. And he is a monkey, too.

The nickname Asfoori means "little bird." The *ibn Arab* called him that because he had spent several years in the state mental hospital, known to them as the *asfoori-veh* or "birdhouse." When he was released he was no good anymore for business, one side of his face frozen in that half-smile, all the English he had learned in America forgotten in the *asfoori-veh*. He had no family, but he was *ibn Arab*, so Amos Salibah set up a cot next to the mops and buckets in the back room of his butcher shop. Asfoori did odd jobs, sweeping, walking the sandwich sign for Braheem Yakoub. They paid him in meals and lodging and spare change. It became his life, and now that he was dead, no one was terribly sad. He's better off, they say, and the arrangements that Taffy the mortician has made are for nothing more than a pauper's funeral.

Zizi, like the others, stands his turn taking coats and leading people to the casket. Asfoori was no relative, but they came nevertheless, out of simple charity, so that his death might not be completely ignored. "God give him rest," they say, and that is all. After the mops and buckets and sandwich sign, what else is there to say? Zizi gives the standard response – "Bless His name" – as he hands the raincoats and umbrellas to his son.

Jameel had been there; he saw how the old man turned the sandwich sign so he could bend down to tie a shoelace, and how he didn't stop bending, but instead made a quiet noise and rolled to the pavement with his mouth open. The boy saw, then he imitated even that. He, too, bent down, made a noise, and rolled sideways on his shoulder. (One of the bums, a war veteran, cried "Sniper!" and two or three others dropped to the ground.) When passersby ran to Jameel first, he abruptly opened his eyes and stood up and walked away.

Since that, Zizi has watched as Braheem instructed him to watch, but still there have been no tears and no bad dreams at night.

"Maybe," Zizi told Braheem, "it won't hit him until after the funeral."

"Maybe," Braheem said. "And maybe it already hit him."

Braheem never came near the casket ("He's dead, right? So where's the coffee?") and all evening he has been sitting in the adjoining room with several of the other older men. As at most funerals, Taffy would have cigars in there, coffee, and always a bottle to lace the coffee.

When Uhdrah arrives, followed briskly down the entranceway by Aunt Afifie, she begins weeping openly before she even reaches the room.

"*Ya Asfoori! Ya Asfoori!*" She launches into the funeral wail, but no one takes up the chant. Instead, the room buzzes as people turn to look and talk among themselves. Some are laughing outright; his real name was not Asfoori, and it sounds funny to wail, "O little bird!" Aunt Afifie grunts an embarrassed warning, and Uhdrah falls silent.

Taking their coats, Zizi leads the two women to the casket. Uhdrah kneels before it, but Aunt Afifie remains standing. The old woman makes a quick sign of the cross, glancing down only once as if to examine the quality of Taffy's work ("Awl ride," she whispers to Zizi), then she turns and walks quickly toward a chair far in the back.

Uhdrah has begun to pray, first only moving her lips, then making the breathy half-sounds of words. Whatever they are, they are not from the Prayers for the Dead. They are not even Arabic. She looks up after a while, listening although no one is talking now. The room has become quiet with watching her. For a full minute the only sounds are rain and the muffled voices of the men in the adjoining room.

"Uhdrah," Zizi whispers, but she ignores him. She separates her hands, like a priest giving benediction, then she places them on Asfoori's chest and begins to stroke back and forth, muttering in that language no one in the room understands. Yet they know what she is doing. One way or another, they've all heard the story of the goat.

Her hands move gently along Asfoori's arm, the shoulder, the neck, the face (and just then Zizi thinks he sees the eyelids flutter – but no, he is staring too hard), the chest, down the belly, the waist.

"What'cha bet," someone says in a loud comic whisper, 'she's gonna crank up his Oldsmobile, too!"

And like a thunderclap everyone is laughing. Then Braheem is there, not laughing. And Aunt Afifie, shaking with anger as she grasps Uhdrah's hands from the corpse and spins her roughly around.

"Wait!" Braheem stares at Aunt Afifie. She understands. She takes the ring from Uhdrah's finger and gives it to him. Then, suddenly, the ring is in Zizi's hand. He does not know how it got there. So many people are talking at once. He puts the ring in his pocket. People chattering and laughing. Then Braheem motions, and Zizi follows him out of the noise.

It seems quiet in the car despite the wipers and the drum of rain on metal. All during the ride home Jameel, huddled alone in the back seat, says nothing. Nor does Braheem, who must have had a great deal of Taffy's "coffee"; he keeps the car at a crawl, weaving it slowly across the center line and then back again toward the curb.

Finally, stalling the engine in front of Zizi's apartment building, Braheem clears his throat to speak. "You're better off," he says. "But you shouldn't 'a let her do that to Asfoori."

"I saw his eyelids move," Zizi says firmly. Then, less firmly: "I thought I did. Besides, what if— "

"What if what? What if it worked? Say she did bring Asfoori back. Okay. But to what? So he can walk around the block some more?"

"God gives the power sometimes." That was how Uhdrah had said it. "To those who believe. And the goat, if it's possible for a goat, then maybe . . . ," Zizi's voice trails off. He is not saying what he means to say. He means to say something for Jameel's sake, so young, sitting back there, listening.

"Goat? If Asfoori got up like the goat, what would people say? Tell me, Cousin. A miracle? How great is God? Not me. I'd say: Bad business." Braheem looks up toward the drumming roof. "Bad business!"

"The boy," Zizi whispers.

"Hah? Never mind, he catches on."

"Please." Then Zizi turns to his son. "Go on upstairs. I'll be up in a minute." Jameel nods but remains where he is.

"Hey–," Braheem says, looking up once more, "–why that old fart Asfoori and not this boy's mama who was young when she died?"

"Go on, Jimmy," Zizi says.

"Or why Asfoori and not Taffy's son who died in Detroit? What do you think, Cousin, would it heal Taffy's heart to see Asfoori jump outta that box?"

"Jimmy."

"Yes, Papa." Jameel opens the car door. He hesitates, then steps out into the rain and disappears beneath the wet shadow of the building. When the hall light winks on, Zizi turns again to Braheem. The old man's head is bobbing slightly, privately, as if in answer to a question nobody asked.

"Yep. But that's the trouble with miracles, Cousin. Wanna know what a practical man would say?" His voice drops, and Zizi has to lean in to hear him. "Why a goat – he would say – a goddamn goat, and not me. You understand, Cousin? Me."

The rain is cold. Zizi stands a while in it, twisting Samira's ring around the knuckle of his little finger. His clothes are getting soaked, but it feels good in a way, the rain dripping cold and clean from his hair. A practical man would laugh.

Going in, he tries to be quiet but the door closes loudly after him and his shoes make sucking noises on the stairs.

"Papa." Jameel stands at the bedroom door, laughing. "Lookit your shoes!"

Zizi looks. There is a puddle where he is standing; the top of one shoe has started to wrinkle, the other is curling up from the sole.

"Sit down, Papa." He takes Zizi's suit coat off. "I'll put this over the kitchen radiator." Zizi sits on the bed. He hears the sounds of the kitchen faucets.

Jameel returns with a clean towel. "Here." He hands Zizi the towel. "I put on some coffee." Then he kneels at his father's feet and begins loosening the shoelaces. Zizi lets him do it.

He lets him pull off the shoes, the stockings, lets him unbutton the wet shirt. The coffee has yet to boil, but already its smell fills the apartment. He swats at the thought of a mama. That is all.

The boy undoes the suspender straps. Then, grinning, he takes the ring from his father's finger and turns aside. When he turns back, the ring is on his thumb. It fits, and he keeps it there.

Zizi lets him. The boy will catch on – monkey see, monkey do. He will be a practical man someday. And that is all.

"Lift your legs." Jameel pulls the trousers off. "Now your arms."

Zizi obeys. Someday the boy will have his own business and sell all the food in waxed paper. And that is all. He will marry and teach his children to speak only English. But that is enough. That, and the smell of coffee in his house.

GAYL JONES

*

Asylum

WHEN THE DOCTOR coming? When I'm getting examined?

They don't say nothing all these white nurses. They walk around in cardboard shoes and grin in my face. They take me in this little room and sit me up on a table and tell me to take my clothes off. I tell them I won't take them off till the doctor come.

Then one of them says to the other, You want to go get the orderly?

She might hurt herself.

Not me, I won't get hurt.

Then they go out and this big black woman comes in to look after me. They sent her in because they think I will behave around her. I do. I just sit there and don't say nothing. She acts like she's scared. She stands next to the door.

You know, I don't belong here, I start to say, but don't. I just watch her standing up there.

The doctor will come in to see you in a few minutes, she says.

I nod my head. They're going to give me a physical examination first. I'm up on the table but I'm not going to take my clothes off. All I want them to do is examine my head. Ain't nothing wrong with my body.

The woman standing at the door looks like somebody I know. She thinks I'm crazy, so I don't tell her she looks like somebody I know. I don't say nothing. I know one thing. He ain't examining me down there. He can examine me anywhere else he wants to, but he ain't touching me down there.

The doctor's coming. You can go to the bathroom and empty your bladder and take your clothes off and put this on.

I already emptied my bladder. The reason they got me here is my little nephew's teacher come and I run and got the slop jar and put it in the middle of the floor. That's why my sister's daughter had me put in here.

I take my clothes off but I leave my bloomers on cause he ain't examining me down there.

The doctor sticks his head in the door.

I see we got a panty problem.

I say, Yes, and it's gonna stay.

He comes in and looks down in my mouth and up in my nose and looks in my ears. He feels my breasts and my belly to see if I got any lumps. He starts to take off my bloomers.

I ain't got nothing down there for you.

His nose turns red. I stare at the black woman who's trying not to laugh. He puts a leather thing on my arm and tightens it. He takes blood out of my arm.

I get dressed and the big nurse goes with me down the hall. She doesn't talk. She doesn't smile. Another white man is sitting behind a desk. He is skinny and about my age and he attaches some things to my head and tells me to lay down. I lay down and see all the crooked lines come out. I stare at circles and squares and numbers and move them around and look at little words and put them together anyway I want to, then they tell me to sit down and talk about anything I want to.

How I do?

I can't tell you that, but we can tell you're an intelligent person even though you didn't have a lot of formal education.

How can you tell?

He doesn't say nothing. Then he asks, Do you know why they brought you here?

I peed in front of Tony's teacher.

Did you have a reason?

I just wanted to.

You didn't have a reason?

I wanted to.

What grade is Tony in?

The first.

Did you do it in front of the little boy?

Yeah, he was there.

He doesn't comment. He just writes it all down. He says tomorrow they are going to have me write words down, but now they are going to let me go to bed early because I have had a long day.

It ain't as long as it could've been.

What do you mean?

I look at his blue eyes. I say nothing. He acts nervous. He tells the nurse to take me to my room. She takes me by the arm. I tell her I can walk. She lets my arm go and walks with me to some other room.

Why did you do it when the teacher came?

She just sit on her ass and fuck all day and it ain't with herself.

I write that down because I know they ain't going to know what I'm talking about. I write down whatever comes into my mind. I write down some things that after I get up I don't remember.

We think you're sociable and won't hurt anybody and so we're going to put you on this floor. You can walk around and go to the sun room without too much supervision. You'll have your sessions every week. You'll mostly talk to me, and I'll have you write things down everyday. We'll discuss that.

I'll be in school.

He says nothing. I watch him write something down in a book. He thinks I don't know what he put. He thinks I can't read upside down. He writes about my sexual amorality because I wouldn't let that other doctor see my pussy.

My niece comes to visit me. I have been here a week. She acts nervous and asks me how I'm feeling. I say I'm feeling real fine except everytime I go sit down on the toilet this long black rubbery thing comes out a my bowels. It looks like a snake and it scares me. I think it's something they give me in my food.

She screws up her face. She doesn't know what to say. I have scared her and she doesn't come back. It has been over a month and she ain't been back. She wrote me a letter though to tell me that Tony wanted to come and see me but they don't allow children in the building.

I don't bother nobody and they don't bother me. They put me up on the table a few more times but I still don't let him look at me down there. Last night I dreamed I got real slender and turned white like chalk and my hair got real long and the black woman she helped them strap me down because the doctor said he had to look at me down there and he pulled this big black rubbery thing look like a snake out of my pussy and I broke the stirrups and jumped right off the table and I look at the big black nurse and she done turned chalk white too and she tells me to come to her because they are going to examine my head again. I'm scared of her because she looks like the devil, but I come anyway, holding my slop jar.

If the sounds fit put them here.
They don't fit.
How does this word sound?
What?
Dark? Warm? Soft?
Me?
He puts down: libido concentrated on herself.
What does this word make you feel?
Nothing.
You should tell me what you are thinking.
Is that the only way I can be freed?

JAMAICA KINCAID

Mariah

ONE MORNING IN EARLY March, Mariah, whose children I
had served as an au pair for three months now, said to me, "You
have never seen spring, have you?" And she did not have to
await an answer, for she already knew. She said the word
"spring" as if spring were a close friend, a friend who had dared
to go away for a long time and soon would reappear for their
passionate reunion. She said, "Have you ever seen daffodils
pushing their way up out of the ground? And then when they're
in bloom and all massed together, a wind without a sharp edge
comes along and makes them do a curtsy to the lawn stretching
out in front of them. Have you ever seen that? When I see that, I
feel so glad to be alive." And I thought, So Mariah is made to
feel alive by some flowers bending in not too chilly a wind. How
does a person get to be that way?

I remembered an old poem I had been made to memorize
when I was ten years old and a pupil at Queen Victoria Girls'
School. I had been made to memorize it, verse after verse, and
then had recited the whole poem to an auditorium full of parents and teachers. After I was done, everybody stood up and applauded with an enthusiasm that surprised me, and later they
told me how nicely I had pronounced every word, how I had
placed just the right amount of special emphasis in places where
that was needed, and how proud the poet, now long dead,

would have been to hear his words ringing out of my mouth. I was then at the height of my two-facedness: that is, outside I seemed one way, inside I was another; outside false, inside true. And so I made pleasant little noises that showed both modesty and appreciation, but inside I was making a vow to erase from my mind, line by line, every word of that poem. The night after I had recited the poem, I dreamed, continuously it seemed, that I was being chased down a narrow cobbled street by bunches and bunches of those same daffodils that I had vowed to forget, and when finally I fell down from exhaustion they all piled on top of me, until I was buried deep underneath them and was never seen again. I had forgotten all of this until Mariah mentioned daffodils, and now I told it to her with such an amount of anger I surprised both of us. We were standing quite close to each other, but as soon as I had finished speaking, without a second of deliberation we both stepped back. It was only one step that was made, but to me it felt as if some motion that I had not been aware of had been checked.

Mariah reached out to me and, rubbing her hand against my cheek, said, "What a history you have." I thought there was a little bit of envy in her voice, and so I said, "You are welcome to it if you like."

After that, each day, Mariah began by saying, "As soon as spring comes," and so many plans would follow that I could not see how one little spring could contain them. She said we would leave the city and go to the house on one of the Great Lakes, the house where she spent her summers when she was a girl. We would visit some great gardens. We would visit the zoo—a nice thing to do in springtime; the children would love that. We would have a picnic in the park as soon as the first unexpected and unusually warm day arrived. An early-evening walk in the spring air—that was something she really wanted to do with me, to show me the magic of a spring sky.

On the very day it turned spring, a big snowstorm came, and more snow fell on that day than had fallen all winter. Mariah looked at me and shrugged her shoulders. "How typical," she

said, giving the impression that she had just experienced a personal betrayal. I laughed at her, but I was really wondering,
How do you get to be a person who is made miserable because
the weather changed its mind, because the weather doesn't live
up to your expectations? How do you get to be that way?

While the weather sorted itself out in various degrees of cold-
ness, I walked around with letters from my family and friends
scorching my breasts. I had placed these letters inside my bras-
siere, and carried them around with me wherever I went. It was
not from feelings of love and longing that I did this; quite the
contrary. It was from a feeling of hatred. There was nothing so
strange about this, for isn't it so that love and hate exist side by
side? Each letter was a letter from someone I had loved at one
time without reservation. Not too long before, out of politeness,
I had written my mother a very nice letter, I thought, telling her
about the first ride I had taken in an underground train. She
wrote back to me a letter, and after I read it I was afraid to even
put my face outside the door. The letter was filled with detail after detail of horrible and vicious things she had read or heard
about that had taken place on those very same underground
trains on which I travelled. Only the other day, she wrote, she
had read of an immigrant girl, someone my age exactly, who
had had her throat cut while she was a passenger on perhaps the
very same train I was riding.

But I already knew fear. I had known a girl, a schoolmate of
mine, and it was well known that her father had dealings with
the Devil. Once, out of curiosity, she had gone into a room
where her father did his business, and she looked into things
that she should not have, and she became possessed. She took
sick and we, my other schoolmates and I, used to stand in the
street outside her house on our way home from school and hear
her being beaten by what possessed her, and hear her as she
cried out from the beatings. Eventually she had to cross the sea,
where the Devil couldn't follow her, because the Devil cannot

walk over water. I thought of this as I felt the sharp corners of the letters cutting into the skin over my heart. I thought, On the one hand there was a girl being beaten by a man she could not see; on the other there was a girl getting her throat cut by a man she could see. In this great big world, why should my life be reduced to these two possibilities?

When the snow fell, it came down in thick, heavy glops, and it hung on the trees like a decoration ordered for a special occasion – a celebration no one had heard of, for everybody complained. In all the months that I had lived in this place, snowstorms had come and gone and I had never paid any attention, except to feel that snow was an annoyance when I had to make my way through the mounds of it that lay on the sidewalk. My parents used to go every Christmas Eve to a film that had Bing Crosby standing waist-deep in snow and singing a song at the top of his voice. My mother once told me that seeing this film was among the first things they did when they were getting to know each other, and at the time she told me this I felt strongly how much I no longer liked even the way she spoke; and so I said, barely concealing my scorn, "What a religious experience that must have been." I walked away quickly, for my thirteen-year-old heart couldn't bear to see her face when I had caused her pain, but I couldn't stop myself.

In any case, this time when the snow fell, even I could see that there was something to it. The day was longer now, the sun set later, the evening sky seemed lower than usual, and the snow was the color and texture of a half-cooked egg white, making the world seem soft and lovely and – unexpectedly, to me – nourishing. That the world I was in could be soft, lovely, and nourishing was more than I could bear, and so I stood there and wept, for I didn't want to love one more thing in my life, didn't want one more thing that could make my heart break into a million little pieces at my feet. But all the same, there it was, and I could not do much about it; for even I could see that I was too young for real bitterness, real regret, real hard-heartedness.

The snow came and went more quickly than usual. Mariah

said that the way the snow vanished, as if some hungry being were invisibly swallowing it up, was quite normal for that time of year. Everything that had seemed so brittle in the cold of winter – sidewalk, buildings, trees, the people themselves – seemed to slacken and sag a bit at the seams. I could now look back at the winter. It was my past, so to speak, my first real past – a past that was my own and over which I had the final word. I had just lived through a bleak and cold time, and it is not to the weather outside that I refer. I had lived through this time, and as the weather changed from cold to warm it did not bring me along with it. Something settled inside me, something heavy and hard. It stayed there, and I could not think of one thing to make it go away. I thought, So this must be living, this must be the beginning of the time people later refer to as "years ago, when I was young."

My mother had a friendship with a woman – a friendship she did not advertise, for this woman had spent time in jail. This woman – her name was Sylvie – had a scar on her right cheek, a human-teeth bite. It was as if her cheek were a half-ripe fruit and someone had bitten into it, meaning to eat it, but then realized it wasn't ripe enough. She had gotten into a big quarrel with another woman over this: which of the two of them a man they both loved should live with. Apparently Sylvie said something that was unforgivable, and the other woman flew into an even deeper rage and grabbed Sylvie in an embrace, only it was not an embrace of love but an embrace of hatred, and she left Sylvie with the marked cheek. Both women were sent to jail for public misconduct, and going to jail was something that for the rest of their lives no one would let them forget. It was because of this that I was not allowed to speak to Sylvie, that she was not allowed to visit us when my father was at home, and that my mother's friendship with her was supposed to be a secret. I used to observe Sylvie, and I noticed that whenever she stopped to speak, even in the briefest conversation, immediately her hand would go up to her face and caress her little rosette (before I knew what it was, I was sure that the mark on her face was a rose she had put there on purpose because she loved the beauty of roses so much she wanted to wear one on her face), and it was as if the mark on her face bound her to something much deeper than its reality, something that she could not put into words. One day, outside my mother's presence, she admired the way my corkscrew plaits fell around my neck, and then she said something that I did not hear, for she began by saying, "Years ago when I was young," and she pinched up her scarred cheek with her fingers and twisted it until I thought it would fall off like a dark, purple plum in the middle of her pink palm, and her voice became heavy and hard, and she laughed all the time she was talking. That is how I came to think that heavy and hard was the beginning of living, real living; and though I might not end up with a mark on my cheek, I had no doubt that I would end up with a mark somewhere.

I was standing in front of the kitchen sink one day, my thoughts centered typically on myself, when Mariah came in – danced in, actually – singing an old song, a song that was popular when her mother was a young woman, a song she herself most certainly would have disliked when she was a young woman and so she now sang it with an exaggerated tremor in her voice to show how ridiculous she still found it. She twirled herself wildly around the room and came to a sharp stop without knocking over anything, even though various things were in her path.

She said, "I have always wanted four children, four girl children. I love my children." She said this clearly and sincerely. She said this without doubt on the one hand or confidence on the other. Mariah was beyond doubt or confidence. I thought, Things must have always gone her way, and not just for her but for everybody she has ever known from eternity; she has never had to doubt, and so she has never had to grow confident; the right thing always happens to her; the thing she wants to happen happens. Again I thought, How does a person get to be that way?

Mariah said to me, "I love you." And again she said it clearly and sincerely, without confidence or doubt. I believed her, for if anyone could love a young woman who had come from halfway around the world to help her take care of her children, it was Mariah. She looked so beautiful standing there in the middle of the kitchen. The yellow light from the sun came in through a window and fell on the pale yellow linoleum of the floor and on the walls of the kitchen, which were painted yet another shade of pale yellow, and Mariah, with her pale yellow skin and yellow hair, stood still in this almost celestial light, and she looked blessed, no blemish or mark of any kind on her cheek or anywhere else, as if she had never quarrelled with anyone over a man or over anything, would never have to quarrel at all, had never done anything wrong and had never been to jail, had never had to leave anywhere for any reason other than a whim. She had washed her hair that morning, and from where I stood I could smell the residue of the perfume from the shampoo in her hair. Then underneath that I could smell Mariah herself. The smell of Mariah was pleasant. Just that – pleasant. And I thought, But that's the trouble with Mariah – she smells pleasant. I knew then that for the rest of my life I would want to have a powerful odor and would not care if it caused offense.

On a day on which it was clear that there was no turning back as far as the weather was concerned, that the winter season was over and its return would be a noteworthy event, Mariah said that we should prepare to go and spend some time at the house on the shore of one of the Great Lakes. Lewis, her husband, would not accompany us. Lewis would stay in town and take advantage of our absence, doing things that she and the children would not enjoy doing with him. What these things were I could not imagine. Mariah said we would take a train, for she wanted me to experience spending the night on a train and waking up to breakfast on the train as it moved through freshly plowed fields. She made so many arrangements – I had not known that just leaving your house for a short time could be so complicated. That afternoon, because the children, my charges, would not return home from school until three, Mariah took me to a garden, a place she described as among her favorites in the world. She covered my eyes with a handkerchief, and then, holding me by the hand, she walked me to a spot in a clearing. Then she removed the handkerchief and said, "Now, look at this." I looked. It was a big area with lots of thick-trunked, tall trees along winding paths. Along the paths and underneath the trees were many, many yellow flowers the size and shape of play teacups, or fairy skirts. They looked like something to eat and something to wear at the same time; they looked beautiful; they looked simple, as if made to erase a complicated and unnecessary idea. I did not know what these flowers were, and so it was a mystery to me why I wanted to kill them. Just like that. I wanted to kill them. I wished that I had an enormous scythe; I would just walk down the path, dragging it alongside me, and I would cut these flowers down at the place where they emerged from the ground.

Mariah said, "These are daffodils. I'm sorry about the poem, but I'm hoping you'll find them lovely in real life all the same."

There was such joy in her voice as she said this, such a music, how could I explain to her the feeling I had about daffodils – that it wasn't exactly daffodils, but that they would do as well as anything else? Where should I start? Over here or over there? Anywhere would be good enough, but my heart and my thoughts were racing so that every time I tried to talk I stammered and by accident bit my own tongue.

Mariah, mistaking what was happening to me for joy at seeing daffodils for the first time, reached out to hug me, but I moved away, and in doing that I seemed to get my voice back. I said, "Mariah, do you realize that at ten years of age I had to learn by heart a long poem about some flowers I would not see in real life until I was nineteen?"

As soon as I said this, I felt sorry that I had cast her beloved daffodils in a scene she had never considered. This woman who hardly knew me loved me, and she wanted me to love this thing that she loved also. He eyes sank back in her head as if they were protecting themselves, as if they were taking a rest after some unexpected hard work. It wasn't her fault. It wasn't my fault. But nothing could change the fact that where she saw beautiful flowers I saw sorrow and bitterness. The same thing could cause us to shed tears, but those tears would not taste the same. We walked home in silence. I was glad to have at last seen what a wretched daffodil looked like.

When the day came for us to depart to the house on the Great Lake, I was sure that I did not want to go, but at midmorning I received a letter from my mother bringing me up to date on things she thought I would have missed since I left home and would certainly like to know about. "It still has not rained since you left," she wrote. "How fascinating," I said to myself, meaning the opposite. It had not rained once for over a year before I left. I did not care about that any longer. The object of my life now was to put as much distance between myself and the events mentioned in her letter as I could manage. For I felt that if I could put enough miles between me and the place from which that letter came, and if I could put enough events between me and the events mentioned in the letter, would I not be free to take everything just as it came and not see hundreds of years in every gesture, every word spoken, every face?

On the train, we settled ourselves and the children into our compartments – two children with Mariah, two children with me. In one of the few films I had seen in my life so far, some people on a train did this – settled into their compartments. And so I suppose I should have felt excitement at doing something I had never done before and had only seen done in a film. But almost everything I did now was something I had never done before, and so the new was no longer thrilling to me unless it reminded me of the past. We went to the dining car to eat our dinner. We sat at tables – the children by themselves. They had

demanded that, and had said to Mariah that they would behave, even though it was well known that they always did. The
other people sitting down to eat dinner all looked like Mariah's
relatives; the people waiting on them all looked like mine. The
people who looked like my relatives were all older men and very
dignified, as if they were just emerging from a church after Sunday service. On closer observation, they were not at all like my
relatives; they only looked like them. My relatives always gave
backchat. Mariah did not seem to notice what she had in common with the other diners, or what I had in common with the
waiters. She acted in her usual way, which was that the world
was round and we all agreed on that, when I knew that the
world was flat and if I went to the edge I would fall off.

That night on the train was frightening. Every time I tried to
sleep, just as it seemed that I had finally done so, I would wake
up sure that thousands of people on horseback were following
me, chasing me, each of them carrying a cutlass to cut me up
into small pieces. Of course, I could tell it was the sound of the
wheels on the tracks that inspired this nightmare, but a real
explanation made no difference to me. Early that morning,
Mariah left her own compartment to come and tell me that we
were passing through some of those freshly plowed fields she
loved so much. She drew up my blind, and when I saw mile after mile of turned-up earth, I said, a cruel tone to my voice,
"Well, thank God I didn't have to do that." I don't know if she
understood what I meant, for in that one statement I meant
many different things.

When we got to our destination, a man Mariah had known all
her life, a man who had always done things for her family, a
man who came from Sweden, was waiting for us. His name was
Gus, and the way Mariah spoke his name it was as if he belonged to her deeply, like a memory. And, of course, he was a
part of her past, her childhood: he was there, apparently, when
she took her first steps; she had caught her first fish in a boat

with him; they had been in a storm on the lake and survival was
a miracle, and so on. Still, he was a real person, and I thought
Mariah should have long separated the person Gus standing in
front of her in the present from all the things he had meant to
her in the past. I wanted to say to him, "Do you not hate the
way she says your name, as if she owns you?" But then I
thought about it and could see that a person coming from Sweden was a person altogether different from a person like me.

We drove through miles and miles of countryside, miles and
miles of nothing. I was glad not to live in a place like this. The
land did not say, "Welcome. So glad you could come." It was
more, "I dare you to stay here." At last we came to a small
town. As we drove through it, Mariah became excited; her voice
became low, as if what she was saying only she needed to hear.
She would exclaim with happiness or sadness, depending, as
things passed before her. Some things had changed, some
things had newly arrived, and some things had vanished completely since she had last been there. When she passed through
this town, it was as if she forgot she was the wife of Lewis and the
mother of four girl children. As we left the small town, a silence
fell on everybody, and in my own case I felt a kind of despair. I
felt sorry for Mariah; I knew what she must have gone through,
seeing her past go swiftly by in front of her. What an awful thing
that is, as if the ground on which you are standing is being
slowly pulled out from under your feet and beneath is nothing, a
hole through which you fall forever.

The house in which Mariah had grown up was beautiful. It
was a large house, and it sprawled out, as if rooms had been
added onto it when needed, but added on all in the same style.
It was modelled on the farmhouse that Mariah's grandfather
grew up in, somewhere in Scandinavia. It had a nice veranda in
front, a perfect place from which to watch rain fall. The whole
house was painted a soothing yellow with white trim, which
from afar looked warm and inviting. From my room I could see
the lake. I had read of this lake in geography books, had read of
its origins and its history, and now to see it up close was odd, for

it looked so ordinary, gray, dirty, unfriendly, not a body of water to make up a song about. Mariah came in, and seeing me
studying the water she flung her arms around me and said,
"Isn't it great?" But I wasn't thinking that at all. I slept peacefully, without any troubling dreams to haunt me; it must have
been that knowing there was a body of water outside my window, even though it was not the big blue sea I was used to,
brought me some comfort.

Mariah wanted all of us, the children and me, to see things
the way she did. She wanted us to enjoy the house, all its nooks
and crannies, all its sweet smells, all its charms, just the way she
had done as a child. The children were happy to see things her
way. They would have had to be four small versions of myself
not to fall at her feet in adoration. But I already had a mother
who loved me, and I had come to see her love as a burden and
had come to view with horror the sense of self-satisfaction it
gave my mother to hear other people comment on her great love
for me. I had come to feel that my mother's love for me was designed solely to make me into an echo of her; and I didn't know
why, but I felt that I would rather be dead than become just an
echo of someone. This is not a figure of speech. These thoughts
would have come as a complete surprise to my mother, for in
her life she had found that her ways were the best ways to have,
and she would have been mystified as to how someone who
came from inside her would want to be anyone different from
her. I did not have an answer to this myself. But there it was.
Thoughts like these had brought me to be sitting on the edge of
a Great Lake with a woman who wanted to show me her world
and hoped that I would like it, too. Sometimes there is no escape, but often the effort of trying will do quite nicely for a
while.

I was sitting on the veranda with these thoughts when I saw
Mariah come up the path, holding in her hands six grayish
blackish fish. She said, "Taa-daah! Trout!" and made a big
sweep with her hands, holding the fish up in the light, so that
rainbowlike colors shone on their scales. She sang out, "I will

make you fishers of men," and danced around me. After she stopped, she said, "Aren't they beautiful? Gus and I went out in my old boat – my very, very old boat – and we caught them. My fish. This is supper. Let's go feed the minions."

It's possible that what she really said was "millions," not "minions." Certainly she said it in jest. But as we were cooking the fish, I was thinking about it "Minions." A word like that would haunt someone like me; the place where I came from was a dominion of someplace else. I became so taken with the word "dominion" that I told Mariah this story: When I was about five years old or so, I had read to me for the first time the story of Jesus Christ feeding the multitudes with seven loaves and a few fishes. After my mother had finished reading this to me, I said to her, "But how did Jesus serve the fish? Boiled or fried?" This made my mother look at me in amazement and shake her head. She then told everybody she met what I had said, and they would shake their heads and say, "What a child!" It wasn't really such an unusual question. In the place where I grew up, many people earned their living by being fishermen. Often, after a fisherman came in from sea and had distributed most of his fish to people with whom he had such an arrangement, he might save some of them, clean and season them, and build a fire, and he and his wife would fry them at the seashore and put them up for sale. It was quite a nice thing to sit on the sand under a tree, seeking refuge from the hot sun, and eat a perfectly fried fish as you took in the view of the beautiful blue sea, former home of the thing you were eating. When I inquired about the way the fish were served with the loaves, to myself I had thought, Not only would the multitudes be pleased to have something to eat, not only would they marvel at the miracle of turning so little into so much, but they might go on to pass a judgment on the way the food tasted. I know it would have mattered to me. In our house, we all preferred boiled fish. I wondered why the people who recorded their life with Christ never mentioned this small detail, a detail that would have meant a lot.

When I finished telling Mariah this, she looked at me, and her blue eyes (which I would have found beautiful even if I hadn't read millions of books in which blue eyes were always accompanied by the word "beautiful") grew dim as she slowly closed the lids over them, then bright again as she opened them wide and then wider.

A silence fell between us; it was a deep silence, but not too thick and not too black. Through it we could hear the clink of the cooking utensils as we cooked the fish Mariah's way, under flames in the oven, a way I did not like. And we could hear the children in the distance screaming – in pain or pleasure, I could not tell.

Mariah and I were saying good night to each other the way we always did, with a hug and a kiss, but this time we did it as if we both wished we hadn't gotten such a custom started. She was almost out of the room when she turned and said, "I was looking forward to telling you that I have Indian blood, that the reason I'm so good at catching fish and hunting birds and roasting corn and doing all sorts of things is because I have Indian blood. But now, I don't know why, I feel I shouldn't tell you that. I feel you will take it the wrong way."

This really surprised me. What way should I take this? Wrong way? Right way? What could she mean? To look at her, there was nothing remotely like an Indian about her. Why claim a thing like that? I myself had Indian blood in me. My grandmother is a Carib Indian. That makes me one-quarter Carib Indian. But I don't go around saying that I have some Indian blood in me. The Carib Indians were good sailors, but I don't like to be on the sea; I only like to look at it. To me my grandmother is my grandmother, not an Indian. My grandmother is alive; the Indians she came from are all dead. If someone could get away with it, I am sure they would put my grandmother in a zoo, as an example of something now extinct in nature. In fact, one of the museums to which Mariah had taken me devoted a whole section to people, all dead, who were more or less related to my grandmother.

Mariah says, "I have Indian blood in me," and underneath everything I could swear she says it as if she were announcing her possession of a trophy. How do you get to be the sort of victor who can claim the soul of the vanquished, too?

I now heard Mariah say, "Well," and she let out a long breath, full of sadness, resignation, even dread. I looked at her; her face was miserable, tormented, ill-looking. She looked at me in a pleading way, as if asking for relief, and I looked back, my face and my eyes hard; no matter what, I would not give it.

I said, "All along I have been wondering how you got to be the way you are. Just how it was that you got to be the way you are."

Even now she couldn't let go, and she reached out, her arms open wide, to give me one of her great hugs. But I stepped out of its path quickly, and she was left holding nothing. At last I said it. I said, "How do you get to be that way?" The anguish on her face almost broke my heart, but I would not bend. It was hollow, my triumph, I could feel that, but I held on to it just the same.

SALVATORE LA PUMA

✳

Inside the Fire

WHERE THE ELEVATED LINE over New Utrecht Avenue curved into the air space over Sixteenth Avenue the three- and four-storied walk-ups on both sides were so close to the train tracks that even the arc light of this August morning couldn't reach Sergio and the others who lived on the sidewalks below. The shops there were also nearly in constant darkness with customers who came in only to look for a bargain or if shops on other streets had closed up for the day.

Besides a lack of light there was also a lack of quiet on the avenue. The noise day and night of train wheels grinding by sounded like prison doors to some of the guys who now lived on the sidewalks. Some of the longtimers had become a little deaf from the train noise and those guys whenever they had something to say would shout it, even if at that moment no train passed by to shout over. In that way too, and with his hands cupped at his mouth for a megaphone besides, Sergio Rinaldo shouted this morning to his friend, Giancarlo, that he would give Becky a party tomorrow on her fortieth birthday. She had told him and others about it over the past few weeks. While Sergio pondered where and how to get the party fixings, Giancarlo should go around to invite the others. Up and down the avenue then Giancarlo shouted the invitation to lots of home-

less guys and to the few homeless women, and some shouted
back that they would come to the party.

"Eight guys and two dames said they'd come," said Giancarlo that night in Sergio's cellar. "You want their names,
Sergio?"

"I don't want their names, Giancarlo. Anyone's welcome to
come to the party. Maybe the people at the party could also be
an audience to hear my jokes. I've been writing some new
jokes."

"Please, don't tell no jokes, Sergio. You ain't funny no
more," said Giancarlo. "Neither is sleeping down here funny
which you think it is. This place is a rat hole, Sergio."

"A cellar has its drawbacks, Giancarlo. But look where you
sleep, in a hallway, when two guys in hallways already got
killed by persons unknown," said Sergio. He grinned over the
candle as they both squatted on the floor. From his years in the
comedy business he knew that candlelight under the chin dis-
torted the face with shadows, but his ghoulish expression didn't
make Giancarlo laugh. "Let me show you what the terrier
caught that I hung up to dry." said Sergio, who liked to see
people react, preferably with a belly laugh, in order for them
and him to know they were all still alive. He lit another squat
candle – he had taken a full box from the candle rack before the
Sacred Heart Shrine at Saint Finbar's. In the light of the second
candle he lured Giancarlo to the back of the cellar despite the
stink and Giancarlo's better judgment. Giancarlo was curious.
Along the back wall Giancarlo saw the dead rats hung heads
down with their tails knotted on a length of clothesline and he
felt queasy.

"You're pretty weird," said Giancarlo, who hunched back
toward the other candle which still flickered on the floor. In the
dark he stepped on the dog's tail. "Sorry, Pagliaccio," he said to
the dog. "Go back to sleep, Pagliaccio."

"A rat ain't stupid," said Sergio, when he too squatted by the
candle on the floor again. "When it sees its buddies hung there,

it will scoot out of this cellar while a guy and his dog try to get some sleep."

"I came here tonight to talk about Becky," said Giancarlo, getting down to business. "Becky ain't so sure she wants to come to her own party in the same old dress she's had on for months now, Sergio." Giancarlo's small body twitched as his eyes failed to poke holes in the cellar darkness all around him as he sat close to the candle. "She said if you're such a great guy, Sergio, who gives a lady a birthday party, then you can also give her the dress to come in. And she needs shoes too. I would know what kind of shoes to get her if you want to." Giancarlo Gargano had been one of five shoe salesmen in a store on Eighty-sixth Street there in Bensonhurst when his wife, Cynthia, decided that he wouldn't ever earn enough money for the family to live decently on so she had moved herself and their two kids in with the owner of the store. After the store owner fired Giancarlo, he couldn't pay his rent and lost the apartment besides and then decided there wasn't anyone to work for anyway, not even for himself, a poor specimen of a man if he had ever seen one. So without a job or savings or an apartment he moved onto the avenue. "You're not going to believe this, Sergio: Becky said what she wants for a present for her birthday—are you listening?—besides the dress and the shoes, is for you to *marry* her, Sergio. Do you believe that? If I was you, Sergio, I wouldn't marry her. On account of I think she has a case of crabs."

"That's an awful lot for a woman to ask a guy for, Giancarlo, for a birthday present. But I just might do it. I had a lot of women in my time, but I never married one which maybe wasn't so nice of me. Now I'm forty-four maybe it's time," said Sergio, who was considered by women to be good-looking despite his long needle nose, because of the way his eyes and mouth twinkled, as they now did. A few people would come to a birthday party but many more would come to a wedding, he thought, so he would have a bigger audience for his jokes, too.

He was hungry for an audience after going a couple of years without one, but he still called his former agent on Seventh Avenue in Manhattan who always told a performer up front how bad he was but never how good he was when he was good. For years Sergio had been very good. The customers had rolled in the aisles. But then Sergio was told on the phone twenty or so times that his light touch had turned into hot lead, and the agent couldn't book him anywhere. Sergio kept his show clothes on under his ragged clothes, though, for when he would go on again, and he called his former agent whenever he had some extra change, which wasn't often. His slightly bonkers form of humor had taken the funnyman over the edge, the agent had decided, so he humored Sergio. "There's a gig up in the Catskills I turned down for you for the lousy money they offered which couldn't hardly cover what they charge for lox and bagels, but another deal that my fingers are crossed about could be your breakthrough shot, Sergio, so call me again in a few weeks." A call like that could give Sergio enough adrenaline to go for a few days without even the thought of food as hope seeped down from his ears into his flesh as far down as his toes which even he couldn't stand the smell of. He didn't take his shoes off now, even when he slept in the wire basket which once had been a city trash container. The wire basket had first been co-opted by some Sicilian in the neighborhood for his personal use as a backyard incinerator, and then it was discarded when some wires had burned through and co-opted this last time by Sergio for him to sleep in in the cellar under the shoe repair shop. In the summer now the shoe repairman didn't come down to the cellar to check on the oil burner, and when he went home to his own apartment on Eightieth Street at the end of the day Sergio went down into the cellar. Before the shoe repairman came back to work in the morning, Sergio would already be gone for breakfast for himself and his dog, Pagliaccio. Sergio thought the terrier had the sad heart of a clown and for that reason named him Clown in Italian, the language Sergio had grown up with and which belonged to the neighborhood. He used Italian as much as his native English now that he was back in Bensonhurst.

"If this is one of your jokes, I'm not playing it on Becky, because she won't laugh at no joke, Sergio. She ain't in her right mind to laugh at anything," said Giancarlo. "If she could be cleaned up with some turpentine like once my Cynthia used to get out the nits from my daughter Angelina's hair, then Becky could look all right and then maybe her mind would come back in one piece."

"After we get married Becky could come down here in the cellar too to sleep at night," said Sergio, his plan for their future as solid proof of his serious intention, that he wasn't just kidding, though often he *was* just kidding. "I even know where there's another wire basket for her to sleep in." He had to laugh out loud right then even though Giancarlo didn't see the joke. Sergio visualized himself and Becky sleeping side by side in wire baskets in the cellar, and he knew that was funny and crazy. But also it wasn't so funny and crazy either, because they wouldn't have any other home to sleep in.

The audience in the nightclub where he had last worked also hadn't laughed when he made up a story about a homeless guy who gave a birthday party for a bag lady, and now he himself was going to be a character in that story except that it wasn't fiction anymore. The audience should have laughed – he had insisted to the nightclub owner – instead of booing him. Boos wouldn't help anyone to feel better the way a few laughs would. Canned from his last club date he stayed in the fleabag hotel on West Forty-seventh Street in the room he shared with Corinne who worked at the same club as a waitress. She wore a tutu to show off in black net stockings the Statue of Liberty long legs he thought she had. Legs which also drove some guys crazy. Corinne kept Sergio around to beat off those crazy guys, but she and Sergio both knew that they were just temporary shelter for each other like the room they had. Nothing was expected or given except a little kindness, a little company, and a roll in the hay. "Personally, Sergio, I think you're the funniest palooka I ever heard in my life, but myself, I don't think no audience wants to hear the awful truth," said Corinne. "What it wants to hear out on a date and having drinks is good news only. Do yourself a favor, pal, go take yourself out of the funny routines. Go get yourself a regular job."

All his life the few people who had really liked him had urged on him grown-up behavior while the others who hadn't liked him had left him alone to be a kid which was the only work he had ever succeeded at. As a teenager he had been foolish and devilish and dangerous without hurting anyone else, a border-line delinquent, but he had no malice, not that his heart was overflowing with the milk of human kindness. Any kid's heart was more or less empty of feelings for others until it could get enough feelings stored away for the kid himself, and Sergio too was still trying to store away feelings for himself. Not only did he get in trouble because of the kid he was, but the kid he was also got him out of trouble when an adult in his shoes would have drawn a blank on what to do next.

For a few months Corinne covered their expenses, but she couldn't convince Sergio to take a job as a short-order cook in a Broadway burger joint or to unload building materials for a new office tower going up on Third Avenue. Corinne had arranged this job through the foreman she was seeing on the side in the process of letting go of Sergio and having someone ready to take his place. When all the signs were clear to Sergio that Corinne wouldn't boot him out but that he wasn't wanted anymore either, he left on his own and went back to Bensonhurst. His widowed mother still lived there, but he wouldn't go to see her until her last days when she would be too sick to tell him what to do.

Seated across from Sergio in the cellar Giancarlo wrapped his arms around his shoulders to protect himself from Sergio, the madman, who laughed for no reason it seemed, and to protect himself too from the darkness down there, and the rats. "You can't get married to Becky tomorrow without a license and a priest," said Giancarlo. "It takes weeks to get a license and a priest and, besides, we don't have any money to get them. And, where, I ask you, are you going to get a dress and shoes from by tomorrow?"

"A license and a priest in order to get married is bullshit, Giancarlo. Let's dispense with the bullshit, especially us in our circumstances. What we have to deal with here, Giancarlo, is two warm bodies to be joined in the married state, Becky because she wants to, and me because I been asked. But do you know what – I'm getting this strange thought in my mind, the way a woman sometimes knows what you're thinking before you do, that I'm the wrong guy she asked. That she should've asked you, Giancarlo. That you're the guy who really wants to marry her. You really go for Becky, don't you, Giancarlo?"

"Me?" said Giancarlo. "No, I don't go for Becky. I think she's nice. I think she was once a beauty. But she's a little wacky, Sergio. Besides, my wife, Cynthia, didn't divorce me yet, on account of it's against the rules of the church. It don't bother her it's against the rules to sleep with that guy. If I married Becky it would be bigamy. I could go to jail for bigamy, Sergio."

"First, Giancarlo, there ain't no bigamy where we are on Sixteenth Avenue," said Sergio. "Second, if *I* married Becky, I would just be doing her a favor, which is the only thing left I can do anymore. But *you* really care about her. That's very touching, Giancarlo. You two could take over this here cellar. I'd move out to your hallway."

"She asked to marry you," said Giancarlo. "She didn't ask to marry me." His hands covered his face to hide the disappointment he had had since he was a kid when the daily routines had already begun to seem too difficult to manage. "In the first place, I didn't have no grand idea like you did to give her a birthday party, Sergio."

"It's settled, Giancarlo. You ask her, and I'm sure she'll say yes," said Sergio. "And I'm going to be the priest myself. And I'm going to prepare the wedding feast too. It'll be a birthday party *and* a wedding feast. So, go ask her, Giancarlo. I'm sure it's you Becky wanted to ask all along, but maybe she thought you were too good for her, which I wouldn't be as a lunatic former funnyman."

"What about the dress and shoes, Sergio? If I believed you'd get them and I could bring her the good news, then maybe she wouldn't mind marrying me instead," said Giancarlo. "But you can't get no dress and no shoes, can you?"

"Yes, I can. I'll tell you how, Giancarlo. I'm going to force my way in where your first wife, Cynthia, lives now by showing her my knife. You know it's a genuine hunting knife," said Sergio. "I'm going to ask her very politely for the favorite dress you used to like to see her in. And she's going to give it to me."

"You'll scare my kids," said Giancarlo.

"When they come out, then I'll go in," said Sergio. "I promise you I won't scare them. Now tell me which dress I should ask her for."

"The ivory satin one with a few pearls sewed on up here," said Giancarlo. "But don't hurt her, Sergio. I still love her, Sergio."

"I know you do, Giancarlo. So I'll be very nice. And she'll be very nice and give me the dress," said Sergio. But it was all a joke for the pleasure of revenge it seemed to give Giancarlo on his wife, and also to urge Giancarlo forward into the marriage with Becky. Sergio saw himself now with a thin Machiavellian heart but he had no remorse. A comedian by nature had to be a certified bastard, in his opinion, which made it possible for him to attack the bad guys. The sweet guys like Giancarlo just didn't have the heart to do it.

Footsteps overhead woke him the next morning in the cellar where he had overslept huddled down at the bottom of the wire basket like a week's accumulated trash, but he was pleased when he opened his eyes that in his sleep his mind had figured out the menu for that night's wedding feast. Promptly he pushed himself up and out of the basket. He said to Pagliaccio that they didn't have time for their usual piss on the back wall to warn the rats not to live in their cellar, but Sergio smelled in the humidity the dog's product. The dog hadn't been able to hold himself. It was a quality a dog was expected to have but not one that had to sleep in a vermin-infested cellar and whose previous owner had arranged for its vocal cords to be surgically cut. Only now had this dog ever been praised for its natural terrier talent as a born ratter. A year ago Sergio had made a dollar deposit at the pound, and for three days he had panhandled on Eighty-sixth Street until he had enough money to pay the fee for the dog. But no money had been left over for a collar and a leash and Sergio knew now that Pagliaccio at least deserved a better life than he was able to give him, including a better collar and leash than a length of clothesline which he now tied to the dog's neck. Without a bark from Pagliaccio they then left the cellar, both on soft paws.

If the dollar in change in his pocket that he had panhandled the day before was enough to buy a thrift-store dress he would give up his and Pagliaccio's breakfast this morning, but more than a dollar was needed – inspiration was needed, and there was no inspiration without coffee first. When the pimple-faced counter kid bagged the coffee and doughnuts, Sergio asked him for ten creams and ten sugars instead of the usual eight. For a moment the kid squinted and seemed poised with an obscenity on the tip of his tongue but instead bagged more creams and sugars than Sergio could count and handed the bag over without a word or a grin. Seated on the curb under the elevated where the darkness and noise comforted him like a blanket he was hiding under with the radio on, he read a discarded copy of this morning's *Daily News,* and with the exception of the coffee which he kept for himself, he shared the doughnuts, creams and sugars with Pagliaccio. The dog had a brown tattered coat of short hair but only half a tail which never wagged. He looked like a joke on all fours, but often Sergio fed him when he himself would go unfed. Not even a square meal made the tail wag, though. Sergio did all the talking, commented on world events, and not even once did Pagliaccio bark back, and when Sergio told his dog a funny story as he did every morning to keep in shape for the time he returned as a top banana, the dog without vocal cords couldn't laugh either. He was a hopeless case.

Inspired by the coffee now, Sergio left Sixteenth Avenue with Pagliaccio on the clothesline leash and they made their way back to Seventy-ninth Street which was a few streets away. He was now unrecognized there by the other kids from his time who had stayed on the street to become adults like their parents and who eyed him suspiciously though once they had been close friends. He and the dog went down the block to the house where he himself had lived and where his mother still lived. After he looked around for a self-appointed spy on his actions, he shrunk to half his size as he crawled under the alley windows to the backyard clothesline where as a high school sophomore he had stolen the upstairs girl's underpants. But at this early hour of the morning there were no drying clothes to be stolen for Becky to wear, so he had to beat a hasty retreat.

His next stop was Saint Finbar's sacristy where he went in, noticed by a young priest who was putting on his cassock to go to offer the sacrifice of the mass in a few minutes, but the priest also *un*noticed Sergio by turning his back on the handout Sergio was expected to ask for. When the priest was gone Sergio helped himself to another priestly garment from a wood peg where the clothes were hung. It looked like a white dress which was usually worn over the black cassock. In this instance the white garment also had a very wide lace border at the bottom which triggered in Sergio's memory a terrifically funny story he used to tell about a priest in lace, and right there in the sacristy he laughed out loud at his own remembered punch line. Then he was out the door with the dresslike surplice when an old woman all in black coming toward him spotted the garment and screamed, "Crook! Crook!" He dropped the priestly dress at her feet, which didn't quiet her so he hotfooted it away from there.

At the Salvation Army store where he went next the clerk gave him a dress at no charge, as simple as that, when he said he had no money to buy one for a bride-to-be. In order to receive the dress he also had to accept a pamphlet about how to save his soul, which seemed very funny to him when he couldn't even save his ass. The dress wasn't ivory satin with pearls but it was pretty close as a sort of yellowed white cotton and it was clean. It was also a bit too spacious as apparently it had been cast off by some well-fed woman while Becky herself was all bones, but the size wouldn't matter. "If you'd let me tell you a funny story it would be my way of paying you for the dress," Sergio said to the clerk who was a glum old man with fallen shoulders. The man said, "I don't have time to laugh. I have to wait on the other customers." He put the dress into a brown sack printed with a supermarket's name. Then Sergio untied the dog from the bike rack by the front door and together they went to find Becky.

To lengthen his own pleasure in the preparation of the feast Sergio had struck a match early, using the trash on the avenue and in the empty lots for his fire, and even some from his cellar. The fire had burned for hours now in the wire trash basket since Giancarlo said he wouldn't want the basket to sleep in with Becky if they moved into the cellar, and Sergio knew the basket wouldn't fit in the hallway where he would move to. Giancarlo said that he and Becky would sleep in sleeping bags in the cellar.

Meat couldn't be barbecued successfully over roaring flames, Sergio knew from his better days. Flames would just scorch the meat but the radiant heat of hot coals would penetrate the meat so it would cook inside too, so he had built up a bed of hot coals. The smell of the meat that roasted on the coals traveled under the elevated to the figures in doorways, sprawled on sidewalks, and huddled in the empty lots. Some of the ragged men and women were so lost in their own nightmares that they had already forgotten that they had been invited to the birthday and wedding party. But their noses reminded them now and they pulled themselves up as if real life called to them once again. They sniffed the night air like animals for the direction the smell was coming from. Starved so often, many had given up even the appetite for food as earlier they had given up the appetites for sex, comfort, and the simple pleasures that sustained normal lives. Still, now, from many small caves in the grand cave under the elevated the figures shuffled unsurely like ghosts in the night toward the red glow in the basket as the memory of what a feast could be came back to them.

Of the two women in the crowd of men, one was the plumpest of them all and had her wits about her to rent a post office box where she received checks which she deposited at a bank and withdrew a few dollars each weekday for food. Somedays she also took out a little money to buy a little gas to move the car she slept in when a notice was posted on the windshield that warned if the car wasn't moved in seventy-two hours it would be towed away. The car's right side was crushed in like a tin can under a heel, but she had bought the car that way from a junk dealer for a hundred dollars to have a place to sleep with locked doors and to get out of the snow in winter. The other woman guest had none of her wits about her at all, evident in the endless loud conversations she had with a man apparently dead before she could tell him everything on her mind. Her speech was in fragments that gaped with holes where the meaning should be and no one had the least idea what she was saying.

Now, close to midnight, a third woman came up the middle of the avenue. It was Becky in the yellowed white cotton dress, holding onto Giancarlo's arm as both took measured steps in time with an organ playing in their minds as they approached the altar and the ceremony. Their path was lighted by twin young men of low intellect who struck and held burning paper matches until their fingers almost caught fire. They then moved a few paces ahead in the summer night to strike more matches for the bride and groom. The avenue was deserted by the other people who had beds to go to, and, as Sergio had anticipated, quite a big crowd of his and Giancarlo's friends had turned out for the party, a much larger crowd than for a birthday alone.

The nuptial couple and all the guests came to stand in a

stretched-out circle around the basket cooker in which the main
course rested on the hot coals themselves, as Sergio hadn't been
able to locate a roasting grate. With a pair of charred wood
sticks Sergio turned the roast for it to cook evenly. The charred
crusty surface of the meat made it tasty. The other morsels of
meat already served to the early arrivals as appetizers on paper
plates had been eaten with the fingers with gusto. Sergio now
turned over the cooking chore to the plump woman. Then he
took off his ragged outer jacket and ragged outer pants. In his
underneath red jacket and black pants he had performed for
paying audiences. But now, without the exaggerated grin with
which he usually warmed up an audience, he came to stand solemnly before Becky and Giancarlo, while he was breaking up
inside over the great joke it seemed to him to get married on the
avenue in desperate straits. "Do you take this man to be your
lawful husband?" he said. "I do," said Becky. "Do you take this
woman to be your lawful wife?" he said. "I do," said Giancarlo.
"Then I pronounce you man and wife. You may kiss the bride,
Giancarlo."

Somehow Becky Rosen had cleaned up immaculately although Sergio thought she did smell a little of turpentine. She
actually looked beautiful as Giancarlo held her loosely about
the waist. A Sicilian man usually didn't show too much affec-
tion for his wife in public, but Giancarlo also wouldn't allow his
wife's tears to go uncomforted even though they were tears of
joy. So as he held her he kissed her cheeks again and again. It
had been easy for Becky to acquire this husband as she had five
previous ones too, just because she always seemed so incredibly
helpless that men tripped over themselves to do things for her
for the reward of her beauty in their beds. But she had also tried
to burn down every apartment and house she had ever lived in
as a wife, and all her previous husbands had bailed out before
they found themselves inside the fire. She had made a clean
breast of all of that to Giancarlo before they took the big step.
Giancarlo figured that there wasn't anything in their circumstances that she could burn down so he wouldn't have to worry

about his own hide, and he took the plunge just so he could watch out for her and have whatever beauty she had left beside him in his bed.

"Don't cry, Becky. Everything's going to be all right," said Giancarlo. "I'm going to take care of you. Tomorrow, I'm going to the church for a bath and clean clothes. Then I'm going to find a job selling shoes again. I was the best damn salesman for ladies' shoes on Eighty-sixth Street. I can do it again, Becky. In the meantime, until I get my first paycheck, Sergio said we can live down in the cellar and he'll move to the hallway." Becky stopped crying and held onto Giancarlo very tight as if he would be the first husband who would truly take care of her, but then they had to let go of each other a little to accept the paper plates Sergio served them. With his hunting knife Sergio sliced the small roast and served thin pieces to all the guests, while he rehearsed in his mind the routine he would perform after everyone had a full stomach.

BHARATI MUKHERJEE

✳

The Tenant

MAYA SANYAL has been in Cedar Falls, Iowa, less than two weeks. She's come, books and clothes and one armchair rattling in the smallest truck that U-Haul would rent her, from New Jersey. Before that she was in North Carolina. Before that, Calcutta, India. Every place has something to give. She is sitting at the kitchen table with Fran drinking bourbon for the first time in her life. Fran Johnson found her the furnished apartment and helped her settle in. Now she's brought a bottle of bourbon which gives her the right to stay and talk for a bit. She's breaking up with someone named Vern, a pharmacist. Vern's father is also a pharmacist and owns a drugstore. Maya has seen Vern's father on TV twice already. The first time was on the local news when he spoke out against the selling of painkillers like Advil and Nuprin in supermarkets and gas stations. In the matter of painkillers, Maya is a universalist. The other time he was in a barbershop quartet. Vern gets along all right with his father. He likes the pharmacy business, as business goes, but he wants to go back to graduate school and learn to make films. Maya is drinking her first bourbon tonight because Vern left today for San Francisco State.

"I understand totally," Fran says. She teaches utopian fiction and a course in women's studies and worked hard to get Maya hired. Maya has a Ph.D. in comparative literature and will introduce writers like R.K. Narayan and Chinua Achebe to three sections of sophomores at the University of Northern Iowa. "A person has to leave home. Try out his wings."

Fran has to use the bathroom. "I don't feel abandoned." She pushes her chair away from the table. "Anyway, it was a sex thing totally. We were good together. It'd be different if I'd loved him."

Maya tries to remember what's in the refrigerator. They need food. She hasn't been to the supermarket in over a week. She doesn't have a car yet and so she relies on a corner store – a longish walk – for milk, cereal, and frozen dinners. Someday these exigencies will show up as bad skin and collapsed muscle tone. No folly is ever lost. Maya pictures history as a net, the kind of safety net travelling trapeze artists of her childhood fell into when they were inattentive, or clumsy. Going to circuses in Calcutta with her father is what she remembers vividly. It is a banal memory, for her father, the owner of a steel company, is a complicated man.

Fran is out in the kitchen long enough for Maya to worry. They need food. Her mother believed in food. What is love, anger, inner peace, etc., her mother used to say, but the brain's biochemistry? Maya doesn't want to get into that, but she is glad she has enough stuff in the refrigerator to make an omelette. She realizes Indian women are supposed to be inventive with food, whip up exotic delights to tickle an American's palate, and she knows she should be meeting Fran's generosity and candor with some sort of bizarre and effortless countermove. If there's an exotic spice store in Cedar Falls or in neighboring Waterloo, she hasn't found it. She's looked in the phone book for common Indian names, especially Bengali, but hasn't yet struck up culinary intimacies. That will come – it always does. There's a six-pack in the fridge that her landlord, Ted Suminski, had put in because she'd be thirsty after unpacking. She was thirsty, but she doesn't drink beer. She probably should have asked him to come up and drink the beer. Except for Fran she hasn't had anyone over. Fran is more friendly and helpful than anyone Maya has known in the States since she came to North Carolina ten years ago, at nineteen. Fran is a Swede, and she is tall, with blue eyes. Her hair, however, is a dull, darkish brown.

"I don't think I can handle anything that heavy-duty," Fran says when she comes back to the room. She means the omelette. "I have to go home in any case." She lives with her mother and her aunt, two women in their mid-seventies, in a drafty farmhouse. The farmhouse now has a computer store catty-corner from it. Maya's been to the farm. She's been shown photographs of the way the corner used to be. If land values ever rebound, Fran will be worth millions.

Before Fran leaves she says, "Has Rab Chatterji called you yet?"

"No." She remembers the name, a good, reliable Bengali name, from the first night's study of the phone book. Dr. Rabindra Chatterji teaches physics.

"He called the English office just before I left." She takes car keys out of her pocketbook. She reknots her scarf. "I bet Indian men are more sensitive than Americans. Rab's a Brahmin, that's what people say."

A Chatterji has to be a Bengali Brahmin – last names give ancestral secrets away – but Brahminness seems to mean more to Fran that it does to Maya. She was born in 1954, six full years after India became independent. Her India was Nehru's India: a charged, progressive place.

"All Indian men are wife beaters," Maya says. She means it and doesn't mean it. "That's why I married an American." Fran knows about the divorce, but nothing else. Fran is on the Hiring, Tenure, and Reappointment Committee.

Maya sees Fran down the stairs and to the car which is parked in the back in the spot reserved for Maya's car, if she had owned one. It will take her several months to save enough to buy one. She always pays cash, never borrows. She tells herself she's still recovering from the U-Haul drive halfway across the country. Ted Suminski is in his kitchen watching the women.

Maya waves to him because waving to him, acknowledging him in that way, makes him seem less creepy. He seems to live alone though a sign, THE SUMINSKIS, hangs from a metal horse's head in the front yard. Maya hasn't seen Mrs. Suminski. She hasn't seen any children either. Ted always looks lonely. When she comes back from campus, he's nearly always in the back, throwing darts or shooting baskets.

"What's he like?" Fran gestures with her head as she starts up her car. "You hear these stories."

Maya doesn't want to know the stories. She has signed a year's lease. She doesn't want complications. "He's all right. I keep out of his way."

"You know what I'm thinking? Of all the people in Cedar Falls, you're the one who could understand Vern best. His wanting to try out his wings, run away, stuff like that."

"Not really." Maya is not being modest. Fran is being impulsively democratic, lumping her wayward lover and Indian friend together as headstrong adventurers. For Fran, a utopian and feminist, borders don't count. Maya's taken some big risks, made a break with her parents' ways. She's done things a woman from Ballygunge Park Road doesn't do, even in fantasies. She's not yet shared stories with Fran, apart from the divorce. She's told her nothing of men she picks up, the reputation she'd gained, before Cedar Falls, for "indiscretions." She has a job, equity, three friends she can count on for emergencies. She is an American citizen. But.

Fran's Brahmin calls her two nights later. On the phone he presents himself as Dr. Chatterji, not Rabindra or Rab. An old-fashioned Indian, she assumes. Her father still calls his closest friend "Colonel." Dr. Chatterji asks her to tea on Sunday. She means to say no but hears herself saying, "Sunday? Fiveish? I'm not doing anything special this Sunday."

Outside, Ted Suminski is throwing darts into his garage door. The door has painted-on rings: orange, purple, pink. The bull's-eye gray. He has to be fifty at least. He is a big, thick, lonely man about whom people tell stories. Maya pulls the phone cord as far as it'll go so she can look down more directly on her landlord's large, bald head. He has his back to her as he lines up a dart. He's in black running shoes, red shorts, he's naked to the waist. He hunches his right shoulder, he pulls the arm back; a big, lonely man shouldn't have so much grace. The dart is ready to cut through the September evening. But Ted Suminski doesn't let go. He swings on worn rubber soles, catches her eye in the window (she has to have imagined this), takes aim at her shadow. Could she have imagined the noise of the dart's metal tip on her windowpane?

Dr. Chatterji is still on the phone. "You are not having any mode of transportation, is that right?"

Ted Suminski has lost interest in her. Perhaps it isn't interest, at all; perhaps it's aggression. "I don't drive," she lies, knowing it sounds less shameful than not owning a car. She has said this so often she can get in the right degree of apology and Asian upper-class helplessness. "It's an awful nuisance."

"Not to worry, please." Then, "It is a great honor to be meeting Dr. Sanyal's daughter. In Calcutta business circles he is a legend."

On Sunday she is ready by four-thirty. She doesn't know what the afternoon holds; there are surely no places for "high tea" – a colonial tradition – in Cedar Falls, Iowa. If he takes her back to his place, it will mean he has invited other guests. From his voice she can tell Dr. Chatterji likes to do things correctly. She has dressed herself in a peach-colored nylon georgette sari, jade drop-earrings and a necklace. The color is good on dark skin. She is not pretty, but she does her best. Working at it is a part of self-respect. In the mid-seventies, when American women felt rather strongly about such things, Maya had been in trouble with her women's group at Duke. She was too feminine. She had tried to explain the world she came out of. Her grand-

mother had been married off at the age of five in a village now in
Bangladesh. Her great-aunt had been burned to death over a
dowry problem. She herself had been trained to speak softly, arrange flowers, sing, be pliant. If she were to seduce Ted
Suminski, she thinks as she waits in the front yard for Dr. Chatterji, it would be minor heroism. She has broken with the past.
But.

Dr. Chatterji drives up for her at about 5:10. He is a hesitant
driver. The car stalls, jumps ahead, finally slams to a stop.
Maya has to tell him to back off a foot or so; it's hard to leap over
two sacks of pruned branches in a sari. Ted Suminski is an ob-
sessive pruner and gardener.

"My sincerest apologies, Mrs. Sanyal," Dr. Chatterji says.
He leans across the wide front seat of his noisy, very old, very
used car and unlocks the door for her. "I am late. But then, I am
sure you're remembering that Indian Standard Time is not at
all the same as time in the States." He laughs. He could be nervous — she often had that effect on Indian men. Or he could just
be chatty. "These Americans are all the time rushing and rushing but where it gets them?" He moves his head laterally once,
twice. It's the gesture made famous by Peter Sellers. When Peter Sellers did it, it had seemed hilarious. Now it suggests that
Maya and Dr. Chatterji have three thousand years plus civilization, sophistication, moral virtue, over people born on this
continent. Like her, Dr. Chatterji is a naturalized American.

"Call me Maya," she says. She fusses with the seat belt. She
does it because she needs time to look him over. He seems quite
harmless. She takes in the prominent teeth, the eyebrows that
run together. He's in a blue shirt and a beige cardigan with the
K-Mart logo that buttons tightly over the waist. It's hard to
guess his age because he has dyed his hair and his moustache.
Late thirties, early forties. Older than she had expected. "Not
Mrs. Sanyal."

This isn't the time to tell about ex-husbands. She doesn't
know where John is these days. He should have kept up at least.

John had come into her life as a graduate student at Duke, and she, mistaking the brief breathlessness of sex for love, had married him. They had stayed together two years, maybe a little less. The pain that John had inflicted all those years ago by leaving her had subsided into a cozy feeling of loss. This isn't the time, but then she doesn't want to be a legend's daughter all evening. She's not necessarily on Dr. Chatterji's side is what she wants to get across early; she's not against America and Americans. She makes the story – of marriage outside the Brahminic pale, the divorce – quick, dull. Her unsentimentality seems to shock him. His stomach sags inside the cardigan.

"We've each had our several griefs," the physicist says. "We're each required to pay our karmic debts."

"Where are we headed?"

Mrs. Chatterji has made some Indian snacks. She is waiting to meet you because she is knowing your cousin-sister who studied in Scottish Church College. My home is okay, no?"

Fran would get a kick out of this. Maya has slept with married men, with nameless men, with men little more than boys, but never with an Indian man. Never.

The Chatterjis live in a small blue house on a gravelly street. There are at least five or six other houses on the street; the same size but in different colors and with different front yard treatments. More houses are going up. This is the cutting edge of suburbia.

Mrs. Chatterji stands in the driveway. She is throwing a large plastic ball to a child. The child looks about four, and is Korean or Cambodian. The child is not hers because she tells it, "Chung-Hee, ta-ta, bye-bye. Now I play with guest," as Maya gets out of the car.

Maya hasn't seen this part of town. The early September light softens the construction pits. In that light, the houses too close together, the stout woman in a striped cotton sari, the child hugging a pink ball, the two plastic lawn chairs by a tender young tree, the sheets and saris on the clothesline in the back, all seem miraculously incandescent.

"Go home now, Chung-Hee. I am busy." Mrs. Chatterji points the child homeward, then turns to Maya, who has folded her hands in traditional Bengali greeting. "It is an honor. We feel very privileged." She leads Maya indoors to a front room that smells of moisture and paint.

In her new, deliquescent mood, Maya allows herself to be backed into the best armchair – a low-backed, boxy Goodwill item draped over with a Rajasthani bedspread – and asks after the cousin Mrs. Chatterji knows. She doesn't want to let go of Mrs. Chatterji. She doesn't want husband and wife to get into whispered conferences about their guest's misadventures in America, as they make tea in the kitchen.

The coffee table is already laid with platters of mutton croquettes, fish chops, onion pakoras, ghugni with puris, samosas, chutneys. Mrs. Chatterji has gone to too much trouble. Maya counts four kinds of sweetmeats in Corning casseroles on an end table. She looks into a see-through lid, spongy, white dumplings float in rosewater syrup. Planets contained, mysteries made visible.

"What are you waiting for, Santana?" Dr. Chatterji becomes imperious, though not unaffectionate. He pulls a dining chair up close to the coffee table. "Make some tea." He speaks in Bengali to his wife, in English to Maya. To Maya he says, grandly, "We are having real Indian Green Label Lipton. A nephew is bringing it just one month back."

His wife ignores him. "The kettle's already on," she says. She wants to know about the Sanyal family. Is it true her great-grandfather was a member of the Star Chamber in England?

Nothing in Calcutta is ever lost. Just as her story is known to Bengalis all over America, so are the scandals of her family, the grandfather hauled up for tax evasion, the aunt who left her husband to act in films. This woman brings up the Star Chamber, the glories of the Sanyal family, her father's philanthropies, but it's a way of saying, *I know the dirt.*

The bedrooms are upstairs. In one of those bedrooms an unseen, tormented presence – Maya pictures it as a clumsy ghost that strains to shake off the body's shell – drops things on the floor. The things are heavy and they make the front room's chandelier shake. Light bulbs, shaped like tiny candle flames, flicker. The Chatterjis have said nothing about children. There are no tricycles in the hallway, no small sandals behind the doors. Maya is too polite to ask about the noise, and the Chatterjis don't explain. They talk just a little louder. They flip the embroidered cover off the stereo. What would Maya like to hear? Hemanta Kumar? Manna Dey? Oh, that young chap, Manna Dey! What sincerity, what tenderness he can convey!

Upstairs the ghost doesn't hear the music of nostalgia. The ghost throws and thumps. The ghost makes its own vehement music. Maya hears in its voice madness, self-hate.

Finally the water in the kettle comes to a boil. The whistle cuts through all fantasy and pretense. Dr. Chatterji says, "I'll see to it," and rushes out of the room. But he doesn't go to the kitchen. He shouts up the stairwell. "Poltoo, kindly stop this nonsense straightaway! We're having a brilliant and cultured lady-guest and you're creating earthquakes?" The kettle is hysterical.

Mrs. Chatterji wipes her face. The face that had seemed plump and cheery at the start of the evening now is flabby. "My sister's boy," the woman says.

So this is the nephew who has brought with him the cartons of Green Label tea, one of which will be given to Maya.

Mrs. Chatterji speaks to Maya in English as though only the alien language can keep emotions in check. "Such an intelligent boy! His father is government servant. Very highly placed."

Maya is meant to visualize a smart, clean-cut young man from south Calcutta, but all she can see is a crazy, thwarted, lost graduate student. Intelligence, proper family guarantee nothing. Even Brahmins can do self-destructive things, feel unsavory urges. Maya herself had been an excellent student.

"He was First Class First in biology science from Presidency College," the woman says. "Now he getting master's in agriculture science at Iowa State."

The kitchen is silent. Dr. Chatterji comes back into the room with a tray. The teapot is under a tea cozy, a Kashmiri one embroidered with the usual chinar leaves, loops, and chains. "*Her* nephew," he says. The dyed hair and dyed moustache are no longer signs of a man wishing to fight the odds. He is a vain man, anxious to cut losses. "Very unfortunate business."

The nephew's story comes out slowly, over fish chops and mutton croquettes. He is in love with a student from Ghana.

"Everything was A-OK until the Christmas break. Grades, assistantship for next semester, everything."

"I blame the college. The office for foreign students arranged a Christmas party. And now, *baapre baap!* Our poor Poltoo wants to marry a Negro Muslim."

Maya is known for her nasty, ironic one-liners. It has taken her friends weeks to overlook her malicious, un-American pleasure in others' misfortunes. Maya would like to finish Dr. Chatterji off quickly. He is pompous; he is reactionary; he wants to live and work in America but give back nothing except taxes. The confused world of the immigrant – the lostness that Maya and Polto feel – that's what Dr. Chatterji wants to avoid. She hates him. But.

Dr. Chatterji's horror is real. A good Brahmin boy in Iowa is in love with an African Muslim. It shouldn't be a big deal. But the more she watches the physicist, the more she realizes that "Brahmin" isn't a caste, it's a metaphor. You break one small rule, and the constellation collapses. She thinks suddenly that John Cheever – she is teaching him as a "world writer" in her classes, cheek-by-jowl with Africans and West Indians – would have understood Dr. Chatterji's dread. Cheever had been on her mind, ever since the late afternoon light slanted over Mrs. Chatterji's drying saris. She remembers now how full of a soft,

Cheeverian light Durham had been the summer she had slept with John Hadwen; and how after that, her tidy graduate-student world became monstrous, lawless. All men became John Hadwen; John became all men. Outwardly, she retained her poise, her Brahminical breeding. She treated her crisis as a literary event; she lost her moral sense, her judgment, her power to distinguish. Her parents had behaved magnanimously. They had cabled from Calcutta: WHAT'S DONE IS DONE. WE ARE CONFIDENT YOU WILL HANDLE NEW SITUATIONS WELL. ALL LOVE. But she knows more than do her parents. Love is anarchy.

Poltoo is Mrs. Chatterji's favorite nephew. She looks as though it is her fault that the Sunday has turned unpleasant. She stacks the empty platters methodically. To Maya she says, "It is the goddess who pulls the strings. We are puppets. I know the goddess will fix it. Poltoo will not marry that African woman." Then she goes to the coat closet in the hall and staggers back with a harmonium, the kind sold in the music stores in Calcutta, and sets it down on the carpeted floor. "We're nothing but puppets," she says again. She sits at Maya's feet, her pudgy hands on the harmonium's shiny, black bellows. She sings, beautifully, in a virgin's high voice, "Come, goddess, come, muse, come to us hapless peoples' rescue."

Maya is astonished. She has taken singing lessons at Dakshini Academy in Calcutta. She plays the sitar and the tanpur, well enough to please Bengalis, to astonish Americans. But stout Mrs. Chatterji is a devotee, talking to God.

A little after eight, Dr. Chatterji drops her off. It's been an odd evening and they are both subdued.

"I want to say one thing," he says. He stops her from undoing her seat belt. The plastic sacks of pruned branches are still at the corner.

"You don't have to get out," she says.

"Please. Give me one more minute of your time."

"Sure."

"Maya is my favorite name."

She says nothing. She turns away from him without making her embarrassment obvious.

"Truly speaking, it is my favorite. You are sometimes lonely, no? But you are lucky. Divorced women can date, they can go to bars and discos. They can see mens, many mens. But inside marriage there is so much loneliness." A groan, low, horrible, comes out of him.

She turns back toward him, to unlatch the seat belt and run out of the car. She sees that Dr. Chatterji's pants are unzipped. One hand works hard under his Jockey shorts; the other rests, limp, penitential, on the steering wheel.

"Dr. Chatterji – *really!*" she cries.

The next day, Monday, instead of getting a ride home with Fran – Fran says she *likes* to give rides, she needs the chance to talk, and she won't share gas expenses, absolutely not – Maya goes to the periodicals room of the library. There are newspapers from everywhere, even from Madagascar and New Caledonia. She thinks of the periodicals room as an asylum for homesick aliens. There are two aliens already in the room, both Orientals, both absorbed in the politics and gossip of their far-off homes.

She goes straight to the newspapers from India. She bunches her raincoat like a bolster to make herself more comfortable. There's so much to catch up on. A village headman, a known Congress-Indira party worker, has been shot at by scooter-riding snipers. An Indian pugilist has won an international medal – in Nepal. A child drawing well water – the reporter calls the child "a neo-Buddhist, a convert from the now-outlawed untouchable caste" – has been stoned. An editorial explains that the story about stoning is not a story about caste but about failed idealism; a story about promises of green fields and clean, potable water broken, a story about bribes paid and wells not dug. But no, thinks Maya, it's about caste.

Out here, in the heartland of the new world, the India of serious newspapers unsettles. Maya longs again to feel what she had felt in the Chatterjis' living room: virtues made physical. It is a familiar feeling, a longing. Had a suitable man presented himself in the reading room at that instant, she would have seduced him. She goes on to the stack of *India Abroad*s, reads through matrimonial columns, and steals an issue to take home.

Indian men want Indian brides. Married Indian men want Indian mistresses. All over America, "handsome, tall, fair" engineers, doctors, data processors – the new pioneers – cry their eerie love calls.

Maya runs a finger down the first column; her fingertip, dark with newsprint, stops at random.

Hello! Hi! Yes, you *are* the one I'm looking for. You are the new emancipated Indo-American woman. You have a zest for life. You are at ease in USA and yet your ethics are rooted in Indian tradition. The man of your dreams has come. Yours truly is handsome, ear-nose-throat specialist, well-settled in Connecticut. Age is 41 but never married, physically fit, sportsmanly, and strong. I adore idealism, poetry, beauty. I abhor smugness, passivity, caste system. Write with recent photo. Better still, call!!!

Maya calls. Hullo, hullo, hullo! She hears immigrant lovers cry in crowded shopping malls. Yes, you who are at ease in both worlds, you are the one. She feels she has a fair chance.

A man answers. "Ashoke Mehta speaking."

She speaks quickly into the bright-red mouthpiece of her telephone. He will be in Chicago, in transit, passing through O'Hare. United counter, Saturday, two P.M. As easy as that.

"Good," Ashoke Mehta says. "For these encounters I, too, prefer a neutral one."

On Saturday at exactly two o'clock the man of Maya's dreams floats toward her as lovers used to in shampoo commercials. The United counter is a loud, harrassed place but passengers and piled-up luggage fall away from him. Full-cheeked and fleshy-lipped, he is handsome. He hasn't lied. He is serene, assured, a Hindu god touching down in Illinois.

She can't move. She feels ugly and unworthy. Her adult life no longer seems miraculously rebellious; it is grim, it is perverse. She has accomplished nothing. She has changed her citizenship but she hasn't broken through into the light, the vigor, the *hustle* of the New World. She is stuck in dead space.

"Hullo, hullo!" Their fingers touch.

Oh, the excitement! Ashoke Mehta's palm feels so right in the small of her back. Hullo, hullo, hullo. He pushes her out of the reach of anti-Khomeini Iranians, Hare Krishnas, American Fascists, men with fierce wants, and guides her to an empty gate. They have less than an hour.

"What would you like, Maya?"

She knows he can read her mind, she knows her thoughts are open to him. *You,* she's almost giddy with the thought, with simple desire. "From the snack bar," he says, as though to clarify. "I'm afraid I'm starved."

Below them, where the light is strong and hurtful, a Boeing is being serviced. "Nothing," she says.

He leans forward. She can feel the nap of his scarf – she recognizes the Cambridge colors – she can smell the wool of his Icelandic sweater. She runs her hand along the scarf, then against the flesh of his neck. "Only the impulsive ones call," he says.

The immigrant courtship proceeds. It's easy, he's good with facts. He knows how to come across to a stranger who may end up a lover, a spouse. He makes over a hundred thousand. He owns a house in Hartford, and two income properties in Newark. He plays the market but he's cautious. He's good at badminton but plays handball to keep in shape. He watches all the sports on television. Last August he visited Copenhagen, Helsinki, and Leningrad. Once upon a time he collected stamps but now he doesn't have hobbies, except for reading. He counts himself an intellectual, he spends too much on books. Ludlum, Forsyth, MacInnes; other names she doesn't catch. She supresses a smile, she's told him only she's a graduate student. He's not without his vices. He's a spender, not a saver. He's a sensualist: good food – all foods, but easy on the Indian – good wine. Some temptations he doesn't try to resist.

And I, she wants to ask, do I tempt?

"Now tell me about yourself, Maya." He makes it easy for her. "Have you ever been in love?"

"No."

"But many have loved you, I can see that." He says it not unkindly. It is the fate of women like her, and men like him. Their karmic duty, to be loved. It is expected, not judged. She feels he can see them all, the sad parade of need and demand. This isn't the time to reveal all.

And so the courtship enters a second phase.

When she gets back to Cedar Falls, Ted Suminski is standing on the front porch. It's late at night, chilly. He is wearing a down vest. She's never seen him on the porch. In fact there's no chair to sit on. He looks chilled through. He's waited around a while.

"Hi." She has her keys ready. This isn't the night to offer the six-pack in the fridge. He looks expectant, ready to pounce.

"Hi." He looks like a man who might have aimed the dart at her. What has he done to his wife, his kids? Why isn't there at least a dog? "Say, I left a note upstairs."

The note is written in Magic Marker and thumbtacked to her apartment door. DUE TO PERSONAL REASONS, NAMELY RE-MARRIAGE, I REQUEST THAT YOU VACATE MY PLACE AT THE END OF THE SEMESTER.

Maya takes the note down and retacks it to the kitchen wall. The whole wall is like a bulletin board, made of some new, crumbly building material. Her kitchen, Ted Suminski had told her, was once a child's bedroom. Suminski in love: the idea stuns her. She has misread her landlord. The dart at her window speaks of no twisted fantasy. The landlord wants the tenant out.

She gets a glass out of the kitchen cabinet, gets out a tray of ice, pours herself a shot of Fran's bourbon. She is happy for Ted Suminski. She is. She wants to tell someone how moved she'd been by Mrs. Chatterji's singing. How she'd felt in O'Hare, even about Dr. Rab Chatterji in the car. But Fran is not the person. No one she's ever met is the person. She can't talk about the dead space she lives in. She wishes Ashoke Mehta would call. Right now.

Weeks pass. Then two months. She finds a new room, signs another lease. Her new landlord calls himself Fred. He has no arms, but he helps her move her things. He drives between Ted Suminski's place and his twice in his station wagon. He uses his toes the way Maya uses her fingers. He likes to do things. He pushes garbage sacks full of Maya's clothes up the stairs.

"It's all right to stare," Fred says. "Hell, I would."

That first afternoon in Fred's rooming house, they share a Chianti. Fred wants to cook her pork chops but he's a little shy about Indians and meat. Is it beef, or pork? Or any meat? She says it's okay, any meat, but not tonight. He has an ex-wife in Des Moines, two kids in Portland, Oregon. The kids are both normal; he's the only freak in the family. But he's self-reliant. He shops in the supermarket like anyone else, he carries out the garbage, shovels the snow off the sidewalk. He needs Maya's help with one thing. Just one thing. The box of Tide is a bit too heavy to manage. Could she get him the giant size every so often and leave it in the basement?

The dead space need not suffocate. Over the months, Fred and she will settle into companionship. She has never slept with a man without arms. Two wounded people, he will joke during their nightly contortions. It will shock her, this assumed equivalence with a man so strikingly deficient. She knows she is strange, and lonely, but being Indian is not the same, she would have thought, as being a freak.

One night in spring, Fred's phone rings. "Ashoke Mehta speaking." None of this "do you remember me?" nonsense. The god has tracked her down. He hasn't forgotten. "Hullo," he says, in their special way. And because she doesn't answer back, "Hullo, hullo, hullo." She is aware of Fred in the back of the room. He is lighting a cigarette with his toes.

"Yes," she says, "I remember."

"I had to take care of a problem," Ashoke Mehta says. "You know that I have my vices. That time at O'Hare I was honest with you."

She is breathless.

"Who is it, May?" asks Fred.

"You also have a problem," says the voice. His laugh echoes. "You will come to Hartford, I know."

When she moves out, she tells herself, it will not be the end of Fred's world.

SUSAN NUNES

*

A Moving Day

ACROSS THE STREET, the bulldozer roars to life. Distracted, my mother looks up from the pile of embroidered linen that she has been sorting. She is seventy, tiny and fragile, the flesh burned off her shrinking frame. Her hair is gray now – she had never dyed it – and she wears it cut close to her head with the nape shaved. Her natural hairline would have been better suited to the kimono worn by women of her mother's genera- tion. She still has a beautiful neck. In recent years she has taken a liking to jeans, cotton smocks, baggy sweaters, and running shoes. When I was a child she wouldn't have been caught dead without her nylons.

Her hands, now large-jointed with arthritis, return to the pile of linen. Her movements always had a no-nonsense quality and ever since I was a child, I have been wary of her energy because it was so often driven by suppressed anger. Now she is making two stacks, the larger one for us, the smaller for her to keep. There is a finality in the way she places things in the larger pile, as if to say that's *it*. For her, it's all over, all over but this last ac- counting. She does not look forward to what is coming. Strang- ers. Schedules. The regulated activities of those considered too old to regulate themselves. But at least, at the *very* least, she'll not be a burden. She sorts through the possessions of a lifetime, she and her three daughters. It's time she passed most of this on. Dreams are lumber. She can't *wait* to be rid of them.

My two sisters and I present a contrast. There is nothing purposeful or systematic about the way we move. In fact, we don't know where we're going. We know there is a message in all this activity, but we don't know what it is. Still, we search for it in the odd carton, between layers of tissue paper and silk. We open drawers, peer into the recesses of cupboards, rummage through the depths of closets. What a lot of stuff! We lift, untuck, unwrap, and set aside. The message is there, we know. But what is it? Perhaps if we knew, then we wouldn't have to puzzle out our mother's righteous determination to shed the past.

There is a photograph of my mother taken on the porch of my grandparents' house when she was in her twenties. She is wearing a floral print dress with a square, lace-edged collar and a graceful skirt that shows off her slim body. Her shoulder-length hair has been permed. It is dark and thick and worn parted on the side to fall over her right cheek. She is very fair; "one pound powder," her friends called her. She is smiling almost reluctantly, as if she meant to appear serious but the photographer has said something amusing. One arm rests lightly on the railing, the other, which is at her side, holds a handkerchief. They were her special pleasures, handkerchiefs of hand-embroidered linen as fine as rice paper. Most were gifts (she used to say that when she was a girl, people gave one another little things – a handkerchief, a pincushion, pencils, hair ribbons), and she washed and starched them by hand, ironed them, taking care with the rolled hems, and stored them in a silk bag from Japan.

There is something expectant in her stance, as if she were waiting for something to happen. She says, your father took this photograph in 1940, before we were married. She lowers her voice confidentially and adds, now he cannot remember taking it. My father sits on the balcony, an open book on his lap, peacefully smoking his pipe. The bulldozer tears into the foundations of the Kitamura house.

What about this? My youngest sister has found a fishing boat carved of tortoise shell.

Hold it in your hand and look at it. Every plank on the hull is visible. Run your fingers along the sides, you can feel the joints. The two masts, about six inches high, are from the darkest part of the shell. I broke one of the sails many years ago. The remaining one is quite remarkable, so thin that the light comes through it in places. It is delicately ribbed to give the effect of canvas pushed gently by the wind.

My mother reaches for a sheet of tissue paper and takes the boat from my sister. She says, it was a gift from Mr. Oizumi. He bought it from an artisan in Kamakura.

Stories cling to the thing, haunt it like unrestful spirits. They are part of the object. They have been there since we were children, fascinated with her possessions. In 1932, Mr. Oizumi visits Japan. He crosses the Pacific by steamer, and when he arrives he is hosted by relatives eager to hear of his good fortune. But Mr. Oizumi soon tires of their questions. He wants to see what has become of the country. It will be arranged, he is told. Mr. Oizumi is a meticulous man. Maps are his passion. A trail of neat X's marks the steps of his journey. On his map of China, he notes each military outpost in Manchuria and appends a brief description of what he sees. Notes invade the margins, march over the blank spaces. The characters are written in a beautiful hand, precise, disciplined, orderly. Eventually, their trail leads to the back of the map. After Pearl Harbor, however, Mr. Oizumi is forced to burn his entire collection. The U.S. Army has decreed that enemy aliens caught with seditious materials will be arrested. He does it secretly in the shed behind his home, his wife standing guard. They scatter the ashes in the garden among the pumpkin vines.

My grandfather's library does not escape the flames either. After the army requisitions the Japanese school for wartime headquarters, they give my mother's parents twenty-four hours to vacate the premises, including the boarding house where they lived with about twenty students from the plantation camps outside Hilo. There is no time to save the books. Her father decides to nail wooden planks over the shelves that line the classrooms. After the army moves in, they rip open the planks, confiscate the books, and store them in the basement of the post office. Later, the authorities burn everything. Histories, children's stories, primers, biographies, language texts, everything, even a set of Encyclopaedia Brittanica. My grandfather is shipped to Oahu and imprisoned on Sand Island. A few months later, he is released after three prominent Caucasians vouch for his character. It is a humiliation he doesn't speak of, ever.

All of this was part of the boat. After I broke the sail, she gathered the pieces and said, I'm not sure we can fix this. It was not a toy. Why can't you leave my things alone?

For years the broken boat sat on our bookshelf, a reminder of the brutality of the next generation.

Now she wants to give everything away. We have to beg her to keep things. Dishes from Japan, lacquerware, photographs, embroidery, letters. She says, I have no room. You take them, here, *take* them. Take them or I'll get rid of them.

They're piled around her, they fill storage chests, they fall out of open drawers and cupboards. She only wants to keep a few things – her books, some photographs, three carved wooden figures from Korea that belonged to her father, a few of her mother's dishes, perhaps one futon.

My sister holds a porcelain teapot by its bamboo handle. Four white cranes edged in black and gold fly around it. She asks, Mama, can't you hang on to this? If you keep it, I can borrow it later.

My mother shakes her head. She is adamant. And what would I do with it? I don't want any of this. Really.

My sister turns to me. She sighs. The situation is hopeless. You take it, she says. It'll only get broken at my place. The kids.

It had begun slowly, this shedding of the past, a plate here, a dish there, a handkerchief, a doily, a teacup, a few photographs, one of my grandfather's block prints. Nothing big. But then the odd gesture became a pattern; it got so we never left the house empty-handed. At first we were amused. After all, when we were children she had to fend us off her things. Threaten. We were always *at* them. She had made each one so ripe with memories that we found them impossible to resist. We snuck them outside, showed them to our friends, told and retold the stories. They bear the scars of all this handling, even her most personal possessions. A chip here, a crack there. Casualties. Like the music box her brother brought home from Italy after the war. It played a Brahms lullaby. First we broke the spring, then we lost the winding key, and for years it sat mutely on her dresser.

She would say again and again, it's impossible to keep anything nice with you children. And we'd retreat, wounded, for a while. The problem with children is they can wipe out your history. It's a miracle that anything survives this onslaught.

There's a photograph of my mother standing on the pier in Honolulu in 1932, the year she left Hawaii to attend the University of California. She's loaded to the ears with leis. She's wearing a fedora pulled smartly to the side. She's not smiling. Of my mother's two years there, my grandmother recalled that she received good grades and never wore a kimono again. My second cousin, with whom my mother stayed when she first arrived, said she was surprisingly sophisticated – she liked hats. My mother said that she was homesick. Her favorite class was biology and she entertained ambitions of becoming a scientist. Her father, however, wanted her to become a teacher, and his wishes prevailed, even though he would not have forced them upon her. She was a dutiful daughter.

During her second year, she lived near campus with a mathematics professor and his wife. In exchange for room and board she cleaned house, ironed, and helped prepare meals. One of the things that survives from this period is a black composition book entitled *Recipes of California*. As a child, I read it like a book

of mysteries for clues to a life which seemed both alien and familiar. Some entries she had copied by hand; others she cut out
of magazines and pasted on the page, sometimes with a picture
or drawing. The margins contained her cryptic comments:
"Saturday bridge club," "From Mary G. Do not give away,"
underlined, "chopped suet by hand, wretched task, bed at 2
A.M., exhausted." I remember looking up "artichoke" in the
dictionary and asking Mr. Okinaga, the vegetable vendor, if he
had any edible thistles. I never ate one until I was sixteen.

That book holds part of the answer to why our family rituals
didn't fit the recognized norm of either our relatives or the
larger community in which we grew up. At home, we ate in fear
of the glass of spilled milk, the stray elbow on the table, the
boarding house reach. At my grandparents', we slurped our
chasuke. We wore tailored dresses, white cotton pinafores, and
Buster Brown shoes with white socks; however, what we longed
for were the lacy, ornate dresses in the National Dollar Store
that the Puerto Rican girls wore to church on Sunday. For six
years, I marched to Japanese language school after my regular
classes; however, we only spoke English at home. We talked too
loudly and all at once, which mortified my mother, but she was
always complaining about Japanese indirectness. I know that
she smarted under a system in which the older son is the center
of the familial universe, but at thirteen I had a fit of jealous rage
over her fawning attention to our only male cousin.

My sister has found a photograph of my mother, a round-
faced and serious twelve or thirteen, dressed in a kimono and
seated, on her knees, on the *tatami* floor. She is playing the *koto.*
According to my mother, girls were expected to learn this difficult stringed instrument because it was thought to teach disci-
pline. Of course, everything Japanese was a lesson in dis-
cipline – flower arranging, calligraphy, judo, brush painting,
embroidery, everything. One summer my sister and I had to
take *ikebana,* the art of flower arrangement, at Grandfather's
school. The course was taught by Mrs. Oshima, a diminutive,
soft-spoken, terrifying woman, and my supplies were provided

by my grandmother, whose tastes ran to the oversized. I re-member little of that class and its principles. What I remember most clearly is having to walk home carrying, in a delicate bal-ancing act, one of our creations, which, more often than not, towered above our heads.

How do we choose among what we experience, what we are taught, what we run into by chance, or what is forced upon us? What is the principle of selection? My sisters and I are not bound by any of our mother's obligations, nor do we follow the rituals that seemed so important. My sister once asked, do you realize that when she's gone that's *it?* She was talking about how to make sushi, but it was a profound question nonetheless.

I remember, after we moved to Honolulu and my mother stopped teaching and began working long hours in administra-tion, she was less vigilant about the many little things that once consumed her attention. While we didn't exactly slide into sav-agery, we economized in more ways than one. She would often say, there's simply no time anymore to do things right.

I didn't understand then why she looked so sad when she said it, but somehow I knew the comment applied to us. It would be terrible if centuries of culture are lost simply because there is not time.

Still, I don't understand why we carry out this fruitless search. Whatever it is we are looking for, we're not going to find it. My sister tries to lift a box filled with record albums, old seventy-eights, gives up, and sets it down again. My mothers says, there are people who collect these things. Imagine.

Right, just imagine.

I think about my mother bathing me and singing, "The snow is snowing, the wind is blowing, but I will weather the storm." And I think of her story of the village boy carried by the Tengu on a fantastic flight over the cities of Japan, but who returns to a disbelieving and resistant family. So much for questions which have no answers, why we look among objects for meanings which have somehow escaped us in the growing up and growing old.

However, my mother is a determined woman. She will take nothing with her if she can help it. It is all ours. And on the balcony my father knocks the ashes of his pipe into a porcelain ashtray, and the bulldozer is finally silent.

MARY HELEN PONCE

Enero

"THE BABY," *la doctora* said, her wide hands pressing lightly on Constancia's protruding belly, "will be born in January. Uh, *Ineerio?*"

"Sí, *Enero.*" Constancia smiled up into the pleasant face of *la Doctora* Greene, then slowly raised her thick body to an upright position. In the clean, uncluttered bedroom the window curtains danced in the morning breeze and cooled Constancia's warm brow. She adjusted her underclothes, smoothed the bedsheet, then sat quietly on a chair, waiting for Doctor Greene to leave.

Constancia felt tired, lethargic. But my day is only half over, she told herself, smoothing down her dark hair. She sat, watching Doctor Greene, who with her customary efficiency, packed the worn stethoscope into her scruffy black bag, jammed a brown felt hat atop her head, and then, in her sensible brown shoes with the wide heels hurried down the porch steps and to her car. Her crisp cotton dress crinkling at the waist, Constancia stood watching the dusty 1938 Dodge as it went past, Doctor Greene at the wheel. On sudden impulse she leaned over the porch railing, her swollen stomach straining, to snap off a pink rambling rose from a nearby bush. She held the dewy soft flower to her nose and inhaled. The sweet fragrance made her dizzy, yet happy. She thought back to what *la doctora* had predicted. *Enero*. It would be a winter baby after all! The first of her ten children to be born in January, during cold weather. The others, born in spring, summer, and early fall, she remembered, had had a chance to thrive before the mild California weather turned cold. She sighed: *Enero*, the first month of the New Year – a month full of promise. *Enero*, the month when winter roses bloomed.

Across the street Constancia spotted a neighbor and waved, the flower clutched in her hand. At thirty-eight Constancia was still a pretty woman. Her olive face was unlined; the black, wavy hair slightly gray. She, like other women in the Mexican neighborhood, spent her days cooking, cleaning, and caring for a large family. She washed on Mondays, ironed on Tuesdays, and each Sunday cooked a pot of stew for supper. Unlike some of her friends, Constancia was not overly religious, although she made certain the children attended catechism and Sunday Mass, and, during Lent, took part in the *Via Crucis*.

She took pride in her clean appearance, knowing that Americans looked down on "dirty" Mexicans who lived in the barrio. She never left the house without first washing her face and combing her hair. She seldom wore an apron without washing it, and wore cotton stockings all year round, even in summer. She disliked wearing the maternity smocks stored in a box under the bed. Throughout her pregnancies she wore starched cotton dresses until her expanded waist literally burst the seams; then she retrieved the cardboard box under the bed, dusted the full-blown cotton smocks, and rinsed and ironed them. They hung in the small closet until the last months.

Constancia no longer tried to guess her unborn child's birth date – or sex. After the first two – a boy and a girl – it no longer mattered, or so she told herself. What did matter was that this baby be healthy, she conceded – healthy and strong enough to fight disease. She leaned against the railing, took a deep breath of the cool October air, pushed a lock of hair off her face, then went indoors.

In the roomy kitchen, Constancia pulled open a drawer

where aprons lay next to snowy dish towels, took one, then slowly tied the flowered apron around her extended belly and began to work. She felt sleepy. The night before, the stirrings of the unborn baby, the rain that hit against the window, and thoughts of Apollonia, her eldest daughter, had kept her awake. Try as she might, she could not close her eyes without seeing the thin, pale face of her tubercular daughter.

The day before, a warm Sunday of blue skies and white clouds, had been busy. Getting the children washed, fed, and then dressed in their good clothes for the short walk to church was a chore. Gabriela, the baby, had fussed at being left behind by the older kids, and had to be held for a time. Aware of the children's disapproval, a stubborn Constancia had forgone Sunday Mass. I'm not in a mood to pray to alabaster saints, or sing hymns of hope and praise, she decided. Nor do I want to squeeze myself into my "good" maternity dress (bought at J.C. Penney). While Gabriela napped, Constancia prepared for the visit to Apollonia. Once the children returned she fed them the usual Sunday fare: *cocido,* stewing beef with carrots, potatoes, and onions. While the older girls washed and rinsed dishes, she packed a bar of Palmolive soap, chewing gum, and lemon drops into a small carton; then, with Justo at her side and Felicitas in the back seat, they drove to visit Apollonia. Later that evening, when they returned, Constancia felt tired and depressed.

But today is another day, she sighed, pushing aside the kitchen curtains to stare out the window, and I must finish my work. She rinsed the breakfast dishes left soaking in the sink, dried them, and put them away in the cupboard above the linoleum-covered counter. *Enero.* Three months left to visit at will the sanatorium where Apollonia, now almost eighteen, lay dying of tuberculosis. Three months to cope with the pain of knowing Apollonia would not live past Easter Sunday. Three months to make arrangements for the inevitable funeral – and to prepare for the child that was coming.

Apollonia, the serious, sulky child born to them in Mexico, had been in the sanatorium close to three years. When in elementary school she was diagnosed with pleurisy, then later with tuberculosis. Soon after, she was sent to a nearby sanatorium. At first her condition had improved. Her youth, and the daily rest and medication, had arrested the fever, but the raspy, dry cough remained. The experimental surgery and the latest drugs have not helped my daughter, Constancia often thought, trying not to be bitter. Last month Apollonia had been moved to the infirmary reserved for critical cases. Two operations had failed to cure her; her weight had recently dropped. She was close to death.

The visit on Sunday had been especially trying. Constancia shivered as she remembered holding Apollonia's thin hands, squeezing fingers too weak to squeeze back. Long past visiting hours she had sat next to the sullen Apollonia, plying an embossed ivory comb through Apollonia's limp, curly hair, hoping to cheer her dispirited, pale daughter. But Apollonia, a bright and studious girl, knew she was not getting better, but worse. She refused to smile or eat the oatmeal cookies baked by Felicitas. Her dark eyes, like those of Constancia, shone bright, a sign not of good health but of the fever that was consuming her. When they left the sanatorium, which was surrounded by a grove of lemon trees, the sun was no longer visible. By the time they got home, a light rain was falling. Now, as she wiped the kitchen counter, Constancia thought once more about Doctor Greene's visit that morning. She sighed, thinking: I must prepare for life . . . and death.

Constancia hitched up her dress, then picked up the wicker basket near the zinc tubs in the washroom, *el llavadero*. The small cluttered room adjacent to the kitchen was a repository for dented tubs and empty glass jars. She walked outdoors, her steps slow yet firm, to the clothesline, where *calzones*, shirts, and pants flapped on the line. She laid the basket on the ground, pulled the clothespin bag toward her, then began to take down the clothes. Back and forth between the lines she moved, strong arms glistening in the sunlight. Constancia glanced up at the sky, never so blue, and at the birds darting here and there. With minimum effort she pulled, folded, and stacked the clean dry clothes inside the basket. Her pliant fingers released the wooden clothespins, then placed them in the faded cotton bag. The sun felt warm on her round face, in which the dark eyes, so like Apollonia's, blinked, then focused on a white cloud floating in the cobalt blue sky. *Enero.* In three months the clothesline would hold cotton diapers, and the *zapetas* would be folded in the trunk, Constancia knew. Once more I'll have a child and be forced to stay in bed for a month. One month without seeing Apollonia! How will I bear it? Constancia felt familiar tears sting her eyes. She took a handkerchief from her apron pocket, wiped her troubled eyes, then continued with her work.

It seemed to Constancia that most of her life had been spent caring for children. As a girl in Mexico, she had helped care for Rito and José, her mischievous younger brothers, a job she hated. The boys outshouted and outran her, slung mud and sticks at each other, and chased after the newborn calves. They refused to obey her and, during harvest time, hid in the haystacks piled along the road. She liked best to sit indoors embroidering linens, or to work in the rose garden that was her mother Martina's pride and joy, but she dared not disobey her parents. And now here I am, she thought, pulling at the clothesline, still caring for children, still chasing after boisterous boys who play with sticks and mud. Still, still. Except that unlike my mother, I have nine children who depend on me and, come January, one more baby to care for.

Constancia lingered by the clothesline, resisting the urge to reenter the confines of the house. She stood on tiptoe, her stomach straining from the effort, to inhale the pungent scent of the green leaves on the walnut tree. The tree, planted when they first moved to the roomy house, was as old as Apollonia. Unlike the sickly, pale girl, the walnut tree had taken root in the rich California soil. It now stood tall, with a thick, gnarled trunk and large branches that sprouted glossy, gray green leaves. Around its base small shoots were beginning to show.

By next year the tree would bear fruit, Constancia knew.

Round, meaty walnuts for the children to roast, and for the Christmas cookies baked by Felicitas. She inspected the tree, her strong hands caressing the veined leaves, unmindful of the laundry in the basket: socks rolled tight as baseballs, under-shirts folded in three equal parts, khaki pants turned inside out-–clothes ready for the hot iron. She stood silhouetted against the walnut tree, her stomach round as a watermelon, brown eyes fastened on the fluffy white clouds that drifted across the pale sky.

It was during fall that Constancia most missed her family in Mexico. She vividly remembered the sudden change in weather with the arrival of the harvest months, when she and her sisters worked alongside their mother. During the peak days of the *cosecha*, (the harvest), they cooked *cocido* in the huge cauldrons set atop open fires, and piled high the large wooden tables with steaming platters of frijoles, *sopa*, and baskets of hot tortillas. Each table held an enamel coffeepot which Constancia kept filled with *café*, the strong chicory-flavored coffee preferred by the ranchhands. Providing for the workers in Mexico was hard work, Constancia remembered, frowning slightly, as is caring for a large family. She sighed, looking up at the sky once more. And having to appear cheerful when I feel like crying is most difficult. But, I must persevere. She picked up the basket and heaved it onto her ample hip. I must not give in to misfortune, illness, or despair but persevere, like all the women in my fam-ily. At least until *Enero*. I must be strong, for the new baby . . . and for Apollonia.

Don Pedro, her father, was often on Constancia's mind. As *gerente* (general manager) of a large hacienda in Leon, Guanajuato, his job was to see that all went smoothly on the ranch. An intelligent, hardworking man, Don Pedro was re-sponsible for the hiring (and firing) of workers, the harvesting of crops, and the replenishing of stock. More importantly, he kept all the business records and submitted monthly reports to the hacienda owner.

As Constancia folded a worn shirt into the laundry basket,

she thought of her father and the many evenings he sat hunched over the kitchen table to enter numbers into the old, dusty ledgers kept on a shelf. With painstaking care he had dipped a quill pen in ink, then entered each transaction into the record. An astute, honest man, don Pedro was known throughout the area for his kindness and integrity. Constancia sighed, her thoughts on the ranch in Mexico, then slowly picked a clothespin off the ground and put it inside the pin bag.

My mother, too, worked hard, Constancia recalled, pulling at her sweater – very hard. As the ranch manager's wife, doña Martina kept the large house allocated to the manager in perfect order; there was never panic or confusion in that busy household. In addition to caring for a family of seven, her mother, an expert with medicinal herbs, often assisted ranch women during childbirth. Doña Martina also supervised the women at numerous chores connected to the ranch: hauling water, making soap, and wrapping goat cheese in muslin squares. During harvest time when the ranch teemed with men, wagons, and oxen, she was at her best.

When older, Constancia was allowed to deliver lunch baskets to the workers in the fields, where the warm sun and clean air beckoned. She enjoyed being outdoors with girls her own age, aware that the young men in the fields were potential *novios* (suitors). The older girls who already had beaus hid extra tortillas in the baskets for their men. Once lunch was delivered the girls, flushed from the long walk – and from being around the young men – were free to walk around at their leisure. Constancia had roamed the lima bean fields, staring up at the sky and clouds, wondering when Justo would return, when they would marry. She envied her sisters whose *novios* lived nearby, and who chided her for choosing to marry a man who wanted to live *en el otro lado*, "on the other side" – a man who would take her far from her family, her roots.

Yes, we women on the ranch worked hard, Constancia groaned, shaking a creamy yellow towel, and so do women in America. But at least I don't have to make stacks of tortillas ev-

ery day, although Justo would certainly like that. Still, there's
nothing wrong with white bread. The *Americanas* buy it, so why
shouldn't I? And besides, she sighed, I've cooked enough in my
lifetime. She pulled the laundry basket close, then yanked down
a pair of socks with bunched toes, rolled them tight, and tossed
them into the wicker basket, her mind still on Mexico.

Harvest time was fun too, Constancia remembered, folding a
pillowcase into a perfect square. Large wooden tables were set
beneath the cottonwoods that stood like sentinels next to the
ranchhouse. There the workers were fed a tasty stew garnished
with chiles grown on the ranch. Constancia and her sisters, gig-
gling and smiling, had helped their mother prepare the food.
She enjoyed the camaraderie among the workers; both the men
and women relished hard work, and the knowledge that they
would be well paid. She recalled how the men attacked the food
with gusto... and smiles of appreciation. She especially liked
being assigned to serve the younger men, many of whom shyly
looked away when *la hija del patrón* (the boss's daughter) approached. But once Justo asked for her hand – and she accepted
his proposal – she stayed behind to help her mother in the
kitchen, trying not to pine over the tall, handsome boy she was
to marry.

At eighteen, Constancia had married Justo de Paz, a man
two years her senior. When seventeen, Justo had emigrated
with an uncle to California, where for three years he worked the
lemon groves that flourished in the damp, cold town of Ven-
tura. He saved money, spending it only for room and board and
an occasional sack of tobacco. His plan was to return to Mexico,
marry, then return to *el norté* accompanied by his bride. He often
worked on Saturdays, too. Now and then he went to town with
his uncle, but for the most part Justo remained at the ranch to
read the Spanish newspaper. Soon he taught himself to write.
He wrote to Constancia, the crude letters smudged across the
lined paper bought at the five-and-dime. He regaled her with
stories of the wonders of her soon-to-be adopted country.

Everyone here owns property, Justo wrote: land, a house...

and an automobile! I earn more money in the lemon groves than I ever dreamed of. He also described what he perceived as "strange American habits." Here everyone brings their lunch to work, he wrote, unlike in Mexico where a rancher feeds his workers. In this country they only give you water, and at times, very little of that. He told of buying a *lonchera* (a tin lunchpail) for his cold tacos. *Aquí todo es diferente,* he noted: "Everything is different." This strange custom, of not feeding workers, was to Constancia appalling; her parents, she knew, took pains to feed the ranchhands. But, Justo insisted, in America each man provides his own work gloves, and his own lunch. He posted the letters, counting the days until his return.

When it was agreed she and Justo would marry, Constancia began to make preparations. She accompanied her mother to Silao, a nearby town, to buy a bolt of muslin for the linens she would take to the new country. She and her sisters sewed tablecloths, *servilletas,* and a simple trousseau. Each afternoon they sat beneath the cottonwoods, assorted pins and needles at their sides, to embroider as a flushed Constancia read Justo's letters aloud. Her sisters were impressed with the reports written in large, round letters. Once read, the letters were stored in a cedar chest. The women all agreed: Justo de Paz was indeed a young man with a future. But that was long ago, Constancia now told herself. . . long ago.

Inside the house Constancia removed her sweater, then arranged the folded sheets inside the *patequilla* (the trunk) that years before had accompanied her from Mexico and now stood at the foot of her bed. In it, between sacks of potpourri, dried rose petals wrapped in faded lace, were sheets, doilies, and assorted baby clothes. At the bottom, wrapped in faded tissue paper, was Apollonia's baptism gown, now thin and worn but with the lace intact. Constancia bent down, took out the potpourri, and brought it to her face. The aroma of dusky roses filled the room. She sighed, thinking back to Sunday's visit to Apollonia.

That day, as a surprise for her sister, Felicitas had wrapped dried flowers in a muslin square, sprinkled it with eau de cologne, then tied a bright ribbon around it. When given the packet, Apollonia had plunged her nose into the fragrant flowers, then smiled happily at her mother, who smiled back. But Apollonia will never return to this house, Constancia reminded herself, nor will she walk in the rose garden. She stood, closed the trunk lid, then returned to the kitchen, the smell of roses in her hair.

On warm summer evenings while the older girls washed the supper dishes, Constancia retreated to the rose garden to snip roses and carnations left to dry outdoors next to bay and mint leaves. When ready, the mixture was crushed, then wrapped in pieces of muslin and stored in the linen closet. But, thought Constancia, as she retied her apron, come next year, when carnations bloom once more, Apollonia will be dead.

Now, as she set up the ironing board in the kitchen, Constancia felt the baby kick. She sat down, held a hand to her stomach, and waited, but the baby was quiet. She continued to sit, hoping once more to feel the child inside her. She pulled at her stockings, then slowly stood, spread a starched pillowcase across the board, and began to iron. As she worked, she thought again of what was uppermost in her mind: Apollonia, and, to a lesser degree, the baby due in *Enero*.

As she ironed Justo's shirt, Constancia recalled how upset she had been to discover, early in May, she was once more pregnant. One time the *doctora* had cautioned her and other neighborhood women not to have so many children. "*No es* good for you!" the good doctor had said, her face agitated. "*No es* good!" And now here I am, Constancia sighed, pregnant with my tenth child. As she grew heavier, and the summer sun became unbearable, the visits to Apollonia tired her more and more. The drive to the sanatorium was neither bumpy nor long and, under different circumstances, it would have been pleasant, what with the orange groves and flowering oleanders along the highway. But Constancia feared catching tuberculosis, the highly contagious disease prevalent among Mexican families. Early on, the public health nurse had instructed her on what precautions to take when visiting Apollonia so as not to endanger the other children – and the unborn baby. Thereafter, upon returning from the sanatorium, Constancia quickly changed her dress and stockings, washed herself carefully, then, prior to cooking, rinsed her hands with alcohol in a tin basin.

After this baby comes I must remain in bed for six weeks, sighed Constancia, spreading a checkered tablecloth across the ironing board, or at least for a month. And I must try to get someone to help with the children. Justo does his share, and the older girls help with the cooking, but I do not want to burden them with my work. Never will I keep Felicitas home from school to do housework. Never. Yet with each baby I feel more tired, and it takes longer to heal. But until *Enero* I'll visit Apollonia every Sunday, and take her lemonade and cookies.

Once the baby is born, Constancia swore, the iron steady in her hand, Justo and I will have to sleep apart again. It will be difficult for him, she admitted, as she slid the iron across the shirt yoke, but it has to be done. She often heard the neighbor women comment on Justo's slim form, his unwrinkled skin. But, she grumbled, bending to retrieve a fallen handkerchief, I shall insist. Surely Justo will understand how weary I am of childbearing.

Soon after Gabriela's difficult birth, Constancia had claimed the sunny bedroom that looked onto the rose garden as her own. Justo now slept alongside his sons in an adjoining room. In Mexico, Constancia knew, couples who wanted to limit their children followed this custom, one more difficult for men than for women, a thing that created strife in a marriage. And Constancia loved her kind husband, keenly aware that at forty, Justo was still a handsome, virile man.

As the afternoon wore on, Constancia continued with her housework; the pressed clothes covered the kitchen table. She looked out the window, thinking of her mother, and of the subject of birth control. It was rarely discussed on the ranch, even among married women. Her mother had made brief references to couples who slept apart, as did she and her husband. According to *la Iglesia,* doña Martina had intoned, her face a bright pink, any kind of birth control is a mortal sin. However, she concluded, one can always sleep apart. *That* the Church will condone. Constancia had heard her mother proudly note that her children, like those of her own mother, were born three years apart. Anything else was said to be *muy ranchero* (too low class).

Now, as she buttoned Justo's shirts, Constancia felt the baby kick again. She sat, waiting for the incessant kicking that often irritated her. She pressed down on her stomach, but the baby refused to move. With a weary sigh Constancia walked to the stove to stir the beans in the blue enamel pot, then returned to the iron. As she worked she thought back to her cousin Amador's last visit, a visit she sensed had contributed to her pregnancy.

Justo was not a drinking man, although he now and then bought a jug of dago red at an Italian market. The wine was stored in the pantry for company, or special occasions. Constancia hated the taste of alcohol, and stuck the jug behind the oatmeal. Like her mother before her, Constancia feared *el viscio,* the alcoholism said to afflict even the best of families. She remembered well her parents' pain when Lucas, her brother, moved to the city and took to the bottle. The shame still rankled. She knew her father approved of her husband because Justo, an anomaly among his friends, rarely drank. He drank only when her cousin, that rascal Amador, visited.

Amador was Constancia's first cousin, a well-built, fair-skinned, vain man who wore a white Panama hat in summer and a grey fedora in winter. He visited often, accompanied by his sour (and homely) wife and three robust sons. Amador liked to drink. He also liked for everyone else to drink. When he visited in his shiny Ford (with a rumble seat) he brought two things: a jug of wine, and roses for his cousin Constancia. As much as she protested his drinking, Constancia's eyes lit up at the sight of Amador, her handsome, flirtatious cousin who throughout the visit chided Justo for having married the boss's daughter. Within minutes of Amador's arrival, Constancia took to the kitchen to prepare his favorite dish of chicken *molé* while the men sat to talk – and drink dago red. By suppertime Amador's fair skin was flushed red, his caramel brown eyes slightly glazed. After the meal, if the weather was warm, the men sat in the small patio covered with palm fronds to eat *capirotada* (bread pudding made with brown sugar, garnished with raisins and almonds) and drink hot coffee. While Justo and Amador ate dessert and drank coffee from the flowered cups given free with Rinso soap powder, Constancia hid the wine in the pantry, a clear sign that all drinking had come to an end.

In early April Amador had visited and, as usual, polished off a jug of wine. Unable to drive, he asked to remain overnight. Much to Constancia's chagrin, he was given her husband's bed. A smiling Justo returned to the double bed. Soon after Constancia knew she was in the family way. A contrite Justo returned to his solitary bed. His loud snores, he carefully explained, made sleep impossible for his pregnant wife.

Inside the large kitchen a flushed Constancia stirred the beans cooking on the stove. By the time the famished children arrived home from school, she knew, the rosy, plump beans would be ready. The bean soup garnished with tomatoes and onions was especially tasty with hot tortillas, and was a favorite of the children, except for Gabriela, who hated onions.

Although she worked hard, Constancia knew enough to pamper herself. She napped most afternoons, and whenever possible, slept in. She no longer cooked tortillas for each meal. She knew the younger children preferred Weber's bread, bought at the corner store. Lately she was too tired to cook even a few tortillas; Justo now ate bread, too. As she added a limp onion to the beans, Constancia stopped to gaze out the window at the graying sky. It will be cold in *Enero*, she sighed, cold and wet.

She was surprised to see birds darting back and forth outside, small twigs in their beaks. The birds are preparing for winter,

Constancia thought – securing nests and storing food. Arms folded across her swollen stomach, she leaned on the window frame, gazing at the clouds.

Her habit of watching cloud formations often irritated Justo.

"*Qué tanto miras en las nubes?*" he often asked. ("What do you see in the clouds?")

"*Nada. Solo me gusta ver para afuera.*" ("Nothing. I just like to look outdoors.")

The clouds remind me of the ranch in Mexico, she longed to say, and of the lazy summers when I played in the open meadows . . . of when I was free. On sudden impulse, she pushed aside the curtain. The sky above, she noted, was almost as blue as the Mexican sky that long ago hovered over her sisters and her as they walked across grassy meadows, kicking at dirt clods. Evenings at the ranch were spent telling stories, while the overhead sky turned a deep, purplish blue. When of late Constancia gazed at the sky, Justo said nothing.

Inside the large kitchen Constancia slowly moved, aware of the baby pushing against her ribs. She wandered outdoors, to the rosebush that bloomed from early summer to late fall, adjusted her cotton dress, then squatted on her bare knees. The soil felt cold and damp against her warm skin. She pulled the dry leaves off the rose plant, then bent low to get at the shoots sprouting at the base. This bush cannot grow with these small suckers, she grumbled, her hands coated with mud. They take the nourishment needed by the plant to grow. If I get rid of them the roses will bloom much bigger, and prettier. Still, I must cover them at night, or the frost will kill them. She remained in the quiet garden, her round form bent low, until Gabriela, in need of a bottle, called her; then she reluctantly went indoors.

Later that evening, as she cleared the crude table made years ago by Justo, Constancia noted the household repairs she wanted done before January. New linoleum would be nice, she murmured: blue with a red border. Two more clotheslines would help, too. And while it was not a priority, a yellow rose plant would be nice. She smoothed her crumpled apron, thinking of the one task she had so far ignored: the sorting of the baby clothes in the trunk, a job she found depressing. Still, I must do it while I have the time, Constancia reasoned, pushing back her dark hair – before Apollonia gets worse... and before *Enero*, while I have the strength. She rinsed her hands, then walked to the bedroom that overlooked the rosebushes.

With each pregnancy Constancia added and discarded baby clothes: undershirts, flannel nightgowns, embroidered sweaters of soft, light colors. The worn diapers were used as cleaning rags and, when handy, by Justo to wipe oil off his hands. But Apollonia's clothes, worn by no one else, lay intact at the bottom of the trunk between yellowed sheets of tissue paper: smocked dresses trimmed in lace, crocheted caps braided with pink ribbons – each item too precious to discard. Each piece had been stitched by her mother and sisters in Mexico. Each buttonhole had been sewn when life had held such promise, such happiness! But now Apollonia is dying, Constancia sighed, fighting back tears. I have no reason to keep them.

In the dim bedroom Constancia pulled close the rocking chair. She heaved her ample body into the chair, then slowly pulled the dented trunk to her feet. She rummaged through the clothes that smelled of dust and roses; her fingers clutched a faded bonnet, then came to rest on a tiny gossamer dress. Constancia's dark eyes brightened at the sight of the silky dress, now a faded rose color. She pressed the tiny gown to her breast, then brought it to her face. Apollonia. *Hija mia,* she sighed, as warm tears streamed down her face to land on her breasts and stomach. I cannot bear to lose you.

In the evening shadows the rose plants visible through the windows shone a deep green, the blossoms closed tight for the night. Constancia sat lost in thought, the baby dress clutched in her hands. Perhaps the baby can wear Apollonia's dress, she decided, wiping her swollen eyes. Perhaps. She held the baptismal dress against her beating heart, leaned back in the rocker, and closed her eyes. She remained motionless for a time. Suddenly Constancia stood up, smoothed her dress, and took a deep breath. I *will* dress the coming baby in Apollonia's clothes, she vowed – in the dresses, booties, and crocheted jackets. I'll wash the baptismal dress and come next Sunday, I'll show it to Apollonia. Knowing her new brother – or sister – will be christened in this gown will make her happy, make her smile. She shook the clothes free of dust and closed tight the metal trunk; then, baby dress clutched in her hands, Constancia went out of the dark room and into the warm kitchen.

*

Journey of Love

BEFORE HE LEFT for the visit, Alexander Litsios had a suit made for himself by the best tailor in Argos, then bought a few ties and a pair of shoes. He had not seen Gregory for eight years. At the beginning, when Gregory first went to the United States, he had come home for visits a few times but then, once he was finished with his studies in medical school, he stopped coming. It was hard for him to take off, he said, while he was trying to build up a practice. When he got married, he wanted to bring his wife over but one thing led to another and they never managed the trip.

On the airplane Alexander stared out the window at the clouds, one moment a sea of gold and the next, foam. His mind kept drifting to Gregory. He had been a lively, curious boy, a sensitive and introspective adolescent and, when a little older, before he left, a sociable, ambitious, and good-natured young man. Now he was married to an American woman and he had set up a house and practice on Long Island. Perhaps he had changed a great deal. Alexander's heart beat with the anticipation of seeing him after all these years.

At Kennedy Airport, going through the customs line, Alexander was apprehensive. The customs officers, tall cold-looking men, searched his suitcases and the inside of his violin case – he had brought his violin because he liked playing it every day.

They opened up the tin box in which he had packed the goat cheese Margarita made. One of the men said something to the other, which Alexander could not understand, and then put the box away on the other side of the counter. But they let him take everything else. As he entered the vast hall beyond the customs line, he looked for Gregory but could not spot him. Panic came over him. At his age of eighty, it was hard to travel so far and he knew very little English. He saw people everywhere, people hurrying, people on phones. . . . He looked this way and that, growing dizzy with the chaos.

Suddenly a man was coming toward him, smiling. "Father," he called.

"Gregory, my son."

Gregory had gained weight and his movements were heavy, Alexander noticed.

The two of them embraced quickly and kissed.

"You look very well," Alexander said, though inwardly he shrank a bit from Gregory's unfamiliar image.

"You look well too," Gregory said excitedly, his voice trembling a little. "It has been so long. . . . I can't believe you're really here. . . . " He moved closer to his father and they embraced again, first hesitantly and then more firmly.

"Susan is waiting in the car," Gregory then said, pulling back. "It was hard to park around here. You have to tell me all about Mother and Carolyn. . . . Susan and I have been looking forward to your coming."

Outside, Susan was standing by the car, a dark blue Mercedes. She and Alexander greeted each other and kissed. She was tall, thin. In the dim light he could see that she was blond. She smiled at him and said something to him in English that he assumed was an expression of welcome. He smiled back and nodded a few times as he got into the back seat.

They drove along vast highways and then through a string of small towns. "That's our house," Gregory eventually said, pointing to a white shingled house set alongside similar homes on a wide, tree-lined street. The street and the houses had an oddly empty and quiet feeling to them, as if they were deserted.

When they got inside, Gregory said, "Let me take you to the room we set up for you. It's the lightest room in the house. I thought you'd like all the sunlight pouring in during the day."

"You shouldn't have gone to any trouble," Alexander said.

"Please, make yourself comfortable," Susan said half in English and half in Greek. "Make this your home."

Gregory carried Alexander's suitcases into the room. Alexander carried the violin.

"I'm glad you brought your violin," Gregory said.

"You used to like me to play it for you," Alexander said, smiling. He began to pull a few things from one of the suitcases – his bathrobe, a pair of slippers.

"There's a bathroom right there if you feel like taking a shower," Gregory said. "Take your time. We'll be waiting for you in the living room."

After Gregory left, Alexander went into the bathroom. His muscles were aching from the plane ride and he stood under the shower for a long time. Margarita must be with Carolyn right now, helping her with the children, he thought, feeling sad that they had not come along on the trip. Carolyn, the daughter, had just had a baby and her other two children were very young. He had been away from them only for a day but it seemed much longer. . . .

The hard drops of warm water on his skin at last had a soothing effect. But as he stepped out of the shower, he was startled – the floor was covered with water, some of it leaking out into the hallway. He realized he should have put the curtain inside of the tub before he turned on the water. At home, their large deep bath had a door on it and the shower was set far in the back of the tub. He stood for a moment, frozen by embarrassment. Finally, he called Gregory.

Gregory came in promptly.

"Look what I've done," Alexander said.

Gregory stared at the floor, then at his father. His heart gave a squeeze at the shame registered on his father's face. "Don't worry about it. It's nothing – it happens all the time. I'll mop it up."

"I'm an old man, I don't know what I'm doing," Alexander said apologetically.

A few moments later Alexander saw Gregory, through the half-open door of the guest room, standing in the hallway and whispering something to Susan – maybe about the flooding. His heart sank lower and lower. . . .

In half an hour the three of them were sitting in the living room talking. They talked about Carolyn and Margarita, reminisced about other relatives and friends Gregory had left behind. One of his high school friends was now in Athens, working for the Ministry of Education, and another owned a vineyard, Alexander told him.

Gregory and Susan's living room was furnished in a modern, functional style. The rug Alexander had brought over as a present, now spread on a couch, stood out vividly because of its bright colors. He had shopped for the rug himself, going from store to store until he had found one in a fine pink and maroon weave. He had also brought two sweaters that Margarita had knitted, one for Gregory and one for Susan, green and blue for him and yellow and blue for her, and some silver jewelry for her. They all lay on the table, looking alien in that room.

"I must get to bed now," Gregory said after they had had a few drinks. "I have to see patients early in the morning. But I've scheduled a few days off at the beginning of November to take you around to see more of the country."

They all got up. Alexander went to bed immediately but he had a hard time sleeping. The bedroom was furnished in dark teak, a contrast to the stark white walls. The blanket on the bed was a khaki color, the kind he had seen in hospitals. In fact, the room, and what he had seen of the house, had an antiseptic look he associated with institutions. The silence was oppressive. Except for an occasional car passing by, there was no hint of human life. His mind filled with worries. Was the baby going to be all right? (He had been a month premature and was delicate for his age.) Did Margarita remember to take the sick goat to the veterinarian? Would the young boy who came to take care of the olive and fruit trees in their yard be neglectful now with Alexander away? He covered his head with the blanket and curled up his body; and in that position he finally fell asleep.

Gregory lay in bed next to Susan, anxious about his father. He had seemed out of his element in the house, like a lost child. It would have been better if he and Susan had gone to Argos instead, Gregory thought. There, the visit would not be so focused and concentrated. His mother, sister, and relatives would be around to absorb them. Yet he had wanted his father to see something of his life. He had wanted to make his family proud by becoming a doctor, a doctor trained in the United States. It had required so many years, so much work and concentration, that it was hard for him to remember who he used to be; the changes that had come over him had been so gradual. For instance, falling in love with Susan and marrying her had been natural at the time, but his marriage was part of losing his old self.

The next day, when Alexander awoke, Gregory had already left for his office. Susan served him breakfast at the kitchen counter and the two of them made attempts to talk, using what they knew of the other's language. After breakfast she drove him around Setauket, passing a post office, a bank, a supermarket, a pond with white ducks floating on its surface, and then to some of the surrounding towns.

At lunchtime they went to Gregory's office, in Setauket also, not far from the house. It was shiny with modern equipment. Gregory introduced him to two young women, a nurse and a secretary. They greeted Alexander with smiles. Then he, Gregory, and Susan went out to eat at a fish restaurant overlooking the Long Island Sound.

"I have a little extra time," Gregory said to him. "A patient cancelled. Maybe you would like to get some clothes."

Alexander was puzzled. "I don't need any clothes," he said. "I brought enough with me."

"It won't hurt to have some more, Dad. Your suit is a little old-fashioned now." Gregory smiled.

So they went to a department store in the mall and managed to find a suit and shirts in his size, though he was shorter and more broadly built than most American men.

"Do you want to get a haircut too?" Gregory asked.

Alexander shrugged. His hair, still reasonably full, was long at the edges, a little disheveled. "Why not?"

There was a salon right next to the department store. Inside, men and women were sitting on plush swivel chairs, their hair being cut. Gregory talked to a man behind a desk. Something was said on a loudspeaker and a young woman came over to lead Alexander to the washing area. Gregory said he had to go back to work but Susan would wait for him. Alexander's hair was washed and then cut by another young woman in less than an hour. At home he went to the local barber, where sometimes it took a whole afternoon to have his hair cut – they gossiped about town events and drank tea.

After the haircut Susan took Alexander home, then left to go to work; she had a parttime job as an interior decorator. Alexander wandered through the empty, unfamiliar house, leafing through magazines and newspapers, listening to music. When Gregory returned home in the evening, he looked exhausted. He hardly talked to him or to Susan. He retired to bed even earlier than the night before. Susan watched television and Alexander sat on the sofa, dispirited, his hands folded on his lap.

A week had gone by... slowly. Gregory was usually gone by the time Alexander awoke. Alexander had breakfast with Susan and then she went about doing the household chores. After she was done with that, she usually did a little gardening, pulling weeds out of the flower beds or turning the water hose on the grass. Once, looking on the refrigerator door, Alexander found a note, held by a magnet, that Susan had left for Gregory. He could read a few of the words: "Try not to be too late tonight." Underneath the note, Gregory had written: "I'll try but you know I can't help it sometimes." The next day he found another note, with Susan saying, "I love you," and Gregory writing back, "I love you too. Be patient." Be patient with what? Anyway, it was odd that they would leave notes to each other. Was their time so precious – or was it hard for them to say certain things to each other? He recalled how shy Gregory had been with women, rarely seeking them out for pleasure as he himself had when he was young, before he got married. Still, Susan seemed difficult to talk to. There was something abrupt and awkward about her. He might not have been comfortable talking with her even if he knew the language better. She was very different from Margarita and Carolyn, with their soft, fleshy bodies, the ease of their movements. Thinking of them, and of home, Alexander tried to pass time by practicing English, using a book Gregory had given to him, or taking walks in the neighborhood, though it was not that pleasant with no sidewalks anywhere and nothing except houses to look at. He thought of playing the violin but he had no desire to.

Gregory rarely came home for lunch – he said he had to be at the hospital to check on patients. Too bad, Alexander thought, lunch was such a joyful event at home. Relatives and friends got together and spent a long time on the meal – five, six courses. They caught up with the events of each other's lives. No matter what problems might weigh on their chests, they would feel lifted after sharing them with others. Annoyances, grudges a person might bear another person, would be at least temporarily forgotten. Alexander was tempted to take Gregory aside and talk to him about all this, the way he used to: Gregory would lie on the sofa and he would sit at its edge, leaning over him a little, and they would talk late into the night. . . .

The days began to blend together. Susan would feed Alexander a light lunch, a sandwich, soup from a can, and then drop him off at the mall before she went to work. He wandered around by himself. He looked into store windows or sat on a bench and watched the shoppers. He wore his own clothes instead of the ones Gregory bought for him. He liked their familiarity but he was now conscious that they made him seem a little out of place, neglectful of his appearance. He sometimes bought fruit from a supermarket, though the cellophane wrapped around it made it look artificial. The market was very different from the one at home, where heaps of fruits and vegetables were displayed on carts and you could touch and pick the ones you wanted. Here, everything was hidden behind something, wrapped up in paper, set behind glass. He was aware of a gulf between himself and the world around him. Every minute crawled, slowly, slowly. "This is like prison," he said aloud once. No one seemed to have heard him. Everyone went by indifferently. Their faces were so dispassionate that a substance other than blood could be running in their veins. There was no public transportation, there were no cabs to hail, so he had to stay in the mall for four hours until Susan was finished with work and picked him up.

What was he going to tell Margarita and Carolyn when he returned home? If he had to describe what he had seen of this country, he would say that it existed in twilight, dim and gray. The trip was supposed to be for three months but Alexander was already doubting that he could last that long. Gregory must have given up a lot of himself to adjust to this world. There was something like denial that went with his attitude. It was as if he were trying hard to conceal a feeling from everyone, maybe unhappiness, a shame of some kind? It was hard to know what went on in his heart and mind—whatever he truly felt seemed deeply buried, unreachable to Alexander, and maybe even to himself. Gregory, the one he knew from the past, simply was not there. Gregory – the child, the adolescent, the young adult – was barely represented in this man. Still, the love Alexander felt for him remained, an entity unto itself, inside his heart.

Growing up, Gregory had imagined a greater happiness for himself than the one he could find in his hometown. And Alexander, caught in Gregory's dream, worked hard and lived for that distant, misty future. Alexander had been a carpenter, going from house to house, building cabinets, restoring old wooden walls or floors. His job had satisfied him, when he could do it in a leisurely manner. It gave him the chance to build things out of pieces of wood and enjoy their completion into shapes, and at the same time left his mind free to contemplate. As Gregory grew older, Alexander had had to work harder, taking on unpleasant jobs in factories or at building sites. He had hoped Gregory would return home, set up an office and buy a house, maybe on a hill. But this had turned out to be that future, a world that did not include him. . . .

As Gregory drove home from his office on a late afternoon, he thought: My poor father, he must be terribly bored, having to spend so much time alone. I must try harder to get home earlier, make attempts to talk to him more. He constantly seems on the verge of wanting to say something to me. But how can he and I have a satisfactory talk? How can I sum up for him what I cannot for myself?

He remembered Susan had left a note for him to get some butter and milk. He parked his car by the supermarket and went in. By the produce counter he noticed bags of dried fruit. His father, and he himself, liked dried cherries. He picked up a couple of bags and put them in the cart.

At home he found his father sitting on the living room sofa while Susan was preparing dinner in the kitchen. After he kissed Susan and unloaded the groceries, he went over to his father and handed him the bags of cherries. "These are for you, Dad."

"Dried cherries," Alexander said, a faint smile coming over his face. He opened the bag and took a few cherries out, giving some to Gregory.

Gregory sat next to his father. "Not as good as the ones at home," he said after eating one. "Remember we used to pick cherries from the orchard? Mother dried them out in the sun."

"Yes," his father said wistfully.

"I wish Mother had been able to come along with you." But, as he said that, Gregory was aware of a pressure on his chest. Having his mother in the house with Susan would have been so difficult. She might have tried to instruct Susan in cooking or walked around the house frowning at the decor. As he imagined this, he could sense how formal and stiff the house truly was. He started to say something about it to his father but it was very hard. He was aware of a pool of tension collecting in the air between them.

"I'd better help Susan set the table," he said, getting up. "We'll be eating soon," he added in a voice that he tried to make robust.

One night after Alexander had been visiting for three weeks, he lay in bed thinking he was an unwanted guest with no one to talk to. He got out of bed and looked at the street. It was completely empty. The lights above the house doors shone, but for what? Not even a car went by. In Argos you could see people at all hours of the night. A woman still awake would look out of a window, a group of restless teenagers would be standing under the streetlights, men singly or together would be returning home from a bar or a coffee shop. A loud argument between a husband and wife or a son and father would rumble out of a house. Music would be playing somewhere.

He listened to see if there were any signs of awakening from

Gregory and Susan's room but the second floor, where they slept, was dark and silent. He paced the room for a moment, back and forth, and in circles. Then, impulsively, he put his long woolen poncho around him and went into the yard, carrying his violin. He suddenly had a strong desire to play it, to penetrate the silence. He sat under a maple tree, above which the moon dangled, and he began to play. He played melodies from his childhood. The strings were already out of tune from lack of use and he could not tighten them just right, but the sound they made gave him pleasure anyway; he had missed it so much. He played softly, using the low scale. Shadows of the trees and the houses cast definite, vivid shapes across the lawn. Every leaf, every flower, was sharply delineated. He could almost hear Gregory's voice as a child, saying to him, "Play more." He began to play louder and louder, using sharper notes.

He saw several windows opening on the houses across the street. He saw heads leaning out of them and pulling back. His heart began to beat with excitement. The melody enveloped him. He was locked inside of it, lifted into another arena, he was not sure for how long. . . .

Gregory was saying, "Father, what's going on? A neighbor just threatened to call the police."

Confusion surrounded Alexander like fog. Gregory seemed like a figure from a bad dram, leaning out of the window, his face glowing with an eerie light, and talking with an abrupt, jerking motion of his hands. Susan came and stood next to Gregory, looking on silently.

Alexander went on playing, though he had begun to shiver. His teeth were chattering.

"Father. . . "Gregory was now walking rapidly toward him. "Come inside, Father, it's the middle of the night."

"I want to go back home, to our own warm sun," Alexander said. "I'm cold, I'm always shivering."

Gregory and Susan tried to talk Alexander into staying a while longer. But he wanted to leave as soon as possible. He was not feeling well, he said; he wanted to be in his own familiar surroundings.

After he saw his father off at the airport, on the way home Gregory burst out crying. He had not done that for a long time, not since he was refused by several medical schools. He could not get over the nagging guilt he felt that the visit had been a failure. What could he have done to improve it? He did not know. Susan must have had similar feelings. "I wasn't a good enough hostess," she had told him ruefully.

He thought of his father on the plane, over the Atlantic, a small old man barely filling the seat. He had no importance in the world; he would be invisible except for the love of his family and fellow villagers. Gregory tried to conjure up memories of his childhood, the long walks in fragrant cherry orchards, hand in hand with his father. But the happy, peaceful thoughts would not come. Instead, he felt a pain unlike any he had ever known. Now he longed to hear his father's violin music once again – even in the dead of the night, even above the shouts of angry neighbors. Gregory had left something behind in Greece, something once tangible and alive but no longer within his reach.

JIM SAGEL

✳

The Holy Cheese

I

IT WAS AN ACT OF God. There was no other way to explain how a halo had appeared over the head of Amos "the Cheese Candidate" Griego in the political ad published in the *Río Bravo Times*.

Yet, there were few valley residents willing to believe that the candidate for the San Gabriel School Board had received the endorsement of the Almighty; in fact, the "Marching Mothers" went so far as to claim that Griego was the Devil himself. These mothers had begun "marching" after "the Cheese Candidate" had been named to fill a vacancy on the board of education. Emily Wolf, owner of a sporting goods store, and Sue Weaver, the widow of the school board member whose death had created the vacancy on the board, had founded the group of mothers fed up with all the politics in the public schools.

For more than two decades, Ferminio Luján—or "Primo Ferminio," as he was better known—had ruled the political roost in Río Bravo County. The Primo had begun his life of "public service" as the county sheriff. Since then, he had consolidated power in the classic manner, granting favors and denying them, until he felt fully justified in claiming, as he had in an interview with the *Río Bravo Times:* "There's not a single family in the whole county that doesn't owe me a favor."

Of course, it wasn't just the humble folks that "owed favors"

to the Primo; the members of the United States Congress themselves were beholden to the *patrón,* for even the most powerful
senator needed the votes the Primo delivered without fail each
and every election, a block of guaranteed ballots that often
meant the difference between victory and defeat. Once the leg-
islators were bridled and the judges and law enforcement officials harnessed up, there only remained the municipal schools
for the Primo to tame (and, of course, the four hundred jobs
controlled by the board of education). And the Primo did take
over the schools, too, when he pulled all the right strings to get
his oldest son, Vicente, elected to the school board.

The "Luján Machine" had been chugging along very
smoothly for some time, running on all eight cylinders, as they
say, but then that engine suddenly choked when Lester Weaver
won a seat on the school board. This owner of an insurance
company had broken up the majority the Machine had main-
tained on the board for years. It was no accident that, year after
year, Weaver sold more insurance policies than any other agent
in northern New Mexico, in spite of the fact that Río Bravo
County had the highest unemployment rate in the state. He was
an amazingly persuasive fellow, as was abundantly clear in the
school board meetings when he would convince Geraldo Gonzales to join himself and Miguel Fernández, the other board
member opposed to the Lujánes, in defeating every motion
Vicente Luján would make.

Naturally, the Primo settled accounts with Geraldo Gonzales, who soon found himself facing an investigation into a number of suspicious loans he had received to finance his mobile
home sales business, 'Sangre de Cristo Mobile Home Sales."
Even though the Primo himself had arranged those interest-free
loans from the bank he controlled as president of the board of
directors, he had now unleashed the wolves in the attorney general's office to gnaw away at the bones of his unfaithful ally.

But, as it turned out, the Primo had not had to worry all that
much about Lester Weaver, since the fool had been kind
enough to cook his own goose. It happened on New Year's Eve,

exactly at midnight, in fact, when all the neighborhood machos were outside shooting off their pistols and shotguns to kill the old year. The guests at the Weavers' annual bash were blowing their noisemakers, exchanging drunken kisses, and offering toast after toast to the newborn year, but Lester Weaver and Laurie McFerson, the wife of Weaver's business partner, Hank McFerson, were enjoying a secret and passionate celebration of their own—suffice it to say they weren't singing "Auld Lang Syne" behind the locked door of one of the three bedrooms in the huge house. When your number comes up, you've got to go, the old ones used to say, and Lester's number surely must have come up, for when he heard the shooting, he decided to peer outside just as a stray bullet came crashing through the bedroom window and his main aorta as well. And even though they rushed him to San Gabriel Presbyterian Hospital, Weaver was dead on arrival.

There were some who observed that Lester had only gotten what he deserved for being such a shameless adulterer, for there weren't many folks around who didn't know about Lester and Laurie, at least among the gang that hung out at the major gossip centers in town: the Cowboy Family Restaurant, the Mexican Image Bar, the Chuckwagon Cafe, and the Saints and Sinners Lounge. Those in favor of gun control—a true minority in Río Bravo County—held that the tragic incident proved once again that it really was guns that killed people and not people who killed people, as the members of the National Rifle Association claimed. But Emily Wolf wasn't concerned about the immorality of the late insurance agent, nor did she care much about the arguments for and against the outlawing of weapons—what she was worried about was the rumor going around that the Luján Machine planned to take advantage of this opportunity to reassert their control over the public schools. Vicente Luján, they said, was prepared to nominate his brother-in-law, Amos Griego, to fill the vacancy on the school board.

That was why Emily Wolf and Lester's widow, Sue Weaver,

had established the "Marching Mothers." The women organized community meetings in the parish hall at the Cristo Rey Church, raised funds to hire a lawyer, wrote letters of protest to the state superintendent of schools, Lawrence DiLorenzo, appeared before the New Mexico State Board of Education with a stack of petitions, and, of course, marched in the streets, chanting, shouting, and carrying their anti-Luján placards. One of those placards which Emily herself had painted ended up pictured in the *Río Bravo Times*. The sign read "The Skunk Underneath the Barracks Is Named Luján," in an allusion to the charge that Emily's son, Tommy, had made in a rally attended by some four hundred valley residents.

Tommy, the president of the senior class and one of the star athletes on the San Gabriel High School football, basketball, and baseball teams, had stood up in front of the crowd to denounce the deplorable condition of the high school. There were countless broken windows in the gym, he said, and never any hot water in the dressing room showers, and the uniforms the San Gabriel Demons played in were so worn-out and tattered that every team in the conference made fun of the poor ragged devils. Furthermore, Tommy had continued, the classrooms were ready to fall down, with heaters that never worked, light fixtures whose bulbs had been burned out for years and bathrooms that were so filthy that you were afraid even to set foot in them. Many students, he said, had to attend classes in decrepit barracks that housed several families of skunks. "I'd like to see if any of you could concentrate on your history lesson in that stench!" the young man shouted to a thunderous roar of applause.

Tommy's speech caused an uproar in the San Gabriel Valley, so it was no surprise when even more people showed up at the meeting the following week when the Lujánes planned to name Amos Griego a member of the school board. In fact, there were so many people – some nine hundred citizens, according to the *Río Bravo Times* – that they had to move the meeting to the gym. In spite of the fact that the Marching Mothers had come for blood – Luján blood, to be specific – the school board president, Vicente Luján, remained regally aloof, arrogantly informing Emily Wolf that inasmuch as the Mothers had failed to make the necessary application to appear on the official agenda of the meeting, which application had to be filed in the office of the superintendent of schools no later than one week in advance of the meeting, they would have to wait until the business of the board was finished before making their presentation. And when Emily tried to raise an objection, Vicente cut her off with the slick syllogisms that seemed to stream endlessly out of his mouth.

When they eventually did yield the floor to Emily, the outraged woman blew her top, loudly declaring that the school board was no more than a gang of bootlickers and brownnosers. As she continued her harangue, the board members, seated beneath the basketball hoop, sank into their chairs like so many turtles trying to crawl into their shells – all, that is, except for Vicente, who remained erect in a posture of lofty rigidity. When Emily and her associates finally finished their speeches, Vicente returned to the microphone to lash back at them in an equally bitter attack.

"My dear neighbors and friends, these women have had a lot to say about 'the people.' Well, I, for one, have had it up to here with this smoke screen – and make no mistake about it, my friends, what we have here is a complete and utter fantasy. Do you really think these ladies who have never left Fairview Heights know anything at all about 'the people?' Well, then where are all of the mothers from Cañoncito, la Canova, and la Cuchilla? They're not here, and I'll tell you why – it's because these so-called 'Marching Mothers' have never even been to most of the hundreds of villages that make up our school system – villages just like yours and mine. What do these highfalutin' socialites really know about our proud people who have been struggling to scratch out an existence on this land where we've lived for three hundred years?

"Here you have before you a man who truly *does* know our people, a neighbor of yours and mine who has spent his entire life struggling right alongside us to improve the lives of our children! Yes, Amos Griego, a self-made man, a man who is proud of his family, proud of his culture, and proud of his community!"

With that, Amos rose and made his way to the podium, accompanied by a chorus of boos and hisses which Vicente answered with a rain of blows from his gavel. When the uproar at last died down, Amos "the Cheese Candidate" Griego began to defend himself.

"All I ask from you is that you give me a chance, the chance to use this book to serve you and all our children!" he declared, holding a Bible aloft in his hand, the same Bible, he said, that his father had given him before passing away.

"King Griego," murmured everybody in the gym in unison, for that had been the nickname of Amos' late father. The retired carpenter had received that title late in life when he had become a self-made biblical "scholar." "King Griego" never tired of telling every poor soul he could corner at the post office or the barbershop that he was a direct descendant of the kings of Israel. And when King Griego died of a heart attack and Father Ramón said, "May he rest in peace," there was no doubt that the priest would finally get a chance to "rest" a little too now that King Griego wouldn't be around to interrupt his sermons and correct his interpretations of the Scriptures.

Amos Griego also interpreted a verse from the Bible that evening before the Marching Mothers and the nine hundred angry spectators when he read from the second Epistle of Saint Paul to Timothy. "Use all care to present thyself to God as a man approved, a worker that cannot be ashamed, rightly handling the word of truth," he quoted.

"And *this* is the truth!" he exclaimed, lifting the Bible high above his head again. "The truth is that I'm going to fight day and night to keep politics out of our schools!"

Luckily, it was wintertime, for if Amos had made that last statement during the harvest season, there's no doubt the Marching Mothers would have peppered him with rotten tomatoes and overripe melons. Instead of vegetables, they showered him with "raspberries," booing him right off the podium. But that presented no problem for Amos, who really didn't have much more to say, either that night or in the two years that he has been sitting on the school board, for that's all he's done – sit, just like a bump on a log. Of course, he never was expected to say much – all he's had to do is vote the way Vicente votes. Miguel Fernández, the only school board member still opposed to the Luján Machine now that Geraldo Gonzales has been "straightened out," finally got so fed up with "the Cheese Candidate" that once, after listening to another one of Vicente's long and incomprehensible speeches, he publicly challenged Amos to give his point of view, his opinion about the motion Vicente had just finished advancing. Amos simply opened his eyes, which always seemed to be half-closed as if he were lost in an endless daydream, and delivered his straightforward answer: "I say the same as Vicente."

When the laughter in the audience at last dissipated – laughter strictly limited to the reporter from the *Río Bravo Times* and a few scattered individuals from the community, inasmuch as the teachers, principals, and other employees of the public schools had long since learned how to suppress their laughter when it was necessary – Miguel Fernández pressed on, telling Amos that if it was true that he was only "saying the same as Vicente," then, what, exactly, was Vicente saying? Once again, Amos rose to the occasion with an observation that was so frank it was impossible to judge whether it had been motivated by simple honesty or even simpler stupidity. "I don't get it all," he said, "but I bite off enough to chew on."

Now that his two-year appointment had expired and Amos was running for his own six-year term on the school board, Emily Wolf and the Marching Mothers also had found plenty to "chew on" and, once again, they found themselves marching in the streets, working for the defeat of Griego in the upcoming election. The Mothers reminded the public in their press conferences and demonstrations that everything they had predicted two years before had come to pass. There was more politics than ever in the schools. The condition of the school buildings had deteriorated right along with the quality of education their children received in those ramshackle classrooms. In fact, the only thing that *had* improved was the office of the superintendent of schools, Josué Garcia, a political kingpin in the Luján Machine and a notorious ally of Primo Ferminio. The superintendent had not approved the purchase of a single textbook in the last two years, but he had ordered the complete renovation of his office. Worst of all – Emily complained – he had redecorated his office with furniture purchased from a business owned by none other than Amos "the Cheese Candidate" Griego.

II

Over the years, the Lujánes had developed thick skins when it came to spurious attacks in the press, but this latest attempt to besmirch the family name went a little too far. Now, Emily Wolf – or "la Loba," as members of the Machine had begun calling the brazen gringa – had charged over the radio that Amos Griego had been warning all the senior citizens in the county that anyone who didn't vote right was running the risk of losing the free cheese that the government distributed to the needy. Even though everybody started calling him "the Cheese Candidate" after that, Amos was reluctant to respond to the charge; however, his wife Mela, Primo Ferminio's only daughter and, in the opinion of most folks, the one who really wore the pants in the family, took it upon herself to defend her silent husband. She even swallowed her pride and submitted to an interview with the *Río Bravo Times* in spite of the fact that she despised the editor, Bill Taylor, who, in the past, had crucified her in an editorial he had written about the Indigent Fund that she administered. Although those public monies were set aside to help the poor pay their hospital bills, Mela only approved ap-

plications when there was an election coming up, apparently to
help the needy decide how to vote. Naturally, one hardly
needed to be impoverished in order to qualify for remuneration
from the fund – that is, unless the vice president of the Río
Bravo National Bank could be considered an indigent, for his
name appeared in the list Taylor published of judges, policemen, city officials, county commissioners, and other subjects of
the Luján Machine who had received money from the Indigent
Fund.

But this tall tale about the cheese – well, aside from the fact
that it was "utterly false," it was also "totally absurd," to use
the words Mela had chosen in her interview with the newspaper. "This cheese program has nothing to do with the Lujánes,"
Mela had declared. "It's the president's program, the same
president who has made the rich richer and the poor a whole lot
poorer. He gives the millionaires a big tax break, but to the poor
he tosses a piece of cheese. *That's* where you ought to be looking
for corruption – at the White House, not here in this poor
county."

But the people of San Gabriel knew there was no need to
leave the valley in order to find plenty of abuses in the political
system; in other words, they agreed with Emily Wolf when she
insisted that Amos had been using that "Reagan cheese" as a
tool of extortion among the county's senior citizens. Emily had
first made that accusation on Filogonio Atencio's program, 'El
Swap Shop del Aigre." The program that aired every Saturday
morning at nine-thirty was, beyond a shadow of a doubt, the
most popular one on Radio KBSO, not solely because people
always love to purchase their neighbors' junk, but also because
Filogonio Atencio had transformed this "flea market of the air-
waves" into a fascinating forum for philosophy, folklore, and
folk wisdom. Filogonio was a true communicator – there was
nothing he loved more than talking with people, asking their
opinions, scrutinizing their thoughts, and challenging their
ideas. And so, if an old lady called up with a wood cookstove for
sale, it wouldn't be long before Filogonio would have her shar-

ing her philosophy about food stamps and whether she thought it was fair that those hippies got food stamps when they were richer than the very people who worked at the welfare office.

As one might expect, the majority of the callers on "El Swap Shop del Aigre" were not terribly entertaining. Yet Filogonio knew just how to orchestrate a conversation so his listeners wouldn't get bored, whether it was with a joke he threw in or an especially appropriate *dicho*, for he knew an amazing number of proverbs and traditional riddles. Sometimes he'd even break out singing, as he usually did when someone called in with an old jalopy for sale; the zany announcer would wrap up the conversation with a verse from the song "Mi Carrito Paseado":

> It's got *dos* fenders *twistiados*
> *Y los* tires *bien gastados* –
>   It's got a roof made of *cartón*.
> It's got a leaky *rayador*
> And a broken *generador* –
>   It's got a messed-up *transmisión*.

Now and then he'd receive a call from a person who was a true original. Filogonio would simply let such a person rattle on, as he had done when Abel Valerio, a rancher from El Rito de los Pinos, had called with his entire herd of livestock for sale – his cattle, calves, bull, Jersey milk cow, and even his forest permits. Having spent his entire life on the ranch, Abel had finally decided to throw in the towel. "They've got us rancheros all *fregaos*," he said, explaining how he made less money every year with his cattle and his harvest, yet his costs just kept going up – especially the price of those "goddamned *permisos*" that one needed in order to run livestock on the National Forest lands, the same mountain land Abel's ancestors had used freely before those "blue eyes" had come to rip it all off.

"Say what you want to – *no me importa*," the indignant rancher declared. "I've got seventy-eight *años*, and I still say Tixerina was right. But we're just a bunch of *pendejos* – fools, I'm telling you. *Mira* – how come we didn't get together with Tixerina – all of us rancheros? *Pos,* maybe then we could've gotten back our *tierra.* That pastureland, it belongs to us, just like Tixerina *dijo,* and not to those snot-nosed rangers. But, what did we do? *Pos,* we went and turned our backs on Tixerina – *sí, nos hicimos nalga, manito* – and just look how we ended up. More *fregaos* than ever!"

Still, it wasn't the "snot-nosed rangers" who had finally forced Abel Valerio to call it quits but, rather, *los mutilators,* as he put it. The elderly rancher was referring to the epidemic of livestock mutilations in northern New Mexico which, in recent years, had left his herd of cattle severely reduced. No one knew the identity of these mysterious criminals who struck at night, leaving behind dead carcasses with the reproductive organs cut out. Some blamed the attacks on a satanist cult that used the organs in its Black Mass, while others were certain it had to be aliens from outer space.

Abel Valerio, for his part, put forward a different and utterly original theory that morning on "El Swap Shop del Aigre" when he claimed that *esos mutilators* were actually scientists from Los Alamos who flew through the mountains in silent helicopters, performing their bizarre experiments. When Filogonio asked him why he thought Los Alamos scientists were cruising around at night, cutting the sex organs out of cattle, Abel replied that he had the whole thing *figurao.* The public wasn't aware of it yet, but those scientists had caused an accident like the one that had taken place in India. All the mountains of northern New Mexico had been contaminated by an invisible cloud of radiation.

"They're doing that to the poor *animales* because they want to *chequiarlos por* radiation," Abel went on explaining, as if the whole matter were as clear as day. "*Pos,* that's why they cut out the *ojete, mano* – that radioactive shit's gotta pass through there."

Another person worried about radioactive contamination was Frances Tapia, an elderly woman from San Pablo Pueblo, one of the three Indian pueblos bordering San Gabriel. She called up "El Swap Shop del Aigre" one morning with a litter of puppies to give away, but, before long, she started talking about a lawsuit that she and the mother of the puppies, a three-year-old Chihuahua named Nyoka, had filed in the federal court against the president of the United States. "Yes, I did – I sued the president to make him stop making all those bombs. And I put my dog in there, too, because all those bombs, they're going to wipe out the animals on this earth too. That's right – you just go over to the courthouse there and you see for yourself – it's got my Nyoka's pawprint right there under where I sign."

When Filogonio, in his customary style, asked the Indian woman to explain the motivation behind her actions, Frances responded without hesitation. "After I'm living for thirty years under the shadow of Los Alamos, I know the time is ripe for me to do something about it, don't you see? I'm no crazy lady – the crazy guy is that one, that old fool we got right now in the White House. He's been living a hundred years ago – that crazy guy thinks he can still win a world war."

For his part, Filogonio didn't know whether it was possible or not to win a world war. Nor did he know whether Frances had found a home for the puppies of the anti-nuclear dog. Clearly, he couldn't keep in touch with all his callers, nor could he accept responsibility for any deals that might or might not be made. Nonetheless, when Filogonio realized what had happened with Dora Toledo, he felt obligated to do something about it.

Dora, a middle-aged divorcée from Otowi, one of the hundreds of small villages in Río Bravo County that Vicente Luján said the Marching Mothers knew nothing about, called "El Swap Shop del Aigre" with a car for sale. She told Filogonio that it was an '81 Pontiac Sunbird, red with a black interior, with good tires and less than fifty thousand miles, and she was selling "very cheap." Naturally, Dora failed to add that the car was bewitched.

She had arrived at that conclusion unwillingly, but there was no way to ignore the awful evidence. The very day she bought the car, Dora had an accident. She was just driving it off the lot of Joe Romero's Oldsmobile-Pontiac-GMC Sales and Service – "Your Little Car Dealer with the Big City Deals" – when some young guy in a Ford truck bashed into the brand-new car. In the four years since then, Dora had had no less than eleven accidents in the car. What was worse, during that same period, five members of her family had died, including her mother, father, two brothers, and her favorite aunt. Naturally, she didn't share all that information with the fellow who had come that same morning to purchase the Pontiac, but it wouldn't have made any difference to Nazario Serrano anyway, because there was no way in hell he would have passed up a deal like that. At any rate, now that he had become a politician, Nazario needed a good used car to travel to the hundreds of small villages in Río Bravo County full of people who refused to sell out for a chunk of cheese. Yes, Nazario Serrano, an engineer who worked at the Los Alamos National Laboratory, had decided to run against Amos "the Cheese Candidate" Griego in the school board election. But neither the support of Miguel Fernández nor all the efforts of the Marching Mothers could save Nazario Serrano once he got into that possessed car.

III

A few short weeks later, Nazario was driving his Sunbird to a Rotary Club meeting at the Cowboy Family Restaurant. Even though he was running late, Nazario was trying his best to drive carefully, for he knew it was Halloween night and all the children in town would be out on the streets, showing off their costumes and asking for their "tricks or treats." But how in the devil was Nazario to know that a dog would suddenly jump into his path, forcing him to slam on the brakes? Luckily, he didn't flatten the dog, for it was expecting – not just another litter, but a legal precedent as well. Yet, Nazario might well have been better off making Vienna sausage out of Nyoka, Frances Tapia's celebrated anti-nuclear dog, for when he veered to his right, brakes squealing and tires laying two strips of rubber on the pavement, he ran right into a group of kids crossing the street. Although these kids were awfully mature to be out trick-or-treating, there was no doubt that Nazario had hit one of them or, rather, the wheelchair that belonged to one of them, for that was the first thing he saw when he leaped out of the car, his heart pounding wildly – an overturned wheelchair whose top wheel was still spinning absurdly in the darkness. Before Nazario could locate the person who had occupied the wheel-chair, a long-haired girl began screaming at him: "Look at what you've done! Look at what you've done, you dumb asshole!"

It was then that Naario did, indeed, look at what he had done, and his blood ran cold, for there was a young girl sprawled out on the street before him. "But... her legs?" Nazario sputtered in a choked voice, for the headlights of his demonic automobile revealed that the girl was missing not one, but both, of her legs.

"Yes, her legs, you *pendejo!* What have you done to her legs?" the enraged teenager continued shrieking. Meanwhile, Virginia Flores was about to burst with laughter, not only because she hadn't really been hurt in her fall, but also because she had never had those legs the driver of the car was searching for while he howled like a madman.

Virginia was the daughter of Urbán Flores, a true madman who was known throughout the valley as "the inventor" because he spent all his time inventing things, though the local gossips claimed the only thing he ever invented was tall tales. Be that as it may, his daughter Virginia, who had been born without legs, had never let the birth defect turn her into a recluse, disabled as much by sadness as by her physical deformity. On the contrary, she had grown up to be a spirited and lively teenager with a friendly disposition, one of the most popular students at San Gabriel High School. What's more, she was physically active and there wasn't a sport she didn't attempt, whether it be basketball, volleyball, or even bowling at the Tewa Lanes in the Black Rock Shopping Center. But the overriding passion of her life was horses. Virginia lived and died for horses and, thanks to a special saddle her dad had invented that cinched her tightly onto the horse's back, the legless girl was able to go riding whenever she pleased.

One of the few things that Virginia enjoyed as much as trotting through the woods on her gray pony was playing practical jokes, and this, without a doubt, was a true classic. Although they might feel sorry someday for this guy, he deserved whatever he got for driving like such a maniac on a night when all the kids in town were out on the streets – why, he might have killed somebody with that damned jalopy of his! When the girls had finally sated their appetite for revenge, Becky picked up Virginia and placed her back in the wheelchair, after which she confessed to the terrified man that all of this uproar had just been a big joke. In spite of the fact that Virginia assured Nazario Serrano – albeit between uncontrollable spasms of laughter – that everything was cool and that she could not possibly have lost the legs she had never had, it was too late for the poor school board candidate, who had come completely unglued; he had lost something far more essential than his legs – namely, his peace of mind. It's not that Nazario went crazy overnight, for he realized the pair of girls had made him the butt of their cruel joke; yet, in spite of all his attempts to convince himself that the entire experience had been nothing more than a ridiculous farce, he seemed unable to put it out of his mind and regain his emotional balance. Then, Dora Toledo, who had read an account of the accident in the *Río Bravo Times*, called up Nazario and told him the terrible and tortured history of the diabolical vehicle, but all she ended up doing was upsetting him even more, this poor fellow who was already finishing off a bottle of vodka every day. Nazario understood all too well that the bewitched car could finish him off as well, but he couldn't sell that tool of the devil to some innocent fool – why, he couldn't even give it away, knowing what he knew. No, what Nazario had in mind was rolling it off the edge of the Río Bravo Canyon, but he never got the chance to do it because his son decided to butt in.

José Climaco Serrano, or "Joe Chamaco," as everyone called him, was a Vietnam vet who still lived at home with his parents. Joe Chamaco couldn't help but laugh when his old man asked him to get some dynamite from his old war buddy, that Eluid Rendón who had been a demolitions expert in Vietnam, because Nazario wanted to blow the Pontiac Sunbird and the devil that possessed it straight to hell. But Joe Chamaco himself had already spent a season in hell, and he was damned if he was going to be afraid of a fucking car after he had shared the trenches with death itself. "If you really wanna get rid of it," he said with a broad grin, "give it to me." Nazario, of course, refused to give his son the keys, but Joe Chamaco simply grabbed them, laughing wildly as he took off in his new wheels.

God only knows where he got the crazy idea of taking a cruise that same afternoon on the iced-over lake at the Gary Lucero Memorial Park. It might have been because of that joint he sparked up, or maybe it was the six-pack of Bud Light he'd also polished off, smashing all the bottles on the "black rock" of the Black Rock Shopping Center which was located in front of the park. His old man, of course, was convinced the whole mess was caused by the bedeviled car, but the truth of the matter is that Joe Chamaco drove on the frozen lake out of sheer stupidity, the same type of stupidity that motivated so many people to paint that famous black rock.

Nobody really knew how that black rock had ended up where it was, though many believed it had once been part of a volcano in the Jemez Mountains that had erupted in prehistoric times, leaving a huge hole in the ground now known as El Valle Grande. What was certain was that the most ancient elders claimed that the most ancient elders they had known had claimed that the black boulder had always been right where it was today, between the lake and the road. So when local businessman Joe Frye, or "José Frito," as the jokers in San Gabriel had baptized him, signed a ninety-nine-year lease with the Indians of San Pablo Pueblo to construct his shopping center, he decided to leave the boulder in its place. The one thing he did do was fence it in with a chainlink fence, after Bill Taylor suggested in an editorial in the *Río Bravo Times* that Frye ought to change the name of his shopping center from "Black Rock" to "Graffiti Rock," since every square inch of the venerable stone had been defaced with the vulgarities of local graffiti artists. The boulder sported more names than "Inscription Rock" down in El Morro, although it didn't have such famous names as "Juan de Oñate," but, rather, the signatures of "Chango," "la Chepa," and "los Homeboys." As well as building the tall fence, Frye covered the entire boulder with several coats of black paint. But the entrepreneur didn't realize that there's nothing in the world more tempting to the "popular artist" than a virginal canvas, and, in the blink of an eye, some anonymous and particularly pernicious vandal had cut a hole in the chainlink fence and painted an inscription in white letters large enough to be seen by even the blindest old bat in the valley: "JOSÉ FRITO SUCKS COCK."

As might be expected, Joe Frye didn't waste much time re-painting the rock, and this time he even hired a night watchman from Khalsa Security, Inc., a private security service run by the community of Sikhs who lived just south of San Gabriel; he had absolutely no confidence in those imbeciles who dressed up in the uniform of the San Gabriel Police, and spent the vast major-ity of their time eating doughnuts at the Chuckwagon Cafe and sipping coffee at the Cowboy Family Restaurant. But not even the scowling guards with the daggers on their belts and the dia-pers on their heads could withstand the forces of popular cul-ture, and, before long, the fence was back on the ground and the hapless boulder was once again plastered with graffiti. José Frito had at last given up and simply allowed the black rock to stand as a monument to the depravity of the public; in fact, the businessman didn't even bother to remove the remains of the mangled fence which, over time, became the receptacle for tumbleweeds, trash, and every other kind of windblown litter.

Of course, the Gary Lucero Memorial Park, which was located behind the Black Rock Shopping Center, was no aesthetic wonder, either. The park, in fact, was no more than a clump of trees by the river. There were no picnic benches, no playground, and no monument to the veterans of the Vietnam War, all of which the city council had promised to build when they dedicated the municipal park to the memory of local war hero Gary Lucero, who had "sacrificed his life in the defense of liberty," to use the words that rolled off the tongue of the mayor of San Gabriel that day. Lucero had been one of Joe Chamaco's classmates back in the days when they both played basketball for the best team in the history of San Gabriel High School, the Division AAA Championship Team of 1968. Naturally, at that time, it would never have occurred to the mighty warriors of the basketball court that John Wayne could die before the movie was over. Joe Chamaco, at least, had lived to see through that patriotic lie – Gary Lucero, on the other hand, still believed he was defending the ideals of democracy in the jungles of Southeast Asia when he stepped on a Vietcong mine.

But Joe Chamaco never thought about the war anymore, for he knew all too well that too much thinking was not a good thing. It was thinking, after all, that had turned his *jefe* into an alcoholic. No, what the Devil knows comes from years of bedevilment and not by virtue of being the Devil, and Joe Chamaco now had enough years under his belt to realize that the best thing was just to kick back and enjoy life, and to hell with anxieties! However, even Joe Chamaco couldn't help but become a little anxious when his old man's bewitched car broke through the ice of the Gary Lucero Memorial Park lake that wasn't quite as frozen as it looked. The car, of course, sank like a torpedoed boat and, inasmuch as Joe Chamaco had long since rejected all that "heroism" crap, he immediately decided against going down with his ship. Even so, he narrowly escaped losing his life in the freezing waters of the lake.

IV

Even though Filogonio "El Swap Shop del Aigre" Antencio knew, along with everybody else, that the teenager who had been pushing the wheelchair of the legless girl last Halloween Eve had been none other than Becky Gonzales, one of Primo Ferminio Luján's illegitimate daughters, he still found it difficult to believe that the Luján Machine could have contrived the chain of events that ended up causing Nazario Serrano to take permanent leave of his senses. Nonetheless, now that Serrano's candidacy had turned into a big joke, Filogonio felt a certain amount of guilt for, after all, Nazario might never have purchased the diabolical car had he not tuned into "El Swap Shop del Aigre." Thus, when Emily Wolf and the Marching Mothers approached Filogonio to urge him to enter the race against Amos "the Cheese Candidate" Griego, the radio announcer had to admit that he had nursed a few political ambitions over the years. Yet, even though he enjoyed tremendous popularity among radio listeners in the valley, everybody knew the Lujánes had plenty of ways to win elections, whether it was with bought votes, stolen votes, or even "miraculous" votes – that is, ballots cast by the dead who, of course, always voted a straight Luján ticket. And, indeed, the Lujánes pulled off yet another "miraculous" election; however, in this case, the "miracle" backfired on them, perhaps because it revealed itself in the page of the *Río Bravo Times*.

As usual, the Luján Machine had filled the newspaper with political ads the week before the election; in fact, one could hardly turn a single page without seeing Amos Griego's puffy face. But there was something very strange in one of the photos; some of the "old regulars" at the Chuckwagon Cafe and the Cowboy Family Restaurant wondered whether their eyes were playing tricks on them, but it was no optical illusion. There, above the head of "the Cheese Candidate," was a huge, glowing halo.

All the barstool philosophers at the Mexican Image Bar and

the Saints and Sinners Lounge had their own ideas about how that halo had ended up there – some blamed it on Filogonio, while others claimed it must have been the editor himself who had sabotaged the ad in his own newspaper. Yet, while Bill Taylor might have loved coming up with such a fine practical joke, the truth of the matter was that he had nothing to do with the strange appearance of the halo. In fact, had he not already grown callous after so many years of reporting such supernatural phenomena as the Lujánes' political power in the other world, Taylor might well have declared the whole incident a miracle, for he could not find a trace of the halo in the original composition of the ad in the galley proofs.

Yet even Taylor couldn't help but believe in miracles after Amos "the Holy Cheese" Griego lost the election. "THE IMPOSSIBLE HAPPENS: ATENCIO WINS!" proclaimed the oversized headlines in that week's edition of the *Times*. And in his editorial entitled "There Must Be a God," Taylor crowed sarcastically, "Every saint has his day, the old saying goes, and this 'holy cheese' has at last met his day of reckoning."

It goes without saying that that edition of the newspaper sold like tickets to the Second Coming, but the strangest thing was that the Lujánes, for some inexplicable reason, simply took Taylor's insults in silence; what was more, the Primo didn't even bother to take his revenge on the "wolf lady" and her band of victorious mothers. Even Mela, a woman not widely known for her kindly disposition, ended up keeping her word about the free government cheese which the Lujánes continued to distribute.

It was true that three old-timers died up in San Buenaventura, one of the twenty-three precincts that Amos failed to carry in the election in spite of the fact that he lived there himself, and there was no doubt that the three had all died from eating bad cheese. But no one made much of that tragic coincidence because, after all, the three seniors had not been killed by the "Reagan cheese," but by a homemade white cheese manufactured by a tiny dairy that didn't pasteurize its milk. While it is undeniable that all three of the dead voted against Amos "the Holy Cheese" Griego, it would be as absurd to blame Primo Ferminio for the presence of the toxic microorganism in the white cheese as it would be to conjecture that he somehow had a hand in the mutilation of Abel Valerio's cattle, which, incidentally, is still going on. The anti-nuclear lawsuit is also pending, albeit in the absence of Frances Tapia who has likewise died, though not from eating poisonous cheese but, rather, from cervical cancer. However, her dog Nyoka is expecting yet another litter of puppies, as well as a favorable decision from the judge.

Meanwhile, Nazario Serrano is still drinking, though he lives out on the street now that the Lab has fired him and his wife has kicked him out of the house. But, as necessity is the mother, or at least the stepdaughter, of invention, Nazario has discovered a rather ingenious way of paying his tab at the Mexican Image Bar. He walks the streets, collecting all the aluminum cans that people throw out without realizing they're throwing away money, and sells them at Safeway, the grocery store in the Black Rock Shopping Center. Every day he hauls in at least one gunnysack full of flattened cans, thereby assuring himself of another day's ration of booze while, at the same time, getting a little exercise and performing a public service. The gang down at the Saints and Sinners Lounge believes that Nazario does more for the community cleaning the streets than he ever would have sitting on the board of education.

As far as Emily Wolf is concerned, the San Gabriel Schools would be better off if *all* the school board members took to the streets, including Filogonio "El Swap Shop del Aigre" Atencio. But it's the Marching Mothers who are back out on the streets, demonstrating and distributing petitions demanding a recall election. They're calling for either the resignation or the expulsion of all five members of the school board for misappropriation of public funds. It seems that the board, in a private session, approved the purchase of three thousand brooms from none other than Amos Griego, "the Holy Cheese." Even Filogonio Atencio went along with the decision to buy the truckload of brooms, easily enough to give two to every student, teacher, principal, secretary, and cook in the entire system. Naturally, Emily Wolf and the Marching Mothers are fuming over the betrayal of "Judas del Aigre," as they now refer to Filogonio in their meetings, but the most seasoned scholars of local affairs, at the Cowboy Family Restaurant and the Chuckwagon Cafe, simply shrug their shoulders and observe that every man can be bought and sold, and there's nobody who can figure out the price better than Primo Ferminio Luján.

AMY TAN

＊

Two Kinds

MY MOTHER BELIEVED you could be anything you wanted to be in America. You could open a restaurant. You could work for the government and get good retirement. You could buy a house with almost no money down. You could become rich. You could become instantly famous.

"Of course you can be prodigy, too," my mother told me when I was nine. "You can be best anything. What does Auntie Lindo know? Her daughter, she is only best tricky."

America was where all my mother's hopes lay. She had come here in 1949 after losing everything in China: her mother and father, her family home, her first husband, and two daughters, twin baby girls. But she never looked back with regret. There were so many ways for things to get better.

We didn't immediately pick the right kind of prodigy. At first my mother thought I would be a Chinese Shirley Temple. We'd watch Shirley's old movies on TV as though they were training films. My mother would poke my arm and say, *"Ni kan"*–You watch. And I would see Shirley tapping her feet, or singing a sailor song, or pursing her lips into a very round O while saying, "Oh my goodness."

"Ni kan," said my mother as Shirley's eyes flooded with tears.

"You already know how. Don't need talent for crying!"

Soon after my mother got this idea about Shirley Temple, she took me a beauty training school in the Mission district and put me in the hands of a student who could barely hold the scissors without shaking. Instead of getting big fat curls, I emerged with an uneven mass of crinkly black fuzz. My mother dragged me off to the bathroom and tried to wet down my hair.

"You look like Negro Chinese," she lamented, as if I had done this on purpose.

The instructor of the beauty training school had to lop off those soggy clumps to make my hair even again. "Peter Pan is very popular these days," the instructor assured my mother. I now had hair the length of a boy's, with straight-across bangs that hung at a slant two inches above my eyebrows. I liked the haircut and it made me actually look forward to my future fame.

In fact, in the beginning, I was just as excited as my mother, maybe even more so. I pictured this prodigy part of me as many different images, trying each one on for size. I was a dainty ballerina girl standing by the curtains, waiting to hear the right music that would send me floating on my tiptoes. I was like the Christ Child lifted out of the straw manger, crying with holy indignity. I was Cinderella stepping from her pumpkin carriage with sparkly cartoon music filling the air.

In all of my imaginings, I was filled with a sense that I would soon become *perfect*. My mother and father would adore me. I would be beyond reproach. I would never feel the need to sulk for anything.

But sometimes the prodigy in me became impatient. "If you don't hurry up and get me out of here, I'm disappearing for good," it warned. "And then you'll always be nothing."

Every night after dinner, my mother and I would sit at the Formica kitchen table. She would present new tests, taking her examples from stories of amazing children she had read in *Ripley's Believe It or Not,* or *Good Housekeeping, Reader's Digest,* and a dozen other magazines she kept in a pile in our bathroom. My mother got these magazines from people whose houses she cleaned. And since she cleaned many houses each week, we had a great assortment. She would look through them all, searching for stories about remarkable children.

The first night she brought out a story about a three-year-old boy who knew the capitals of all the states and even most of the European countries. A teacher was quoted as saying the little boy could also pronounce the names of the foreign cities correctly.

"What's the capital of Finland?" my mother asked me, looking at the magazine story.

All I knew was the capital of California, because Sacramento was the name of the street we lived on in Chinatown. "Nairobi!" I guessed, saying the most foreign word I could think of. She checked to see if that was possibly one way to pronounce "Helsinki" before showing me the answer.

The tests got harder – multiplying numbers in my head, finding the queen of hearts in a deck of cards, trying to stand on my head without using my hands, predicting the daily temperatures in Los Angeles, New York, and London.

One night I had to look at a page from the Bible for three minutes and then report everything I could remember. "Now Jehoshaphat had riches and honor in abundance and... that's all I remember, Ma," I said.

And after seeing my mother's disappointed face once again, something inside of me began to die. I hated the tests, the raised hopes and failed expectations. Before going to bed that night, I looked in the mirror above the bathroom sink and when I saw only my face staring back – and that it would always be this ordinary face – I began to cry. Such a sad, ugly girl! I made high-pitched noises like a crazed animal, trying to scratch out the face in the mirror.

And then I saw what seemed to be the prodigy side of me – because I had never seen that face before. I looked at my reflection, blinking so I could see more clearly. The girl staring back at me was angry, powerful. This girl and I were the same. I had new thoughts, willful thoughts, or rather thoughts filled with lots of won'ts. I won't let her change me, I promised myself. I won't be what I'm not.

So now on nights when my mother presented her tests, I performed listlessly, my head propped on one arm. I pretended to be bored. And I was. I go so bored I started counting the bellows of the foghorns out on the bay while my mother drilled me in other areas. The sound was comforting and reminded me of the cow jumping over the moon. And the next day, I played a game with myself, seeing if my mother would give up on me before eight bellows. After a while I usually counted only one, maybe two bellows at most. At last she was beginning to give up hope.

Two or three months had gone by without any mention of my being a prodigy again. And then one day my mother was watching "The Ed Sullivan Show" on TV. The TV was old and the sound kept shorting out. Every time my mother got halfway up from the sofa to adjust the set, the sound would go back on and Ed would be talking. As soon as she sat down, Ed would go silent again. She got up, the TV broke into loud piano music. She sat down. Silence. Up and down, back and forth, quiet and loud. It was like a stiff embraceless dance between her and the TV set. Finally she stood by the set with her hand on the sound dial.

She seemed entranced by the music, a little frenzied piano piece with this mesmerizing quality, sort of quick passages and then teasing lilting ones before it returned to the quick playful parts.

"*Ni kan,*" my mother said, calling me over with hurried hand gestures. "Look here."

I could see why my mother was fascinated by the music. It was being pounded out by a little Chinese girl, about nine years old, with a Peter Pan haircut. The girl had the sauciness of a

Shirley Temple. She was proudly modest like a proper Chinese child. And she also did this fancy sweep of a curtsy, so that the fluffy skirt of her white dress cascaded slowly to the floor like the petals of a large carnation.

In spite of these warning signs, I wasn't worried. Our family had no piano and we couldn't afford to buy one, let alone reams of sheet music and piano lessons. So I could be generous in my comments when my mother bad-mouthed the little girl on TV.

"Play note right, but doesn't sound good! No singing sound," complained my mother.

"What are you picking on her for?" I said carelessly. "She's pretty good. Maybe she's not the best, but she's trying hard." I knew almost immediately I would be sorry I said that.

"Just like you," she said. "Not the best. Because you not trying." She gave a little huff as she let go of the sound dial and sat down on the sofa.

The little Chinese girl sat down also to play an encore of "Anitra's Dance" by Grieg. I remember the song, because later on I had to learn how to play it.

Three days after watching "The Ed Sullivan Show," my mother told me what my schedule would be for piano lessons and piano practice. She had talked to Mr. Chong, who lived on the first floor of our apartment building. Mr. Chong was a retired piano teacher and my mother had traded housecleaning services for weekly lessons and a piano for me to practice on every day, two hours a day, from four until six.

When my mother told me this, I felt as though I had been sent to hell. I whined and then kicked my foot a little when I couldn't stand it anymore.

"Why don't you like me the way I am? I'm *not* a genius! I can't play the piano. And even if I could, I wouldn't go on TV if you paid me a million dollars!" I cried.

My mother slapped me. "Who ask you be genius?" she

shouted. "Only ask you be your best. For you sake. You think I want you be genius? Hnnh? What for! Who ask you!"

"So ungrateful," I heard her mutter in Chinese. "If she had as much talent as she has temper, she would be famous now."

Mr. Chong, whom I secretly nicknamed Old Chong, was very strange, always tapping fingers to the silent music of an invisible orchestra. He looked ancient in my eyes. He had lost most of the hair on top of his head and he wore thick glasses and had eyes that always looked tired and sleepy. But he must have been younger than I thought, since he lived with his mother and was not yet married.

I met Old Lady Chong once and that was enough. She had this peculiar smell like a baby that had done something in its pants. And her fingers felt like a dead person's, like an old peach I once found in the back of the refrigerator; the skin just slid off the meat when I picked it up.

I soon found out why Old Chong had retired from teaching piano. He was deaf. "Like Beethoven!" he shouted to me. "We're both listening only in our head!" And he would start to conduct his frantic silent sonatas.

Our lessons went like this. He would open the book and point to different things, explaining their purpose: "Key! Treble! Bass! No sharps or flats! So this is C major! Listen now and play after me!"

And then he would play the C scale a few times, a simple chord, and then, as if inspired by an old, unreachable itch, he gradually added more notes and running trills and a pounding bass until the music was really something quite grand.

I would play after him, the simple scale, the simple chord, and then I just played some nonsense that sounded like a cat running up and down on top of garbage cans. Old Chong smiled and applauded and then said, "Very good! But now you must learn to keep time!"

So that's how I discovered that Old Chong's eyes were too slow to keep up with the wrong notes I was playing. He went through the motions in half-time. To help me keep rhythm, he stood behind me, pushing down on my right shoulder for every beat. He balanced pennies on top of my wrists so I would keep them still as I slowly played scales and arpeggios. He had me curve my hand around an apple and keep that shape when playing chords. He marched stiffly to show me how to make each finger dance up and down, staccato like an obedient little soldier.

He taught me all these things, and that was how I also learned I could be lazy and get away with mistakes, lots of mistakes. If I hit the wrong notes because I hadn't practiced enough, I never corrected myself. I just kept playing in rhythm. And Old Chong kept conducting his own private reverie.

So maybe I never really gave myself a fair chance. I did pick up the basics pretty quickly, and I might have become a good pianist at that young age. But I was so determined not to try, not to be anybody different that I learned to play only the most earsplitting preludes, the most discordant hymns.

Over the next year, I practiced like this, dutifully in my own way. And then one day I heard my mother and her friend Lindo Jong both talking in a loud bragging tone of voice so others could hear. It was after church, and I was leaning against the brick wall wearing a dress with stiff white petticoats. Auntie Lindo's daughter, Waverly, who was about my age, was standing farther down the wall about five feet away. We had grown up together and shared all the closeness of two sisters squabbling over crayons and dolls. In other words, for the most part, we hated each other. I thought she was snotty. Waverly Jong had gained a certain amount of fame as "Chinatown's Littlest Chinese Chess Champion."

"She bring home too many trophy," lamented Auntie Lindo that Sunday. "All day she play chess. All day I have no time do nothing but dust off her winnings." She threw a scolding look at Waverly, who pretended not to see her.

"You lucky you don't have this problem," said Auntie Lindo with a sigh to my mother.

And my mother squared her shoulders and bragged: "Our problem worser than yours. If we ask Jing-mei wash dish, she hear nothing but music. It's like you can't stop this natural talent."

And right then, I was determined to put a stop to her foolish pride.

A few weeks later, Old Chong and my mother conspired to have me play in a talent show which would be held in the church hall. By then, my parents had saved up enough to buy me a second-hand piano, a black Wurlitzer spinet with a scarred bench. It was the showpiece of our living room.

For the talent show, I was to play a piece called "Pleading Child" from Schumann's *Scenes from Childhood*. It was a simple, moody piece that sounded more difficult than it was. I was supposed to memorize the whole thing, playing the repeat parts twice to make the piece sound longer. But I dawdled over it, playing a few bars and then cheating, looking up to see what notes followed. I never really listened to what I was playing. I daydreamed about being somewhere else, about being someone else.

The part I liked to practice best was the fancy curtsy: right foot out, touch the rose on the carpet with a pointed foot, sweep to the side, left leg bends, look up and smile.

My parents invited all the couples from the Joy Luck Club to witness my debut. Auntie Lindo and Uncle Tin were there. Waverly and her two older brothers had also come. The first two rows were filled with children both younger and older than I was. The littlest ones got to go first. They recited simple nursery rhymes, squawked out tunes on miniature violins, twirled Hula Hoops, pranced in pink ballet tutus, and when they bowed or curtsied, the audience would sigh in unison, "Awww," and then clap enthusiastically.

When my turn came, I was very confident. I remember my childish excitement. It was as if I knew, without a doubt, that the prodigy side of me really did exist. I had no fear whatsoever, no nervousness. I remember thinking to myself, This is it! This is it! I looked out over the audience, at my mother's blank face, my father's yawn, Auntie Lindo's stiff-lipped smile, Waverly's sulky expression. I had on a white dress layered with sheets of lace, and a pink bow in my Peter Pan haircut. As I sat down I envisioned people jumping to their feet and Ed Sullivan rushing up to introduce me to everyone on TV.

And I started to play. It was so beautiful. I was so caught up in how lovely I looked that at first I didn't worry how I would sound. So it was a surprise to me when I hit the first wrong note and I realized something didn't sound quite right. And then I hit another and another followed that. A chill started at the top of my head and began to trickle down. Yet I couldn't stop playing, as though my hands were bewitched. I kept thinking my fingers would adjust themselves back, like a train switching to the right track. I played this strange jumble through two repeats, the sour notes staying with me all the way to the end.

When I stood up, I discovered my legs were shaking. Maybe I had just been nervous and the audience, like Old Chong, had seen me go through the right motions and had not heard anything wrong at all. I swept my right foot out, went down on my knee, looked up and smiled. The room was quiet, except for Old Chong, who was beaming and shouting, "Bravo! Bravo! Well done!" But then I saw my mother's face, her stricken face. The audience clapped weakly, and as I walked back to my chair, with my whole face quivering as I tried not to cry, I heard a little boy whisper loudly to his mother, "That was awful," and the mother whispered back, "Well, she certainly tried."

And now I realized how many people were in the audience, the whole world it seemed. I was aware of eyes burning into my back. I felt the shame of my mother and father as they sat stiffly throughout the rest of the show.

We could have escaped during intermission. Pride and some strange sense of honor must have anchored my parents to their chairs. And so we watched it all: the eighteen-year-old boy with a fake mustache who did a magic show and juggled flaming hoops while riding a unicycle. The breasted girl with white makeup who sang from *Madame Butterfly* and got honorable mention. And the eleven-year-old boy who won first prize playing a tricky violin song that sounded like a busy bee.

After the show, the Hsus, the Jongs, and the St. Clairs from the Joy Luck Club came up to my mother and father.

"Lots of talented kids," Auntie Lindo said vaguely, smiling broadly.

"That was somethin' else," said my father, and I wondered if he was referring to me in a humorous way, or whether he even remembered what I had done.

Waverly looked at me and shrugged her shoulders. "You aren't a genius like me," she said matter-of-factly. And if I hadn't felt so bad, I would have pulled her braids and punched her stomach.

But my mother's expression was what devastated me: a quiet, blank look that said she had lost everything. I felt the same way, and it seemed as if everybody were now coming up, like gawkers at the scene of an accident, to see what parts were actually missing. When we got on the bus to go home, my father was humming the busy-bee tune and my mother was silent. I kept thinking she wanted to wait until we got home before shouting at me. But when my father unlocked the door to our apartment, my mother walked in and then went to the back, into the bedroom. No accusations. No blame. And in a way, I felt disappointed. I had been waiting for her to start shouting, so I could shout back and cry and blame her for all my misery.

I assumed my talent-show fiasco meant I never had to play the piano again. But two days later, after school, my mother came out of the kitchen and saw me watching TV.

"Four clock," she reminded me as if it were any other day. I was stunned, as though she were asking me to go through the talent-show torture again. I wedged myself more tightly in front of the TV.

"Turn off TV," she called from the kitchen five minutes later.

I didn't budge. And then I decided. I didn't have to do what my mother said anymore. I wasn't her slave. This wasn't China. I had listened to her before and look what happened. She was the stupid one.

She came out of the kitchen and stood in the arched entryway of the living room. "Four clock," she said once again, louder.

"I'm not going to play anymore," I said nonchalantly. "Why should I? I'm not a genius."

She walked over and stood in front of the TV. I saw her chest was heaving up and down in an angry way.

"No!" I said, and I now felt stronger, as if my true self had finally emerged. So this was what had been inside me all along.

"No! I won't!" I screamed.

She yanked me by the arm, pulled me off the floor, snapped off the TV. She was frighteningly strong, half pulling, half carrying me toward the piano as I kicked the throw rugs under my feet. She lifted me up and onto the hard bench. I was sobbing by now, looking at her bitterly. Her chest was heaving even more and her mouth was open, smiling crazily as if she were pleased I was crying.

"You want me to be someone that I'm not!" I sobbed. "I'll never be the kind of daughter you want me to be!"

"Only two kinds of daughters," she shouted in Chinese. "Those who are obedient and those who follow their own mind! Only one kind of daughter can live in this house. Obedient daughter!"

"Then I wish I wasn't your daughter. I wish you weren't my mother," I shouted. As I said these things I got scared. I felt like worms and toads and slimy things were crawling out of my chest, but it also felt good, as if this awful side of me had surfaced, at last.

"Too late change this," said my mother shrilly.

And I could sense her anger rising to its breaking point. I wanted to see it spill over. And that's when I remembered the babies she had lost in China, the ones we never talked about. "Then I wish I'd never been born!" I shouted. "I wish I were dead! Like them."

It was as if I had said the magic words. Alakazam! – and her face went blank, her mouth closed, her arms went slack, and she backed out of the room, stunned, as if she were blowing away like a small brown leaf, thin, brittle, lifeless.

It was not the only disappointment my mother felt in me. In the years that followed, I failed her so many times, each time asserting my own will, my right to fall short of expectations. I didn't get straight A's. I didn't become class president. I didn't get into Stanford. I dropped out of college.

For unlike my mother, I did not believe I could be anything I wanted to be. I could only be me.

And for all those years, we never talked about the disaster at the recital or my terrible accusations afterward at the piano bench. All that remained unchecked, like a betrayal that was now unspeakable. So I never found a way to ask her why she had hoped for something so large that failure was inevitable.

And even worse, I never asked her what frightened me the most: Why had she given up hope?

For after our struggle at the piano, she never mentioned my playing again. The lessons stopped. The lid to the piano was closed, shutting out the dust, my misery, and her dreams.

So she surprised me. A few years ago, she offered to give me the piano, for my thirtieth birthday. I had not played in all those years. I saw the offer as a sign of forgiveness, a tremendous burden removed.

"Are you sure?" I asked shyly. "I mean, won't you and Dad miss it?"

"No, this your piano," she said firmly. "Always your piano. You only one can play."

"Well, I probably can't play anymore," I said. "It's been years."

"You pick up fast," said my mother, as if she knew this was certain. "You have natural talent. You could been genius if you want to."

"No, I couldn't."

"You just not trying," said my mother. And she was neither angry nor sad. She said it as if to announce a fact that could never be disproved. "Take it," she said.

But I didn't at first. It was enough that she had offered it to me. And after that, every time I saw it in my parents' living room, standing in front of the bay windows, it made me feel proud, as if it were a shiny trophy I had won back.

Last week I sent a tuner over to my parents' apartment and had the piano reconditioned, for purely sentimental reasons. My mother had died a few months before and I had been getting things in order for my father, a little bit at a time. I put the jewelry in special silk pouches. The sweaters she had knitted in yellow, pink, bright orange—all the colors I hated—I put those in moth-proof boxes. I found some old Chinese silk dresses, the kind with little slits up the sides. I rubbed the old silk against my skin, then wrapped them in tissue and decided to take them home with me.

After I had the piano tuned, I opened the lid and touched the keys. It sounded even richer than I remembered. Really, it was a very good piano. Inside the bench were the same exercise notes with handwritten scales, thee same secondhand music books with their covers held together with yellow tape.

I opened up the Schumann book to the dark little piece I had played at the recital. It was on the left-hand side of the page, "Pleading Child." It looked more difficult than I remembered. I played a few bars, surprised at how easily the notes came back to me.

And for the first time, or so it seemed, I noticed the piece on the right-hand side. It was called "Perfectly Contented." I tried to play this one as well. It had a lighter melody but the same flowing rhythm and turned out to be quite easy. "Pleading Child" was shorter but slower; "Perfectly Contented" was longer but faster. And after I played them both a few times, I realized they were two halves of the same song.

YOSHIKO UCHIDA

*

Tears of Autumn

HANA OMIYA stood at the railing of the small ship that shuddered toward America in a turbulent November sea. She shivered as she pulled the folds of her silk kimono close to her throat and tightened the wool shawl about her shoulders.

She was thin and small, her dark eyes shadowed in her pale face, her black hair piled high in a pompadour that seemed too heavy for so slight a woman. She clung to the moist rail and breathed the damp salt air deep into her lungs. Her body seemed leaden and lifeless, as though it were simply the vehicle transporting her soul to a strange new life, and she longed with childlike intensity to be home again in Oka Village.

She longed to see the bright persimmon dotting the barren trees beside the thatched roofs, to see the fields of golden rice stretching to the mountains where only last fall she had gathered plum white mushrooms, and to see once more the maple trees lacing their flaming colors through the green pine. If only she could see a familiar face, eat a meal without retching, walk on solid ground, and stretch out at night on a *tatami* mat instead of in a hard narrow bunk. She thought now of seeking the warm shelter of her bunk but could not bear to face the relentness smell of fish that penetrated the lower decks.

Why did I ever leave Japan? she wondered bitterly. Why did

I ever listen to my uncle? And yet she knew it was she herself who had begun the chain of events that placed her on this heaving ship. It was she who had first planted in her uncle's mind the thought that she would make a good wife for Taro Takeda, the lonely man who had gone to America to make his fortune in Oakland, California.

It all began one day when her uncle had come to visit her mother.

"I must find a nice young bride," he had said, startling Hana with this blunt talk of marriage in her presence. She blushed and was ready to leave the room when her uncle quickly added, "My good friend Takeda has a son in America. I must find someone willing to travel to that far land."

This last remark was intended to indicate to Hana and her mother that he didn't consider this a suitable prospect for Hana, who was the youngest daughter of what once had been a fine family. Her father, until his death fifteen years ago, had been the largest landholder of the village and one of its last samurai. They had once had many servants and field hands, but now all that was changed. Their money was gone. Hana's three older sisters had made good marriages, and the eldest remained in their home with her husband to carry on the Omiya name and perpetuate the homestead. Her other sisters had married merchants in Osaka and Nagoya and were living comfortably.

Now that Hana was twenty-one, finding a proper husband for her had taken on an urgency that produced an embarrassing secretive air over the entire matter. Usually, her mother didn't speak of it until they were lying side by side on their quilts at night. Then, under the protective cover of darkness, she would suggest one name and then another, hoping that Hana would indicate an interest in one of them.

Her uncle spoke freely of Taro Takeda only because he was so sure Hana would never consider him. "He is a conscientious, hardworking man who has been in the United States for almost ten years. He is thirty-one, operates a small shop, and rents some rooms above the shop where he lives." Her uncle rubbed his chin thoughtfully. "He could provide well for a wife," he added.

"Ah," Hana's mother said softly.

"You say he is successful in this business?" Hana's sister inquired.

"His father tells me he sells many things in his shop – clothing, stockings, needles, thread, and buttons – such things as that. He also sells bean paste, pickled radish, bean cake, and soy sauce. A wife of his, would not go cold or hungry."

They all nodded, each of them picturing this merchant in varying degrees of success and affluence. There were many Japanese emigrating to America these days, and Hana had heard of the picture brides who went with nothing more than an exchange of photographs to bind them to a strange man.

"Taro San is lonely," her uncle continued. "I want to find for him a fine young woman who is strong and brave enough to cross the ocean alone."

"It would certainly be a different kind of life," Hanna's sister ventured, and for a moment, Hana thought she glimpsed a longing ordinarily concealed behind her quiet, obedient face. In that same instant, Hana knew she wanted more for herself than her sisters had in their proper, arranged, and loveless marriages. She wanted to escape the smothering strictures of life in her village. She certainly was not going to marry a farmer and spend her life working beside him planting, weeding, and harvesting in the rice paddies until her back became bent from too many years of stooping and her skin was turned to brown leather by the sun and wind. Neither did she particularly relish the idea of marrying a merchant in a big city as her two sisters had done. Since her mother objected to her going to Tokyo to seek employment as a teacher, perhaps she would consent to a flight to America for what seemed a proper and respectable marriage.

Almost before she realized what she was doing, she spoke to

her uncle. "Oji San, perhaps I should go to America to make this lonely man a good wife."

"You, Hana Chan?" Her uncle observed her with startled curiosity. "You would go all alone to a foreign land so far away from your mother and family?"

"I would not allow it." Her mother spoke fiercely. Hana was her youngest and she had lavished upon her the attention and latitude that often befall the last child. How could she permit her to travel so far, even to marry the son of Takeda who was known to her brother?

But now, a notion that had seemed quite impossible a moment before was lodged in his receptive mind, and Hana's uncle grasped it with the pleasure that comes from an unexpected discovery.

"You know," he said looking at Hana, "it might be a very good life in America."

Hana felt a faint fluttering in her heart. Perhaps this lonely man in America was her means of escaping both the village and the encirclement of her family.

Her uncle spoke with increasing enthusiasm of sending Hana to become Taro's wife. And the husband of Hana's sister, who was head of their household, spoke with equal eagerness. Although he never said so, Hana guessed he would be pleased to be rid of her, the spirited younger sister who stirred up his placid life with what he considered radical ideas about life and the role of women. He often claimed that Hana had too much schooling for a girl. She had graduated from Women's High School in Kyoto, which gave her five more years of schooling that her older sister.

"It has addled her brain – all that learning from those books," he said when he tired of arguing with Hana.

A man's word carried much weight for Hana's mother. Pressed by the two men, she consulted her other daughters and their husbands. She discussed the matter carefully with her brother and asked the village priest. Finally, she agreed to an exchange of family histories and an investigation was begun into Taro Takeda's family, his education, and his health, so they would be assured there was no insanity or tuberculosis or police records concealed in his family's past. Soon Hana's uncle was devoting his energies entirely to serving as go-between for Hana's mother and Taro Takeda's father.

When at last an agreement to the marriage was almost reached, Taro wrote his first letter to Hana. It was brief and proper and gave no more clue to his character than the stiff formal portrait taken at his graduation from middle school. Hana's uncle had given her the picture with apologies from his parents, because it was the only photo they had of him and it was not a flattering likeness.

Hana hid the letter and photograph in the sleeve of her kimono and took them to the outhouse to study in private. Squinting in the dim light and trying to ignore the foul odor, she read and reread Taro's letter, trying to find the real man somewhere in the sparse unbending prose.

By the time he sent her money for her steamship tickets, she had received ten more letters, but none revealed much more of the man than the first. In none did he disclose his loneliness or his need, but Hana understood this. In fact, she would have recoiled from a man who bared his intimate thoughts to her so soon. After all, they would have a lifetime together to get to know one another.

So it was that Hana had left her family and sailed alone to America with a small hope trembling inside of her. Tomorrow, at last, the ship would dock in San Francisco and she would meet face to face the man she was soon to marry. Hana was overcome with excitement at the thought of being in America, and terrified of the meeting about to take place. What would she say to Taro Takeda when they first met, and for all the days and years after?

Hana wondered about the flat above the shop. Perhaps it would be luxuriously furnished with the finest of brocades and lacquers, and perhaps there would be a servant, although he had not mentioned it. She worried whether she would be able to manage on the meager English she had learned at Women's High School. The overwhelming anxiety for the day to come and the violent rolling of the ship were more than Hana could bear. Shuddering in the face of the wind, she leaned over the railing and became violently and wretchedly ill.

By five the next morning, Hana was up and dressed in her finest purple silk kimono and coat. She could not eat the bean soup and rice that appeared for breakfast and took only a few bites of the yellow pickled radish. Her bags, which had scarcely been touched since she boarded the ship, were easily packed, for all they contained were her kimonos and some of her favorite books. The large willow basket, tightly secured by a rope, remained under the bunk, untouched since her uncle had placed it there.

She had not befriended the other women in her cabin, for they had lain in their bunks for most of the voyage, too sick to be company to anyone. Each morning Hana had fled the closeness of the sleeping quarters and spent most of the day huddled in a corner of the deck, listening to the lonely songs of some Russians also travelling to an alien land.

As the ship approached land, Hana hurried up to the deck to look out at the gray expanse of ocean and sky, eager for a first glimpse of her new homeland.

"We won't be docking until almost noon," one of the deckhands told her.

Hana nodded, "I can wait," she answered, but the last hours seemed the longest.

When she set foot on American soil at last, it was not in the city of San Francisco as she had expected, but on Angel Island, where all third-class passengers were taken. She spent two miserable days and nights waiting, as the immigrants were questioned by officials, examined for trachoma and tuberculosis, and tested for hookworm by a woman who collected their stools on tin pie plates. Hana was relieved she could produce her own, not having to borrow a little from someone else, as some of the women had to do. It was a bewildering, degrading beginning, and Hana was sick with anxiety, wondering if she would ever be released.

On the third day, a Japanese messenger from San Francisco appeared with a letter for her from Taro. He had written it the day of her arrival, but it had not reached her for two days.

Taro welcomed her to America, and told her that the bearer of the letter would inform Taro when she was to be released so he could be at the pier to meet her.

The letter eased her anxiety for a while, but as soon as she was released and boarded the launch for San Francisco, new fears rose up to smother her with a feeling almost of dread.

The early morning mist had become a light chilling rain, and on the pier black umbrellas bobbed here and there, making the task of recognition even harder. Hana searched desperately for a face that resembled the photo she had studied so long and hard. Suppose he hadn't come. What would she do then?

Hana took a deep breath, lifted her head and walked slowly from the launch. The moment she was on the pier, a man in a black coat, wearing a derby and carrying an umbrella, came quickly to her side. He was of slight build, not much taller than she, and his face was sallow and pale. He bowed stiffly and murmured, "You have had a long trip, Miss Omiya. I hope you are well."

Hana caught her breath. "You are Takeda San?" she asked.

He removed his hat and Hana was further startled to see that he was already turning bald.

"You are Takeda San?" she asked again. He looked older than thirty-one.

"I am afraid I no longer resemble the early photo my parents gave you. I am sorry."

Hana had not meant to begin like this. It was not going well.

"No, no," she said quickly. "It is just that I . . . that is, I am terribly nervous. . . . " Hana stopped abruptly, too flustered to go on.

"I understand," Taro said gently. "You will feel better when you meet my friends and have some tea. Mr. and Mrs. Toda are expecting you in Oakland. You will be staying with them until . . . " He couldn't bring himself to mention the marriage just yet and Hana was grateful he hadn't.

He quickly made arrangements to have her baggage sent to Oakland then led her carefully along the rain-slick pier toward the streetcar that would take them to the ferry.

Hana shuddered at the sight of another boat, and as they climbed to its upper deck she felt a queasy tightening of her stomach.

"I hope it will not rock too much," she said anxiously. "Is it many hours to your city?"

Taro laughed for the first time since their meeting, revealing the gold fillings of his teeth. "Oakland is just across the bay," he explained. "We will be there in twenty minutes."

Raising a hand to cover her mouth, Hana laughed with him and suddenly felt better. I am in America now, she thought, and this is the man I came to marry. Then she sat down carefully beside Taro, so no part of their clothing touched.

ABOUT THE AUTHORS

KIM CHI-WŎN was born in 1943 in Kyŏnggi Province in Korea, and is the daughter of Ch'oe Chŏng-hŭi, one of the most popular women writers in twentieth-century Korea. Since the 1970s, Kim has been living in the New York City area, and much of her work describes the tribulations of Korean immigrant women in an American city.

EKONESKAKA is the true and Kickapoo name of Aurelio Valdez García, who lives on the new Kickapoo land near Eagle Pass, Texas. He has published stories in *Rolling Stock*, the *Northwest Review*, and *New Blood*.

LOUISE ERDRICH is a Turtle Mountain Chippewa. Her first novel *Love Medicine* won the National Book Critics Circle Award in 1984. Her other novels include *Beet Queen* and *Tracks* and she is the author of *Jacklight*, a collection of poetry.

K.C. FREDERICK grew up in Detroit and currently teaches at the University of Massachusetts. His short stories have appeared in numerous publications as well as *Best American Short Stories* and *Pushcart Prize: X* (1986).

JOSEPH GEHA was born in Zahleh, Lebanon, and moved with his family to Toledo, Ohio, in 1946. He is currently teaching at Iowa State University in Ames, Iowa. *Through and Through: Toledo Stories* (Graywolf Press, 1990) is his first book.

GAYL JONES was born in Lexington, Kentucky. She writes from the African-American female perspective. Her publications include *Corregidor* and *Eva's Man*.

JAMAICA KINCAID was born in St. John's, Antigua, West Indies. She is the author of *At the Bottom of the River*, *Annie John*, *A Small Place*, and *Lucy*. She lives with her family in Vermont.

SALVATORE LA PUMA was born in 1929 in Bensonhurst, Brooklyn, New York, and is descended from a long line of Sicilians. He made his living as a copywriter and real estate agent until a few years ago when he began writing fiction full-time. His book *The Boys of Bensonhurst* (1987) won the Flannery O'Connor Award for Short Fiction.

BHARATI MUKHERJEE was born and educated in Calcutta and earned her Ph.D. at the University of Iowa. She is the author of two novels, *Wife* and *The Tiger's Daughter;* two works of nonfiction, *Days and Nights in Calcutta* and *The Sorrow and the Terror;* and two collections of short stories, *Darkness* and *The Middleman and Other Stories,* the latter of which won the 1988 National Book Critics Circle Award for fiction. She is currently teaching creative writing at Columbia University and City University of New York.

SUSAN NUNES was born and raised in Hilo, Hawaii, and now lives in Honolulu. She grew up in two worlds, those of her Japanese mother and Portuguese father, and much of her fiction is about piecing together the scattered impressions of a divided yet doubly rich family. Her collection of short stories is called *A Small Obligation and Other Stories,* and she is the author of two children's books.

MERRIHELEN PONCE writes under the name Mary Helen Ponce. She teaches Chicana literature at the University of New Mexico in Albuquerque. She is currently working on an autobiography based on her childhood in a Mexican-American barrio during the 1940s.

NAHID RACHLIN was born in Iran. She is the author of two novels, *Foreigner* and *Married to a Stranger.* She teaches writing at New York University in Manhattan where she lives with her husband and daughter.

JIM SAGEL is of Russian-American descent and has lived in the Spanish-speaking community of Espanola, New Mexico, for two decades. He has published three short story collections and five books of poetry, including *On the Make Again: Otra Vez en la Movida* and *Mas Que No Love It.*

AMY TAN was born in Oakland, California, in 1952, two and a half years after her parents immigrated to the United States. She visited China for the first time in 1987. She is the author of *The Joy Luck Club,* and lives in San Francisco.

YOSHIKO UCHIDA was born in California. During World War II she and her family were relocated, first to a horse stall at Tanforan Race Track and then to the barracks at a concentration camp in Topaz, Utah. She has published more than twenty-five books, including *Picture Bride, Journey to Topaz,* and *Desert Exile.*